CITRON
PRESS

Fresh ideas from

NEW AUTHORS
CO-OPERATIVE

Published by Citron Press
Connors Corp. Ltd., Suite 155, Business Design Centre,
52 Upper Street, Islington Green, London N1 0QH, Great Britain
www.citronpress.co.uk

This Book is a Work of Fiction. Names, Characters, Places and Incidents are either products of the author's imagination or are used fictitiously. Any resemblance to actual events or locales or persons, living or dead, is entirely coincidental.

ISBN 0754400018

Printed and bound in Great Britain by The Bath Press, Bath.

A copy of this book is held at the British Library.

■ **TOILET** ELEPHANT

NICK **JOHNSTON-JONES** ■

PART ONE

FAST-MOVING CONSUMER GOODS

CHAPTER ONE

I hate telephones. I hate their insistency, their spoilt-brattishness. You can't ignore a telephone. The one in my office gives out a syncopated electronic wail, as if it's announcing a bomb scare or a nuclear strike. But what I really hate about telephones is that some oaf can take it into his head to call up, and all of his problems suddenly take priority over all of yours.

It was getting on for twelve thirty and I was on the point of going out for a sandwich when the telephone brayed in my ear. I picked it up and said, 'Brodie.'

It's taken time to perfect my answering technique. When I first came here I would deploy my full name whenever answering the phone, thus identifying myself to the caller. But this had its drawbacks. Most of my calls are from clients, for whom 'William Brodie' is good enough for a kick-off. But a number are from friends or colleagues, for whom 'William Brodie' is, for reasons unclear to me, a source of rich comedy. I got cheesed off with having to bat through five minutes of '*The* William Brodie?' and 'Hello, William Brodie', or 'Ah, William Brodie, this is Charles James Arthur McKeown.' Office camaraderie is built on this kind of tomfoolery, but fuck it, leave me out.

For an experimental period I tried straight 'William', but this failed to satisfy more querulous callers ('William who?'), and wasn't really right anyway, as hardly anyone I know calls me William, except my father, and he often forgets or gets it wrong. Besides, I don't want to encourage any of this Will or Bill business. The doorman's already taken to calling me Willie, which I can definitely do without.

'Brodie' is good. I like the way it can be spat, tersely, police department-style, into the receiver.

It was Cressida, Mike Sharp's secretary: could I pop round? Mike Sharp being our managing director, the reply to this tends to be along the lines of 'Certainly' or 'Right away'. So round I popped, quelling the small voice of paranoia that whispers in my insides whenever the management express an interest in me.

Everyone in this business is paranoid. About getting fired. Some marketing director somewhere cuts his budget and – what do you know? You're under Waterloo Bridge staking out your cardboard box. I find the insecurity is somehow reinforced by the physical layout of the office, an open-plan affair dotted with stockades for the execs, and little kinds of dugouts for the secretaries. Trench warfare sound effects of chattering keyboards and printers further contribute to an air of reduced life expectancy.

Mike Sharp's office, by contrast, is a haven of chrome, pouffe and pot plant. Mike Sharp's an old-style ad man: fat, ruthless, and full of shit. Like most high-flyers in the business he isn't all that bright (you don't need to be if you're brash and pushy enough). It was Mike Sharp who gave me this job, and lets me tell people I work in advertising. (You'd be surprised: to a lot of people it's a big deal – a lot of people want to do it too.) The problem I have with Mike Sharp – aside from the problem of him giving me the willies – is that I despise him. I particularly despise the way he smokes his cigarettes. He smokes some indescribable continental brand that smells like brake fluid, or rather he doesn't smoke them, he *puffs them about*. He makes a big deal of popping the pack, tamping the cig. and lighting up with a frown of concentration, cheeks tubing inwards...but does he inhale? Nope. He lets the smoke spill and spew out of his mouth in great wreaths before *pretending* to catch an inhalation on the last whisp. Afraid of cancer, probably – and why not? But this exercise in simultaneous ostentation and risk-avoidance really gets my goat. If you're going to smoke, smoke! Live dangerously. Don't do Thomas the Tank Engine impersonations.

'Brodie,' he said. 'Take a seat.'

He was riffing through a document, swiping at sections with a Stabilo. I sat down in an oozing leather settee and stared at the awards racked up on the opposite wall.

A word about my place of work. All the agencies I've ever heard of have deeply silly names, like firms of solicitors on acid. (A friend of mine, I swear to you, works at one called Molesworth, Duckworth, Grub, Beaver & Beardsley.) Ours is merely deeply corny: Short Sharp Advertising. Short and Sharp are the co-founders, creative and managing directors respectively. Paul Short, funnily enough *is* short – very short – about five-three – a fact that clearly pisses him right off. Consensus in the industry is that Shortie is talented, but a bit of a shit. A talented shit. Myself, I'm not so sure about the talented part. True, his office is wall to wall with Honours and Plaudits, but take a closer look and you'll find most of them are of the crappier, less prestigious variety – Reader's Digest Special Award for Typography, sort of thing. Only a couple, D&AD Silvers, *really* count, and they're from the late seventies, in recognition of Paul's work for the British Hat Council (remember that one? 'Get ahead. Get a hat'). Nowadays Paul plays a lot of tennis and knocks out the odd ad, tending to leave most of the creative output (the bread and butter stuff, not the interesting bits) to a handful of starvation-waged college leavers and boozy old art directors.

And me? I'm an account exec. I talk to clients over the telephone.

Mike Sharp tossed aside the document, lit another cigarette and eyed me speculatively through the miasma. 'How long have you been with us now, Brodie?'

'Nearly a year.'

'And how's it going? How do you feel you're getting on?'

'It's going fine. I really like it.'

'It's time you had a change,' said Mike Sharp. He smiled – a power smile. 'I'm going to put you onto a new project. A very important one too. Raise your profile. How do you feel about that?'

Well, naturally I agreed like billyo. It's a good policy to appear keen about anything in the profile-raising line; and it also sounded like the end of a nine-month stint working on Carpet Mania.

It has to be said I've never been exactly wild about Carpet Mania. Advertising's a lot of fun when it's for cars, or jeans, or lager. Less so when it's for discount carpets. And for every ad man jetting off to Monaco to shoot a beer commercial there are fifty driving round the M25 with the artwork for a discount carpet ad that should have been at the publication last Tuesday. You know the sort – great slap-ups of Lowest Prices Ever's and Unbeatable Reductions, with twenty separate products shoehorned into a page at the arse-end of the paper. This is *retail*. No one likes retail, but it pays.

'What you need,' said Mike Sharp, 'is FMCG experience. Packaged goods. Things people buy in supermarkets.'

He launched off on a tutorial on the subject of the supermarket, the revolution it has faced in the last ten years, the explosion of choice facing every housewife pushing a trolley down the aisle, the psychology of the purchasing decisions going through her head.

'Tell me,' he asked suddenly, 'what brand of washing up liquid does your mother buy?'

As a matter of fact my mother's dead, so she doesn't. But not wanting to introduce a negative note at this early stage I hazarded the name of a major brand.

'*Exactly*,' said Mike Sharp. 'She goes for the brand leader. Shall I tell you why? It isn't that she thinks it's better than the others. She *likes* it more than the others. People will never admit what we do influences them. It doesn't – not overtly. But advertising has imbued that brand with emotional values more relevant to her needs than the competition.'

He took a suck at his cigarette and the phone went off.

'Yes?...oh. Tell him two minutes. Two minutes.'

Turning back to me: 'What was I saying?'

'Er – emotional values,' I said. 'Of advertising.' Mike Sharp looked completely blank. 'Supermarkets,' I ventured.

'Right, right. Listen, I have to go.' He stood up. 'I want you to talk to Miles Fraser. He'll fill you in on what this is about. What are you working on at the moment?'

'Carpet Mania.'

'Jesus. Are you? Well this will hot up your CV a bit. Talk to Miles.'

'Thanks very much.'

He crushed out his butt, gave me a matey little sort of half-punch, and said, 'Go for it.' Then he went out for lunch.

Things people buy in supermarkets... Well, I didn't need Mike Sharp to fire me up about supermarkets. Supermarkets, the cathedrals of capitalism, the ad man's playground... It was the best news I'd had in nine months.

'You're cheerful,' said Cressida, as I emerged, a few minutes later. I'd been sitting in a halfwit trance, staring out the window at distant aeroplanes bisecting the blue. The moment one exited the window frame another would take its place on the same trajectory. The regularity was obscurely pleasing, adding in no small measure to my good mood.

'Cressida,' I said, 'You're right. Come and have a sandwich.'

'No, ta. I've got to go shopping.'

Cressida does a lot of shopping. It's kind of a hobby of hers. I strolled back to my desk, where the phone was tolling away beside a great pile of artwork for the weekend's Carpet Mania ads. A hugely long fax had been draped over my chair like a roll of toilet paper. Later, I thought, and scooped up my jacket.

So now – how about that sandwich?

Outside, London cringed in the early summer heat – June and its joke temperatures. Mercifully the agency's computer-cooled. Out on the street the air was the temperature of the car exhaust. Most of the air *was* car exhaust, blue and all-encompassing. What's it going to be like next month? And the one after that? People have stopped taking their clothes off to go brown. The big thing now is to put clothes on, like Arabs, to escape the rays. Isn't it *hot*? people say to each other. There is much talk of global warming. Myself, I love it. Sunshine makes you happy. It means you can wear sunglasses.

I put on my sunglasses and made my way down Bolton Street into Piccadilly and the lunch hour riot. Workmen with shiny orange backs were tearing the pavement up into great slabs. Why? Last time it was new phone lines. 'New phone lines, mate,' shouted the one I asked this time, leaning into his pneumatic. The din was fantastic. Those phones, they really have got a lot to answer for...I stormed the opposite pavement, the hot breath of a BMW practically igniting my trouser ends. Clearly pressed for time to cover the fifteen yards between the end of the last queue and the start of the next. I walked past The Ritz, Hatchards, Fortnums. A keen sense of excitement at the prospect of my sandwich was adding to my stock of sunshine and supermarket-induced optimism. I felt quite unreasonably cheery. A good long queue had formed outside Mario's, the sandwich house I consistently patronise. I considered and dismissed the notion of calling instead at the Peach Melba off Devon Street. Mario is worth a wait.

I fell into line behind a rhubarb-faced businessman with a prodigious drinker's tummy. In front of him a flock of girls in primary colours tried on each other's sunglasses, preening and shrieking with mirth. Everyone's a film star in sunglasses. I hung about thinking about aeroplanes, the weekend, fast moving consumer goods... I wondered idly what exactly it would be. Food? Cosmetics? Booze? Booze would be good. Booze would be brilliant. And no more carpets.

Inside at last, and the air conditioning buzzed in overload, focusing a single hot spot by the door where a medley of odours assaults the nostrils. Elsewhere all is underwater cool. Banked up behind the glass is an Aladdin's cave of delicately sculpted sandwich fillings, flanked with fruit, cakes, macaroons, savouries... Mario himself, that saint-like man, stands at the centre of the counter working at furious speed, surrounded by his lieutenants. The air is thick with exhortation and command. Over their bent and bobbing heads hangs a banner reading simply 'MARIO'S', with the subtext: *We make excellent sandwiches.* This is objective truth. Mario does make excellent sandwiches. Fifteen seconds inside the door your whole body is trembling with appetite.

But what's this? An innocuous Chinese boy, a student by the looks of him, causing chaos with his order, fruitlessly attempting to specify some anarchic combination (I think, half prawn mayonnaise, half pastrami on brown with salad) to Mario's deaf old pa. No chance. 'Ah wan' huff praw, huff pustrum-a'-salad...' – '*Wha*'?'– 'Huff *praw*, huff pustrum...' – '*Wha*'?' and so on, a potentially infinite dialogue, with old Mario making numerous false starts and sorties into the filling bowls, to little cries of protest from the student. Simultaneously, to his right, a loud cockney was dealing with the girls' order, a staggeringly long inventory of baps and cakes and crisps and drinks, bellowing back every request and change of mind across the counter with plenty of pets and loves and sweethearts, compounding the hearing difficulties of Mario Senior. It was at least ten minutes before I escaped with my tuna-bean mix on a giant wholegrain salad bap and stood dithering in the carbon monoxide. Green Park, or the office? A look at the park decided me. Green Park's a bit of a misnomer since the hosepipe ban. Brown Park, possibly; Gobi Desert Park... A solitary lunatic in a singlet jogged sluggishly amongst the trees and deck chairs. God it was hot.

I bought a tinnie from an enterprising rasta ambling with a bucket in and out of the thwarted traffic and drank it straight off. I bought another and drank that straight off too, punctuated by a volley of burps from the first. Holding my sandwich close, like a prayer book, I threaded back through the side streets.

The agency was quiet. Most people seemed to have gone out, or down the pub. Unsurprisingly for a Friday lunchtime. Unsurprising for any lunchtime. Only one secretary, Melissa, and her boyfriend Tod, from accounts, were still about. Tod was stroking Melissa's bare thigh with an air of concentration, while Melissa yawned into a book. They both glanced up as I came in, so I called, 'All right?', and Tod called back: 'Got a phone message for you.'

'Yeah? Who?'

'It was a woman.'

'Yes?'

'That's it. Didn't get her name.'

'Oh. Thanks.'

Nice one, Tod. Good phone message. Next time give it to the milkman. Not that I really cared. I had a sandwich to see to.

I hit the fan, dropped my jacket on a chair and hunkered down for the first bite. The telephone squatted redly, waiting for me to start. I unconditionally promise you that the telephone goes every time I start eating a sandwich. So what, you might think?. Swallow and answer. But eating one of Mario's sandwiches is no simple affair. For a start, it entails taking *the* most gigantic mouthfuls. Chunks of filling slither in all directions as the teeth apply pressure to the bun; the mouth, consequently, has to do some pretty fast work rounding up a tomato segment here, a bit of tuna there, here a bean, there a nut, everywhere the lettuce. As it is, a fair amount inevitably splats back onto the deli paper. The resultant mouthfuls are enormous. Eating Mario's sandwiches takes practice and talent. You have to concentrate. You can't just shovel it down any old how.

And these phones, oh these phones! The big drawback of staying in at lunchtime is that the phones go *all* the time. Plus they have this system of *tripping* if you don't answer. If, after four rings, you don't pick it up (dropping everything), it *trips* to another phone, and thence, presently, to another. Bite – *brrrang!* They're off! It's a race between man and telephone! And if you do manage, chewing like a madman, to pick it up in time, eyes watering, ostrich-throated, the all-important 'Brodie' is invariably converted to a piping wheeze by a segment of celery caught in the windpipe. Besides, all this accelerated chomping and masticating makes it genuinely difficult to breathe. The nostrils, even at peak, uncongested efficiency, are delicate little apertures; ill designed to deliver great whooshes of air to the lungs. And this kind of eating, believe me, constitutes serious cardio-vascular exercise. Breathing, thus, must take place in mid-chew, displeasingly, through a fudge of tuna bean salad. Breathless, empurpled, you cheep into the mouthpiece. The bloke at the other end thinks he's onto some heart-attack case.

So in I bit, wolfishly, keeping a weather eye on the phone, which played it all off hand for at least five seconds before going off in my face.

'...Brodie,' I burped, three and a half rings later.

'Brodie, Miles here. I gather Mike's told you about the new project. We ought to...are you all right?'

'Fine, fine.'

'I need to brief you. Can you come up?

'Ten minutes okay? I'm tied up at the moment.'

'Mmn. No, I'm due in a presentation at two fifteen. Then there's the new business review. Then the creative briefing on fertilisers. Then I've got a client in till seven. Unless you want to make it after that.'

Miles is a great believer in getting the most out of his afternoons. I located a rogue cell of sweetcorn lodged in the mouthpiece, swallowed, pinged it at the bin and said, 'All right. See you in a minute.'

Parking the remains of my sandwich in a drawer, I hooked a note pad off the shelf and mounted the stairs to the directors' floor.

I've never properly worked with Miles before, except one week during my training when I trailed round after him watching him in action. Miles is old captain efficiency personified. He certainly impresses the crap out of me. I'm especially impressed – who isn't? – by the way he manages to keep his office, namely, *totally bare*. Miles keeps, or so it would appear, nothing in his office. Everything has its place, and that place is out of sight. His desktop is a polished slab. Written matter he dictates into a little hand-held machine. Even the phone is kept, thoroughly cowed, in a drawer next to his right leg, whence it petitions him at intervals.

Didn't Mussolini keep a blank desk? Or was it Hitler? There's a dash of both in Miles. Except I get the feeling if Miles had taken matters in hand he'd have had a Reichstag on both poles by 1943, and done it at seventy-five per cent return on capital employed.

Miles continued dictating without glancing at me when I came in. Another thing about Miles: he's obviously gone on a course in power furniture. Not for Miles the winded settees and clapped-out swivel chairs of the other offices. For a start he has a solid mahogany desk. For visitors there is only one place to sit, and that's in a kind of deflated leatherette bag, not quite a chair, not quite a sofa. Not quite anything, really. An osteopathic nightmare. Its function is purely to keep you much much lower than Miles up at the desk there. You practically crick your neck getting a view of his kneecaps.

Here I sagged and wallowed until Miles finished his memos. I listened in for a bit, lapsing after a while into a mild stupor.

'Do you own a flat, Brodie?' Miles had put away his dictaphone and was looking down at me dispassionately.

'I do, yes. Bought three months ago.'

'What kind of toilet cleaner do you use?'

'Toilet cleaner?'

'Toilet cleaner.'

I gave the matter some thought. Not only could I not bring to mind what kind of toilet cleaner I used, I couldn't, at that moment, recall ever having bought a toilet cleaner – or, for that matter, ever having cleaned the toilet.

Come now.

'While we're young, Brodie.'

'I think I use bleach,' I said eventually.

Miles seemed dissatisfied.

'Have you ever bought a toilet cleaner,' he demanded, 'as opposed to bleach?'

'Yes. I suppose so.'

'Which one, then?'

Again, blank. Then a brand name came to me.

'Fresh,' I said wildly.

'*Fresh*? You mean Frish.'

'Frish, yeah.'

'Any idea who manufactures it?' continued Miles remorselessly.

'I haven't the faintest.'

The phone bleeped faintly, interrupting this exchange. Miles frowned, then answered. I searched my brain for toilet memory. It's a characteristic of people like Miles that they can make you feel incredibly stupid and inadequate, incredibly quickly. But I wasn't going to be made to feel small about this. Why should I know all about manufacturers of toilet cleaner? It's not something that comes up much in conversation.

Miles came off the phone and re-garaged it carefully in its drawer. Instead of continuing the interrogation, however, he opened a lower drawer, considered for a moment, then reached inside.

Onto the shiny surface of his desk he placed a translucent blue plastic bottle full of dark fluid. It was nine or ten inches high, with a long, sharply curving spout capped by a yellow spigot top. Either side of the spout were round, moulded Mickey Mouse ears.

He contemplated this slightly obscene object for a moment before returning his gaze to me.

'See this?' he said. 'You're looking at four and a half million pounds of R and D. You're looking at a fifty million pound brand – potentially.'

I read the name embossed on the label: 'Toilet Elephant'.

'What is it?' I said.

'This,' said Miles, 'is the next brand leader in the European lavatory cleaner market.'

Lavatory cleaner. Sod it, it could be worse.

Miles briefed me. He gave me the lot, from soup to nuts. Go on, ask me anything. William Brodie is an encyclopaedia of toilet knowledge. Boy, do I know about toilets. Years of research and market data sits in fat wads on my desk. I know the size of the market, key manufacturers, key brands, key trends, key this, key that. *Key* is a buzz word of Miles'. For Miles, key is a key word. Miles stressed to me the vastness of this market (think about it: everybody has a toilet), and the importance of focusing only on what is key. Miles also believes in knowing more about your market (the key bits) than your client. Not a bad policy, and frankly not as hard as it sounds. I, for example, already know more about the UK carpet market than Carpet Mania. This is not to say I know very much about the UK carpet market, just more than Carpet Mania. It would surprise me to learn that Carpet Mania know anything about the UK carpet market. They just pile them up and flog them cheap to anyone who's interested.

The lavatory cleaner market, now that's a different matter. Here is where strategy comes into play, where nuances of product difference and brand imagery spell success or disaster. Plus it's a tough old market, lavatory cleaner. Own label, says Miles, is putting the squeeze on branded products. Competition is fierce. The way he talked about it made it sound like a bloodbath. I emerged from his office, following a protracted and undignified wrestle with the leather bag, fired up with the scent of combat, gripping my briefing documents like battle orders.

This elephant business. The elephant angle. It's quite straightforward. It's so straightforward it's breathtaking. There is only one truly *key* dynamic in the lavatory cleaner market. The key dynamic in the lavatory cleaner market is...

'Directionality,' said Miles. '*Getting under the rim.*'

'Is that why it's shaped like an elephant?'

He gave me a withering look. 'No, it's shaped like an elephant so it will appeal to three-year-olds. What do you think?'

'But all the other loo cleaners and bleaches I've seen go under the rim too.'

'Not like this they don't.' He tapped the trunk. 'AKL have spent years getting this right. Sure, the others are directional. But no one brand has ever come along with a totally single-minded under the rim proposition backed up with a product like this. This gets *right* under, no fucking about.'

We both looked reverentially at the product.

'What are the ears for?' I asked.

'Watch,' said Miles. He gripped the bottle and turned it upside down. The ears filled, like an optic. 'Holds one application. Secondary consumer benefit. Unique competitive feature.'

'Beautiful,' I said. I meant it.

'There's more. Read the label.'

He passed me the pack. The label was a crudely artworked depiction of an elephant blowing coloured liquid through its trunk under the rim of a giant lavatory bowl. Above it appeared: 'NEW TOILET ELEPHANT', and beside that, 'THE REVOLUTIONARY NEW TOILET CLEANER THAT GETS RIGHT UNDER THE RIM.' Then it read: 'From AKL – The Professionals.' At the bottom was a single line in smaller type: *'Environment Friendly'*.

'Is it? Environmentally friendly?'

'No of course it isn't. But they've managed to remove two of the seven pollutant agents. It's less harmful than anything currently on the market.'

'Well, shouldn't it be – I don't know – "Environmentally Friendlier", then, or "Less Environmentally Harmful"?'

This time Miles laughed in my face. 'Wake up, Brodie. This is advertising. *Never* flag a negative. A glass is always half full, never half empty. That's a key principle of this industry.

'I have another meeting. Read up on that stuff over the weekend. I'll fill you in on the company background on Monday.'

I took Toilet Elephant with me and went to the toilet. It got under the rim all right. If it did anything it got under the rim.

The rest of the afternoon I alternated between my research reports and the increasingly petulant demands of the telephone. For purposes of secrecy the elephant project had, rather wittily, been code-named Project Camel. Miles stressed the confidential nature of the work. If a whiff of this gets out, it's over. Nobody, bar nobody, is to know of it. Hence the codename. Feeling like an FBI agent I cracked open a file marked 'Attitudes to Household Hygiene' and read.

The housewife segments into five clusters by attitude to routine household cleaning. These we have classified: Mrs Anxious Easy Work; Mrs Anxious Hard Work; Mrs Average Contented; Mrs Spick and Span; and Mrs Minimum Bother. Reviewed below are the key attributes of each.

Then the phone went.

It was Vivienne, assistant ad manager at Carpet Mania, with revisions to this weekend's Everything Must Go ad. We run these every Saturday, and everything does go. Then they restock and we do it again the next week.

'Hi, Vivienne. Yes, sorry I haven't returned your calls... hang on while I dig out the artwork.'

I rummaged through the litter on my desk and tugged out a bromide.

'Firstly, can we have "Fantastic Unbelievable Bargains" rather than "Fantastic Bargains" on line two?'

'It doesn't really make sense,' I objected.

'Yes it does. The bargains are fantastic and unbelievable: fantastic unbelievable bargains.'

'You'd need to say, "Fantastic *and* Unbelievable Bargains". The point size on the type would have to be reduced to make it fit.'

'Look, can't you just do it like I want it, Brodie? I really don't think you should get hung up on it.'

'We can *do* it. I just don't think we ought to.'

'Thank you. Now on the next line. Next to the illustration of the thick pile co-ordinates range. Could you...?'

I took down the changes, objecting to the more preposterous. The ad looked like a dog's breakfast. Feeling bullish, Vivienne finished up with an oft-repeated plea to make the logo bigger. Already the Carpet Mania logo seemed to fill the page. There was barely room to illustrate the fantastic unbelievable bargains.

'Oh come *on*,' I said.

'I'm sorry, Brodie,' she said primly, 'but Mr Rigby requested it specifically and I don't think we can just refuse.'

I phoned the revision through to Roy in the studio, who acceded listlessly to all but the last.

'No way.'

'Sorry, mate. We haven't got an option on this one.'

'Course we've got a fucking option. How about telling the client to fuck off for an option?'

This is why account execs exist. To stop art directors telling clients to fuck off for an option. I talked him over. I promised him a beer. Roy does very nearly anything for a beer. And so back to my housewife clusters. Interestingly, I discover, single men living on their own are classified as housewives. Consequently, I am a housewife. What do you know?

I wonder what kind?

Mrs Minimum Bother is characterised by a slack and feckless approach to household cleaning. She will put off tasks to the very last moment, preferring to live in relative squalor rather than face the drudgery of housework where it can be avoided...

Next to the text was a little cartoon of Mrs Minimum Bother with her feet up on a chair, smoking a fag and watching TV. Behind her, toddlers rolled bawling in the mire and a cat dipped its face into a saucepan. She looked content, old Mrs Minimum B. She looked okay. She looked a bit like me, feet up here in the rubble of my office, enjoying a late afternoon cup of tea with the telephone bawling over my shoulder. Mrs Spick and Span, by way of contrast, stood self-righteously in a gleaming hallway, bristling with dusters and aerosols. Mad old bitch.

The phone went again as I was getting into Mrs Anxious Hard Work, depicted face down in a lavatory bowl.

It was Keith 'Hippo' Boothby, my media buyer.

'Brodes, you homosexual. Come down the juicer.'

'Can't be done. I'm busy right now.'

'But it's half five. Come *on*.'

Half five is official going-home time, but nobody in my department goes home then, except particularly brazen temps or half-witted secretaries. Half five is when senior management usually start to get back from lunch, so it isn't such a good time to be seen by the lift. Half five, in fact, is when the office comes to life, as people who've been picking their noses all afternoon burst forth holding pieces of paper, striding hither and thither. Who me? Go home before nine at night? No way.

Hippo, working in media, has no such problems. Working in media the pub is practically the office anyway.

'I'll be down later. Get me a...get me a lime and soda. With ice.'

'Get you a what?'

'I've kicked drinking,' I said. 'For the summer.'

'*Yeah yeah*,' said Hippo.

This is a decision that had come to me a few nights back, late on, whilst throwing up on the steps to my front door. Since starting work back in September

I've found my drinking's gone up appreciably. The office seems to develop a collective thirst about going-home time, the quenching of which can – and usually does – last all evening, and involve an almost indefinite quantity of lager. I thought I might try giving it a rest for a while. Save the money, get fit, that kind of thing.

I didn't realise what tough work not drinking is, mind you. In this profession, for a start, it's tantamount to wearing a pink triangle or a badge saying 'Kiss me, sailor.' You are, additionally, cut off from a rich line of chat based around getting drunk stories. 'I had seven grapefruit juices and went home' doesn't have any swing to it. And have you ever tried drinking seven grapefruit juices and going home? Drink seven grapefruit juices and go home and the next morning you'll feel like *shit*. That's the main problem with not drinking – it's not that I miss the alcohol, I just can't stomach the alternatives. All those sticky-sweet little bottles and fizzy drinks. *Alcohol-free* lager... Ever tried that stuff? Don't. Just don't.

Hippo and the rest were pretty well oiled when I got down the pub at quarter to seven and bought Roy his pint. To loud and derisory commentary I quaffed off a lime juice and soda; and then I went home.

'Hey, Brodie,' called Hippo as I jostled for the door. 'What did Sharpy want to see you 'bout?'

With a couple of pints in me I'd have spilled the news. The place would have rang with toilet talk and elephant chuckles. Instead I grinned enigmatically and barged on out. Not drinking's got some things to recommend it – like keeping your head while everyone else gets out of theirs. If only...if only it was slightly more *interesting*.

I walked home. Took me three quarters of an hour. How come? I have a little flat in Bloomsbury. Quite a posh address, furthermore: 22a Regents Square, WC1. The reality's more prosaic. The reality is three sides fifties' council blocks, garishly painted and covered with satellite dishes, to one side shabby-genteel Edwardian terrace. That's my bit. The terrace faces north, towards St Pancras and its fumy spires. To the rear is an old cemetery with a few benches and some swings and slides. The square itself, a slab of turd-strewn grass with a tree or two, is much frequented by winos and loonies. There are lots of these. There are so many I think some of them must commute in from the suburbs. Most, though, are clearly indigenous. Most I recognise from day to day: the old black guy who shuffles around with a plastic bag on his head; the Irish brothers, Tattoo Charlie, the Professor... They cluster round the benches locked into debate, fierce with gesture and denial. The more clearly barmy ones wander about barking and swiping at the air. These I feel sad for. The winos have their sherry, their cigs. and Superstrong, plus a certain down-and-out solidarity, but the mad ones, what is there for them? Just their obscure anger, and nobody giving a fuck.

But I like it here, I really do. I bought this place with some money my father gave me and a ball-breaking mortgage from a dodgy Mick bank calculated on three and a half times my falsified earnings. The consequence is that I have a flat for one in the heart of town and the lifestyle of a monk saving up for retirement. But so what? Everyone else who lives here is poor too, or old, or both. It would be different in – I don't know – Knightsbridge. It would be unbearable.

A month after I moved here I had an unlucky break. The agency, formerly located ten minutes away off Gower Street, up-sticked for nobbier premises off Piccadilly. Getting to work now constitutes, frankly, something of a pain in the arse. Getting across London seems to be infinitely slower than getting in or out. But I'm stoical. I don't use the tube – largely because I've always thought being packed into a tin and shot through tunnels is a dreadful way of getting about; but also because I have an aversion to being mugged, following an incident on the Northern line last November where I parted company with twenty quid and approximately as many teeth. I could always walk, but I don't have the energy in the mornings. So I catch the bus, the 189. God Bless you, 189 bus, and all who ride upon you. The 189 picks me up from Southampton Row, the merest step from my front door, and puts me down again practically opposite the agency. How about that? The only drawback being that it can take anything from twenty-five minutes to three and a half hours. But this is cool. I use the time productively. I read books and newspapers. I look out of the windows. I rough out sexual fantasies. I think about sandwiches and fret about carpets. I have a deep affection for the 189 bus. I watch it nosing out of Euston and lumbering up to my stop with something approaching paternal fondness. When I get on I sit right at the front, on the top, like a kid. Every journey has thrilling episodes of acceleration and recklessness. Untethered from the surrounding traffic by a propitious bus lane in Kingsway, the 189 plunges off on a heartstopping downhill hurtle towards the Aldwych. Overhead the knuckles of branches thrash and crack on the roof. How it stays vertical as, at practically terminal velocity, it negotiates the bend at the bottom, I have never understood. Seasoned passengers shuffling to get off on the Strand brace themselves like tiller men in a gale. Gaily trousered Americans out for a bus ride disembark queasily at this stage; pointlessly, since the following hundred yards is covered in a series of two-inch lurches.

But what I really like about buses is the chumminess of one's co-passengers. Nice people ride buses. Opting to bus it back home the other night I found both of the front seats occupied, one by a pair of stolid Germans, one by the fattest man I'd ever seen in my life. Puzzling cursorily how he'd got up the stairs (or conceivably he'd been lowered in through the roof), I eyed the unoccupied sliver of seat to the right of his torpedo thigh. The bus was pretty full, and I didn't fancy retreating amongst the smokers in exile at the rear of the top deck. As I vacillated the fat man caught my eye. He gave me this smile, this great big beam. Another front seat charioteer! 'I'm getting off in a minute,' he said, heaving himself upright. 'Sit here.'

We shook hands in mock-formality. He held me hard with his frankfurter fingers. 'You're a gentleman,' I said; *'My pleasure,'* he replied, grinning beatifically. When he got off at Charing Cross the bus seemed perceptibly lighter, cannoning friskily into the Strand. I watched him manoeuvering his bulk amongst the crowds until he was lost from sight.

When I got back I met Connie, owner of the flat below me, a great tank of a woman, enjoying a fag and a cough by the window on the half landing, angling her powdery old face at the departing rays.

'Hi, Connie.'

'All right, love? How's your adverts coming along?'

'Motoring. How are you?'

'Can't complain.'

Good neighbourly stuff, eh? I went on up, and up, eventually getting to my front door in the attic. Five locks later I was within.

I changed, had a rinse, made tea, went to the toilet. Ha! The toilet. It didn't look too grubby, but I gave it a prod with the lavatory brush and a quick squirt of bleach. The bottle was half empty, or alternatively half full, and I had difficulty aiming the thick liquid at low pressure up under the rim. A function of the viscosity of the bleach or the nozzle design? This should be investigated.

Overcome suddenly by hunger I ate half a packet of digestives, four slices of toast with peanut butter, and a cold sausage roll. Jesus, the crap I eat. If it wasn't for Mario I'd probably have rickets. But cooking for yourself is just such a drag. Occasionally I give it a go, but I always fall back on toast, biscuits, packets of things. Most of the time I can't even be arsed to open a tin. Minimum bother. Well, you know where you are with toast and biscuits.

I took a second mug of tea and a paperback and went up onto the roof. I have this little trapdoor leading to a narrow parapet between the chimney stacks. A slightly tricky six feet, wobbly slates on left, chasm on right, and you're in the open by the skylight. Here, in the temperate seasons, my deck chair awaits me, flapping idly in the warm air. And here I sat, thinking toilet thoughts, levelling my gaze at the winking eye of the Telecom Tower in the dregs of the evening.

CHAPTER TWO

Saturday I went shopping. To be more specific, I went shopping in a supermarket, or *major multiple*. It wasn't that I particularly needed to buy anything – I wanted to see the people that buy things in supermarkets.

Hard by Regent's Square is a great bunker of a shopping centre, deep in the bowels of which lurks a supermarket. It sounds silly, indeed I'm obscurely ashamed of the fact, but I haven't been in a supermarket more than half a dozen times in my life. As a kid and a student I ate refectory food (for which I retain a deep passion), and my current set-up doesn't call for the purchase of anything more demanding than bread, tea, and so forth, which I get from a twenty-four hour Asian place up the road.

I liked it. I liked it a lot. What have I been missing here? Before I knew it, wandering up and down the aisles, my cart was stacked with goodies. The stuff you can get in these places! Speciality soups, in cartons. Exotic teas. Amazing biscuits. Vegetarian cheese. Wide-eyed I piled it in. All around me professional shoppers wielded their cages, brooding suspiciously over tomatoes and special offers. The air rang with the demands of children and the roars of clouted toddlers.

I parked strategically near a gondola of lavatory paper to cast an eye over the punters. Only you can't park strategically in a supermarket, or major multiple. It's like parking strategically on the M1. Desperate shoppers baulked and nudged at me with their loads. A woman with the largest and most eclectic collection of cat food I've ever seen on wheels requested me in no uncertain terms to get moving. I checked out, tenner in hand... Thirty-five notes! The queue at my tail heaved with impatience as I rummaged for credit cards. This was the first of my problems. Those soups and drinks and tins of things, the weight of the bastards! Balanced by two pendulous carrier bags I waded out into the open, snagging and goosing passers-by with a protruding roll of cling film. (What had I bought *cling film* for, for Christ's sake?) Half-way home my starboard bag burst spectacularly, sending fast moving consumer goods bowling in all directions. Half-way up my stairs the handles co-instantaneously snapped on the other bag, writing off the yoghurt and mineral water. Inside at last I set out a little row of toilet cleaners on the lavatory window sill for trial. The rest of the stuff I stashed in the fridge. It looked good once it was inside. It looked homely. I have to say that in the past I've entertained ideas of getting rid of the fridge. It never had anything in it except the odd tub of margarine or can of lager, and fridges can get you down when they're perpetually bare. But I didn't have the courage. It wasn't pragmatic considerations that stopped me, like where to keep the milk. I just couldn't face the visitor's unspoken question: nice kitchen – where's the fridge?

Poor old Brodes. Lives on his own and he *doesn't have a fridge*.

In the afternoon I caught a bus to Camden to buy a little pot with a devil on it I'd spotted a couple of Sundays back. I thought it might do for my father's birthday. Only when I got to the shop it was shut, so instead I visited Edward.

Edward is my sole surviving friend from boarding school in Scotland. I'd been bundled off there after my mother died to get out of my father's hair and be near to aunts and uncles in Edinburgh. Edward arrived the following term having been expelled from a public school in Kent. He'd stabbed an older pupil with a blackboard compass after the latter had made an unwelcome sexual advance. Edward was quite unrepentant. He had a truly patrician disregard for the consequences of his actions. Initially we loathed one another, but after a spell we became very close. Our situations drew us together – both English on firmly Scots territory; both in exile for special reasons. We spent the next five years together, both obstreperously at odds with the archaic culture of the school. I have a great affection for Edward. These days he's a full-time bum. He left university after a year and went abroad. Then he came to London to mess around in a band; which soon afterwards fell apart. Since then he's done various things. He makes a bit of dough despatch riding, but he doesn't seem bothered about money. His old man's a big cheese in newspapers, so presumably one day he'll come into something. But I'm sure he'd be the same if his dad was a dustman. He'd be the same if he was a dustman. It's just how he is.

When I arrived he was still in bed. He peered out at me from an upstairs window, hair on end.

'What time is it?'

'Nearly three.'

'Three?' He pondered the fact. 'I'd better make some coffee.'

Presently the door opened. He gave me a mug of incredibly black and gritty coffee and we went into the back yard to sit in the sun.

'Is it Saturday today? Yes it must be. I was out rather late last night.'

'What you get up to?'

'Oh, I took a ride.'

'Where to?'

'Yorkshire.'

'*Yorkshire?*'

'It's a big bike,' said Edward simply.

Edward had recently acquired a new motorbike, a gleaming red Italian number. It *is* a big bike. It's a snortingly big bike.

'I tell you what,' Edward said, when we'd finished the coffee. 'Let's go to Brighton.'

'Now?'

'Why not?'

'All right,' I said. So we did.

I've never trusted myself on a motorcycle since the first time I tried riding one and pulled a wheelie into a hedge. But I'd ridden pillion with Edward many times, from early, hairy escapades on an illicit 125 at school, to longer jaunts on subsequent, bigger machines. But I'd never been with him on anything like this. We cleared London in a matter of minutes, me hanging on for very life while Edward snapped upwards through the gears and the traffic sprinted past us in reverse. When we hit the trunk roads Edward opened up the throttle to the full. Peeping past his shoulder at the vibrating instrument panel I thought I read a hundred and thirty on the clock. Or it could have read two hundred and thirty. What's the difference? Extremely fast is what it read. It was equal parts frightening and exhilarating, though fear's a bit of an irrelevance at that speed. If you come off you're dead, if you don't you aren't. Enjoy the ride.

We got there in less than an hour. Predictably, Brighton was heaving with crowds and traffic. So we carried on instead up the coast to a tiny seaside town my grandparents used to take me to when I was a little kid. Here the daytrippers were thinner on the ground. We parked the bike, went for a swim and lay on the shingle to dry off.

'I've got an idea,' said Edward after a while.

'Yes?'

'Let's go and have some beers.'

'I can't. I've kicked drinking.'

'*Yeah yeah,*' said Edward.

We went to a bar off the sea front and had some beers. After that we had some fish and chips. Then we had some more beers.

This not drinking business, like I've said: it's very hard.

'So tell me,' said Edward some time later, 'how are you getting by at Short Shit Adverts? Selling many carpets?'

'I'm coming off the carpets.' I felt thick with pride saying it. 'I'm working on a highly secret new product launch in the field of packaged goods.'

'Yeah? What?'

'I can't tell you. It's highly secret.'

'Tell me.'

'It's a toilet cleaner shaped like an elephant.'

Edward frowned. 'Like an elephant?'

'Like an elephant.'

'Why,' said Edward at length, 'is it shaped like an elephant?'

'So that the trunk,' I curved my index finger upwards, 'can get *under the rim.*'

He stood up unsteadily. 'That reminds me,' he said, and went off to the lavatory. When he came back he said, 'It won't work.'

'It will.'

'No-one *needs* a lavatory cleaner shaped like an elephant.'

'So? You can make people want it.'

'You've got to get out of advertising, Brodie,' said Edward. 'It'll fuck your brain.'

None of the bed and breakfasts would accommodate us when, around eleven thirty, we made a hopeful round of the darkened and shuttered premises, despite, or perhaps because of our formal good evenings and carefully enunciated enquiries. In the end Edward hauled a hairy old blanket out of some compartment on the bike and we slept side by side on the still warm shingle.

In the morning we bathed again then ate a big yob breakfast of fried everything and tea at a deserted café Edward smoked and read the Sunday Mirror. I browsed through a little catalogue in the colour supplement advertising motorised tie-racks, egg-massagers and computerised pets. At eight thirty the place began to fill and we went up on the cliffs.

'Tell me,' I asked, 'Did you mean what you said last night?'

'What did I say last night?'

'I should get out of my job.'

'Of course. I've thought that ever since you started.'

'Come on, Edward. It's not that bad. As jobs go.'

'Yes it is. As jobs go it sucks.'

'I won't necessarily stay in it, you know.'

'You will. You'll stay in it for years and years and end up managing some horrid company and getting fat and collecting boring bits of art. Then you'll have your kids when you're forty-five. They'll grow up never seeing you and treating you like a rich vicar.'

'Balls.'

'It happened to my father,' said Edward.

'It didn't happen to mine.'

'Exactly. Because he's never worked for some shitty corporation that changed his head.'

Edward sees the office as the root of all evil. He's never been in one in his life.

'Okay,' I said, amicably, 'I'll bear it in mind.'

We walked on for an hour or so before Edward said he had to head back.

'I said I'd meet Lucy for lunch.'

'Lucy?'

'This girl I met.' Edward's perpetually meeting girls. As if to fill out the picture he added, 'Her father's a trampolinist.'

'No kidding?'

'Yup.'

'Check it out. What about her?'

He gave a lop-sided grin. 'She works at Saatchi and Saatchi.'

He dropped me back at the flat at eleven thirty, whereupon I went up on the roof and promptly fell asleep.

*

Some time later I became aware of the phone ringing persistently in the bedroom underneath. It's difficult not to become aware of the phone ringing in my flat, equipped as it is with a bell, not a bleep. It makes a noise like a fire engine. I made my way down in no particular hurry, thinking it would stop before I got there. But it carried on, and on, eventually prompting me into a little last minute dash to the bedroom, not wanting to miss it after all, wherein I stubbed my toe viciously on the bed leg. I picked it up gasping, eyes watering with the quite extraordinary pain.

'Is that Kev?' said the receiver.

Ever since I bought this property I've been taking calls for Kev. I don't know the said Kev. The bloke I bought the flat from wasn't Kev. I can only conclude Kev lived here at some point in the not-so-distant past, or that Kev's number closely resembles mine.

All I definitely know of Kev is that he is, or was, a plumber, and judging by the calls I get a fairly crappy one at that.

'No,' I said, 'no Kev here.'

'What?'

'I said there's no Kev here. You've got the wrong number.'

'Kev the plumber?' said the voice.

'No-one of that name here.'

'Thing is,' persisted the voice, 'the boiler went on the blink Thursday. Only Kev did the fitting and –'

'Look, I really can't help you. He isn't here.'

'Oh.' said the voice. There was a grudging pause. 'It's left me right in the cart. Know where I can get him?

'No.'

Still he wouldn't hang up. I got the feeling he was prepared to believe I wasn't Kev, but not, as yet, that I wasn't a *plumber*. He kept giving me details of his boiler's ailment. In the end, to get him to go away, I actually made a few suggestions: was the pilot on? had he looked at the flue? I swear it took ten minutes to get off the phone. The tyranny of the machine! I really do have better things to do with my Sunday evenings.

Like what?

I ambled in and out of the dusty rooms, scratching my bum. I contemplated making some toast but I wasn't peckish. I contemplated going back to sleep but I wasn't tired. I contemplated reading my book but I couldn't be arsed. I looked out the window. I looked at my watch: seven thirty! I turned on the TV.

I watched a programme about people with curious hobbies. John, from Birmingham, had a curious hobby. John's hobby was jumping over cars driven towards him at seventy miles an hour. There was John, limbering up on the track with a karate kick or two. There was the car, getting up speed. Insert shot of accelerator needle touching seventy. Shot of John. Shot of car. Car, John, John, car. Then John jumped in the air and the car whizzed beneath. Now let's have another look in slo-mo: John's technique is to jump kind of *at* the car in order to propel himself forward and over. Nice one. But hold! He's going for the double – two cars, nose to bumper, at ninety miles an hour...

Something in the commentator's voice told me John wasn't going to pull this one off: I hit the remote control a second before the leap... Momentarily the screen filled with a bawling opera singer. Sure enough, when I flipped back, there was the ambulance, the people milling about. But John was all right! He'd only broken his toe on the spoiler of the second car. Next month he's going to try it again.

I switched off before Dave the scuba-diving vicar did the underwater wedding. I went out for a walk instead, stepping through the turds and lolly wrappers in the velvety evening air. Here and there the winos grouped in the fuzzy glow of the street lamps, brandishing cans in a litany of assertion. 'I'll tell ya... I'll *tell* ya...' Odd, however much they jab and point and emphasise their military training, they never seem to come to blows. On the contrary, regularly – but seldom coincidentally – they will lapse into maudlin outbreaks of affection. Their accents hung in the air around the crumbly old squares: 'Naaa, pal – y're a greet bloke, greet...' – '*Away and fuck, ya bastard!*' One peeled off to ask the wherewithal for a cup of tea, so I gave him fifty pee and he said 'Arright son!', grinning lewdly in my eye. Mad old buffer. Then fifty yards on another, a sandblasted old woman girt round with plastic bags asked me for a quid – a quid! Just like that! 'Gis a poond, son.' I declined. 'Gis a smoke then.' 'I don't have any.' She wheeled away in disgust.

I walked on slightly more quickly, avoiding an old boy in leather trousers and a combat jacket who was denouncing a tree in Tavistock Square, completing a loop round the University buildings and back home again, picking up a pie and some chips on the way. The phone was going when I got back. (Why do I have a phone in the flat at all? Same as the fridge: you have to – you just do.) This time, I decided, if it was for Kev I'd hang straight up.

But it was my father.

'William? Hello?'

My father always approaches the phone as if it's a defective loud-hailer where a little extra volume wouldn't go amiss. He also harbours deep uncertainties as to its power to link up with the person he's calling, not unreasonably given that he specialises in wrong numbers and, consequently, it very seldom does. Half the time he calls me it's the wrong number and who he really wants to talk to is the vet, or my brother, or the bank manager.

'Hi, dad.'

'Hello?'

'Hello.'

'Oh, hello, William.' He seemed relieved to have sorted out my identity and his voice relaxed. We talked about our weekends. He'd been pottering around. I'd been pottering around. He filled me in on what my brother's been up to. My father makes a point of this when he calls. Sometimes he gets carried away and fills me in on what I've been up to as well. All comes of living on his own surrounded by woolly old academics. Dad's a lecturer at Cambridge, although he doesn't lecture much any more. He spends most of his time researching little-known French authors. The rest of the time he, well, potters around. He takes his pug dog Toby for walks; he writes; he goes to the pub. He filled me in on what Toby had been up to, which being a pug wasn't all that much, before asking if he could meet me for lunch next Friday.

'I'll be in town for a seminar. I thought we could get together – I've got some news to tell you.'

'Really? Tell me now.'

'I think I'll wait. I'd rather see you. You don't mind?'

'Of course not. I'll look forward to it.'

Mysterious old bugger. I wonder what he's up to? He rang off with obvious relief the moment we'd agreed to meet. He doesn't like the telephone either. Possibly it's hereditary. I started to make myself ready for the night.

Sometimes, particularly when I go to bed in the empty flat and lie there in the gap between waking and sleeping, listening to the little noises of the darkness, I reflect on the way things are shaping up for me here. On paper it's pretty good – job, flat, independence. In reality it's good too, all things considered. I like how I live. But there's something about turning the light out in an empty flat that is irrevocably solitary. You get a similar feeling occasionally when you put something down and think, that'll stay there, exactly there, until I move it again. Do you know what I'm getting at? And then you think, fuck it, living alone's got a million things going for it. As long as you don't reckon on doing it for ever.

Dad's doing it for ever. I wonder how he feels when he turns out the light?

My dreams were full of motorcycles and fast-moving consumer goods.

CHAPTER THREE

'Morning, Willie.'

'Morning.'

'You're a bit bleeding previous, incha?'

'Oh, you know. Stuff to do.'

'Cheers, Willie.'

This Willie business. Does anyone have any suggestions? Perhaps I should just raise it with him, have it out. Listen – would you mind not calling me Willie? I don't mind the racing tips, the laboriously related anecdotes, the dirty jokes, the obsessive commentary upon my clothes, my hair, my comings and goings (well I do) – but I object to being called *Willie*.

Ken, the doorman, as I think I've mentioned, treats me with a wholly unwelcome matiness. He particularly likes it if I come in early. I think he sees it as a gesture of solidarity with his ghostly doormanly hours. Talking to him as I wait for the lift I have the uneasy feeling he's on the point of asking me out for a pint, or the weekend.

I had in fact come in fiendishly early to get my act together before the progress meeting. Every Monday we have a progress meeting on Carpet Mania, at nine thirty. It lasts hours. It lasts so long we sometimes have another when we finish to catch up on all the progress we've missed while it's been going on. But halfway through my first cup of tea I got abducted by Miles and taken upstairs for a loo cleaner interrogation. Had I thought about the project over the weekend? Had I looked at those documents? Had I got any key thoughts on the key trends?

At ten past eight in the morning I don't have any key thoughts on anything, but I bodged and bluffed to Miles' partial satisfaction, or at least until he got bored. He seemed to approve of my having bought those competitive products on Saturday, and asked me questions about *'stocking strategy'* and *'facings'*. Then he went on to talk about *'weighted rate of sale'* and *'forward out of stock'*.

After a while I said, 'Sorry, Miles... what are you talking about?'

'...what?'

'I'm afraid I'm not familiar with some of those terms.'

'What terms?'

'All those ones you were using. I haven't come across them.'

This clean-chestedness didn't go down as well as it might. Miles rolled his eyes and requested of the potted fern why they sent him children to work with.

'What do you work on at the moment, for Christ's sake?'

'Carpet Mania.'

'Is that it? Nothing else?'

'That's it.'

'Right.' He got brisk again. 'You'll have to go on an FMCG data course. I'll talk to Mike. Meantime, find out what you can from these books. It won't be much; they're all crap. Just keep your mouth shut when you meet the client, all right? He'll think he's walked into a kindergarten, not an advertising agency. Which reminds me. Scott and Jerry are coming in at three, so get a room set up. And run a check on the competitive marketing spends over the last two years. Get the American data too. And the Asian. We'll need the competitive products – did you bring them in?'

'No.'

'Get hold of them. And make sure you've got all the briefing notes from last week, especially the qualitative research. Get your secretary to fix some refreshments; Jerry likes chocolate biscuits – the oaty kind, not the plain ones.'

'Who are Scott and Jerry?'

'Scott's the marketing manager; Jerry's the product manager for bleaches and colorants. You'll be dealing with both of them. There are biographies in the company literature.' He tapped a thick booklet marked *'AKL: Professionals in the Lavatory'*.

'What does AKL stand for?' I asked.

'Originally, Arthur Kessler Lavatory Products. Founded in 1967; went public four years ago. Big in public sector and industrial hygiene. They make a lot of paper products, also lavatory brushes. And they source bleach, rim blocks and so on for some of the key multiples.'

'What about this "Professionals in the Lavatory" business?'

'Corporate slogan. Ignore it.'

'Right,' he said, snapping open a thick file: 'UK consumer penetration audit.'

Half an hour later I came out practically on my hands and knees under half a hundredweight of additional documentation. Now I know how Miles keeps his office so clear – there really is nothing in there. It's all somewhere else. It's all in my office.

I got to my progress meeting ten minutes late, apologising in all directions. When I emerged again at five to twelve Miles was standing by my partition with a stack more data.

'I found this in archives. You should go through it – mostly sales, but you never know what else might have got chucked in.' He dumped it on my desk, already submerged under a yard of shit accumulated since breakfast. As if in response the phone sang out lustily from behind a thicket of letters and internal memos. Executive stress!... Miles was hovering impatiently to tell me something else. I fished out the receiver. It was Hippo to tell me that all the space he'd booked in Saturday's papers had accidentally gone into Sunday's papers instead. He wasn't altogether clear why. The rep had been drunk. So had Hippo. He was negotiating for compensation. The second I put down the phone it went off again with a cackle. Miles exhaled noisily. It was my secretary, Vanessa.

'Brodie? I've got Mike Rigby on the line from Carpet Mania. Says he's been trying to reach you all morning.'

'Right. Put him on.'

'He sounds ever so pissed off,' said Vanessa, putting him on.

'Hello? Hello? William Brodie? Where have you been all morning? Did you see Sunday's papers? Hello?'

Fed up waiting, Miles began to talk simultaneously into my other ear.

'Have you got that attitudinal research in here? Jerry's been on the phone about it.'

'Hello? Hello?'

'Is this it?'

'What I'd like to know is, what the bloody hell is the point of advertising a sale on Saturday on Sunday? What you supposed to do when you see the ad? Get in a time machine?'

'Ah – it was a computer error,' I said. 'We're negotiating for a full refund.'

'I'll take this,' said Miles, reaching in front of my nose.

'I don't want a fucking refund! I want them in court!'

There was a crash, followed by the dialling tone's derisory raspberry. My client had terminated the call. Conceivably, judging by the crash, he'd terminated the telephone. Miles had gone. I sat back in the chair staring moodily at the detritus around me. My desk looked like an unlit bonfire. Then I tittered. It was rather comical, running all those ads designed to goad the nation into buying discount carpets, the day after the sale ended. All those hysterical headlines, those never to be repeated bargains...

'What you laughing at?' enquired Vanessa, sticking her head over the top of my parapet. I told her. 'Fuck!' she said. 'No wonder he was peeved.'

She tripped back up the floor, a line of snorts and guffaws announcing the spread of the story. Everyone loves a fuck-up. I have to get off this account. I don't have *time* for it any more. If I don't get off it I'm going to fuck it up. I'll talk to Mike Sharp about it. Yeah, that's what I'll do. Better still, I'll talk to Miles about it. Better yet, get Miles to talk to Mike about it.

Digging around in my drawer to find a note pad I encountered my sandwich from Friday nestling fruitily in a bed of paper clips and bits of fluff. It put ideas in my head.

Twenty minutes later I was bolted into a disused conference room taking record-breaking mouthfuls of curried turkey on granary with mango chutney.

'Let me introduce your account manager,' Miles was saying: 'William Brodie.'

I stepped up self-consciously, hand outstretched. Unbeknown to me at the time of eating, a large portion of curried turkey had exited my sandwich via, in order, my collar, my tie, my crotch and my right kneecap. Miles drew my attention to the muddy smears a minute before the meeting, and also directed me to the offending chunk sitting brownly in my turn-up. I seemed to be basted in curried turkey. I did what I could with a hanky, but the traces lingered.

Scott gave me a stare and a good hard executive handshake. He was youngish, about thirty-one or thirty-two, quite slim and well turned out, with that fishy, ambitious look you see in the eyes of determined careerists. He had black springy hair and a little freshly grown moustache. I've never really understood moustaches. What is it that prompts people to train those little grubs under their noses? I think it's to make them look mature. I know Edward gave it a go once.

But it didn't make him look mature. It made him look ridiculous. It used to make him sneeze.

Jerry formed a distinct contrast. For one thing he was enormously fat, in a roly-poly, eat-too-much-drink-too-much way (as opposed to the genetic joke or glandular accident kind of way). I'd seldom seen so much product manager all in one place. He looked like a down-at-heel Emperor Nero dressed up in a suit like a badly wrapped parcel. We shook hands: it was like gripping a parcel of liver. 'Very pleased to meet you,' he enthused, standing on my toe. 'Funny, I've got a friend called William Brodie. Used to play rugby together – I'll have to introduce you. Ha ha.'

'Ha ha.'

'Brodie, this is Katherine Napier, Jerry's assistant,' said Miles.

'Slave!' said Jerry.

'Katherine's training with us,' said Scott.

Katherine Napier was about my age. She seemed to be carrying all Jerry's things, like a porter or concubine. Jerry wrestled a bursting briefcase from her and planked it down on the table. He began to delve around inside. Scott sat down and got out a little electronic organiser. I fooled around with coffee and teaspoons.

Scott said, 'Let's begin.'

Scott began by informing the meeting that last Thursday's board meeting had acceded to his recommendation to change the company slogan from 'Professionals in the Lavatory' to '*The* Professionals in the Lavatory.' This, he emphasised, was the direction the company was going. It was a mission statement for the new millennium. He looked at each of us in turn as he said it, as if to make sure everyone was taking it seriously and not bursting into giggles. Miles said it was obviously a key development and we'd keep it uppermost when developing advertising. Jerry smoked and nodded and ate biscuits. Katherine Napier seemed to be in a trance. I wrote it down on my little pad.

Next, Scott enjoined the meeting to dire security. He didn't, he said, want to *hear* the word elephant from now on. Understood? Solemn nodding. It was like being at a masonic initiation. I thought he might want us to swear, like boy scouts, but he seemed satisfied. He launched off into a heavily caveated timetable of development for Project Camel. If such and such was ready by x, then so and so could be ready by y. If this research was positive we could go on to that. Otherwise we'd have to go back to the other.

I hadn't the faintest what he was on about, except that a lot hung on the outcome of a whole series of devilishly complicated bits of research. Miles piled in and talked at length about *'key development programmes'* and *'critical path structures'*. Then Jerry joined in too, muddying the water still further with a string of ifs and buts and what ifs and on the other hands. After a while Miles looked up at me and asked if I'd made a note of all that. Note of all what? I flourished my pad, covered in scribbled contingencies and crossings out. After that I lost track of things altogether. I have this tendency to blank out if I don't do or say anything for more than half an hour. Also, I was feeling unaccountably drowsy and kept floating in and out of consciousness. Why? I'd spent virtually all weekend asleep. Maybe that's why. Sleep's *tiring*. Luckily Jerry overturned the milk jug at a key juncture or I swear I'd have dropped off. Not that anyone paid any attention. After the first couple of minutes all the talk took place between Scott at one end of the table and Miles at the other, with Jerry in between like an umpire, chipping in with contributions that the others barely even acknowledged. I didn't say anything. Nor did Katherine. We sat like children at a dinner party with nothing to do and no one to talk to, waiting for the grown ups to finish the meal. And something of a meal it was in many ways, with Jerry hoovering down the chocolate biscuits and Scott grimly lowering cup after cup of bitter black coffee.

At four o'clock Mike Sharp and Paul Short made a state appearance. Mike talked powerfully about the retail environment for five minutes. He mentioned the explosion of choices facing the housewife as she walked down the aisle. He asked Jerry what brand of washing up liquid his mother bought. Jerry couldn't immediately recall and spent half a minute humming and hawing and changing his mind, so I acted as stooge for a second time. *'Exactly,'* said Mike, 'she goes for the brand leader.' Paul yawned and fidgeted and looked out the window. Clearly he'd heard it before. When Mike ran out of things to say Scott thanked them both formally and they went away again.

The meeting was evidently over.

'What about a drink?' said Miles.

'No thanks,' and 'Love one,' said Scott and Jerry simultaneously. There was a moment's embarrassed pause.

'We need to get back to Bristol,' said Scott.

'Yes, we need to get back to Bristol,' said Jerry, emphatically, as if someone was trying to stop them.

'I'll get you a cab,' said Miles. 'Brodie – get a cab.'

We trooped out and stood by the lifts.

'Till Wednesday,' said Scott. The lift arrived and opened with a *bing bong*. ('Blimey!' said Jerry. 'Space age!') I went down with them to hail a taxi, wedged between the controls and Jerry and his briefcase. Then I spent a diverting ten minutes on tip-toe in the street waving at stony-faced cabbies. At last an amber lozenge hove into view.

'Bye then.'

'Nice to meet you,' called Jerry from inside, a very large goldfish in a small black tank.

'Bye, William,' said Scott, getting in.

'Bye, Brodie,' said Katherine. They were the only words she'd uttered all afternoon.

Then she did the oddest thing. Turned as she was with her face momentarily away from the others, she gripped the bridge of her nose, looked me in the eye and blew, comically puffing out her cheeks. It was like, I don't know, like she was saying: '*Christ*!' Either that or Scott had just farted, and he didn't look the type.

What was all that about? I thought as the lift sucked me back into the building.

I left the office just before eight. All the pubs on the way home were turned inside out: perspiring businessmen in wool suits littered the pavements, clutching glasses and briefcases, shouting stories at one another. In every crowd there were a dozen Jerries and a dozen Scotts. The Jerries were the shiny faced ones with rolled up sleeves and ties undone, shirts coming untucked at the back, tummies leering over their waistbands. They ate great fistfuls of dry roasted peanuts and drank pints of lager, smoking cigarettes and small, smelly cigars. The Scotts kept their jackets on and their ties done up and drank prissy little halves out of designer bottles.

Scott only joined AKL a month ago. He got the job that Jerry wanted. Jerry was too untalented. Not like Scott. Scott's a whizz kid. He trained at some whopping pan-European conglomerate as brand man on their cat food division. According to Miles, Scott was the man behind the launch of 'Puss E Cat', the cat food developed *specifically* for the small cat. Nice one, Scottie. If I ever get a small cat I'll buy some. Come to think of it, do I remember seeing a tin in my father's fridge once upon a time just after it was launched? He can't have thought Toby was a small cat? Small yes, cat no. Though Toby's diet always has been a haphazard affair. He tends to get a bit of whatever Dad's eating at any particular time – here a sausage, there a sandwich, the occasional cup of tea. What's more he thrives on it. So does Dad. The pair are a picture of quite unreasonable good health.

On Oxford Street I took to the road, bypassing the frotteurs and pickpockets competing on the pavement. Buses trundled past like great chunks of Lego, giving me a wide berth; taxis veered and tooted testily. Then into Tottenham Court Road with its three furious lanes of one way traffic, like a section of motorway ripped up and planked down between the exploding bins and Hi Fi stores. And thence, presently, Bloomsbury with its shabby little hotels full of wilting tourists, the broken pavements and scrofulous pigeons, the beggars, the tramp fraternity. I met one or two regulars. There was the black chap with the plastic bag on his head. He was also wearing a long woollen overcoat, which he seems to keep especially for hot weather. I keep wanting to ask him, how did it work out like this – for you? How did events arrange themselves? And why, specifically, the plastic bag on the head? I'd like to know just in case it happens to me. I mean, who knows?

I ventured a hello, which he returned with a gape. Perhaps he's one of those guys who's been put back into the community. If so, why? I don't think he's up to it, if you want my frank opinion. Come to that the community isn't in such great shape either. Both could use a bit of rehabilitation.

That evening I sat pondering on the roof. I watched the sun setting, not a very pretty sight. Sunsets should not be brown. Orange, yes. Pink I'll buy. But not *brown*. Fair enough, there was a hint of pink, a touch of orange, but the overall effect was one big dirty smear the size of the city. Exhaust fumes. We'd have less of that if everyone caught the bus. But less and less people are catching the bus. The buses are unreliable. They're unreliable on account of all the cars. The cars get in the way of the buses. Hence the unreliability. So people use their cars. Hence the brown sunsets. It's a problem. Then there's the garbage, the litter. It is getting worse, isn't it? Or isn't it? Not to mention the dogshit. By any standards, actually, London's disgusting. The place is a toilet. The thing is, *I like it here*. I deplore the filth, the squalor, the down and outedness, but I also crave it.

Perhaps I just like living in a toilet?

Actually, I know I haven't been doing this elephant business all that long – and I'd hate you to start drawing conclusions from this – but I think I may be developing something of a toilet fixation. To be truthful, it always has been an area of some interest for me. Some of my happiest moments have been on the toilet. Be honest – haven't yours? No one can get at you when you're on the toilet. This afternoon, after the meeting, when Carpet Mania were baying for the head of the person who ruined their weekend, I retreated for a quiet quarter of an hour to the gents next to the lifts. Inside the cool cubicle I could just hear the uproar from beyond the double doors and the snuffle of the traffic without. The hiss and sputter of the cleaning sluices was very calming. I had a sit and contemplated the tiles, the paper dispenser, so excellently stocked up, the little gap between the wall and the floor (why do they have that gap? has anyone ever worked it out?)... And the wonderful thing about it is, the unbeatable fact of the matter is that *nobody minds!* Nobody objects! How can they? They could object if you went for a walk. They could object if you had a lie-down, or a massage, or a game of darts... *but they can't object if you go to the toilet.* It's foolproof! Give it a go if you don't believe me. Go on. Go into work tomorrow. As soon as you fancy a breather, go to the toilet. Stay there for, ooh, half an hour. When you come out and your boss asks where you've been for the last half an hour, look him – or her – in the eye and say, fearlessly: 'In the toilet.' I guarantee it. The longer, in fact, the better. You don't ask too many questions of someone who's just been in the toilet for half an hour. You don't want the details.

I didn't just loaf about in there, mind you. I took a file in with me. I sat on the toilet and boned up on The Toilet, its history and development. I discovered – and this you will never believe – that the toilet as we know it today, or water closet, was invented by a German by the name of Thomas Crapper. How about that? God's honest truth. Well good on you, Thomas. Mankind salutes you. I also read that in an average lifetime of seventy-five years, the average human being will spend, on average, *over nine thousand hours* on the toilet, or roughly speaking, a year. A year! On the toilet! And get through, furthermore, in the region of fifty-seven miles of lavatory paper. That's here to Brighton. And that's just on average. It doesn't take into account curry or medical disorders.

It isn't very grown up, all this, is it? Perhaps I *am* getting obsessed with the lavatory... But I need to know this stuff. I need to know it so I can do my job. I need to steep myself in it. It *isn't* very grown up, but the job I do isn't very grown up. Who cares?

Oh and get this: the Japanese have invented the paperless toilet. I read it in a magazine. It's all done by jets of water and hot air. Not only that, your efforts are analysed by the in-toilet computer and a read-out is supplied giving blood pressure, pulse, urine acidity, etc. You can even get ones that fix an appointment with your doctor as the need arises. (I wonder how I'd get on in one of those? It'd probably fix an appointment directly with the undertaker: *You died half an hour ago...*) You can see why they're taking over the world.

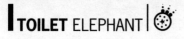

I have to say that my competitive loo cleaner comparisons put Elephant a mile out ahead of the rest. There's something about the way the trunk curves so invitingly from the ears that just begs you to go and stick it up your lavatory. In my opinion AKL have come up with a winner. Further to recommend it, it really does get the loo clean, with, what's more, a pleasant aroma to boot. Kind of zesty, with a hint of pine. I wouldn't half mind wearing it as aftershave. I've smelt worse. (I've worn worse.) Yes, overall, taking everything into consideration, in the final analysis and at the end of the day, Elephant will do the business.

Don't believe me? *Watch*.

CHAPTER FOUR

The presenter was having difficulty with his slides, which kept going backwards or popping up in the wrong order.

'Now let's have a look at the results of the odour check,' he said. The screen read: 'EXPECTATIONS OF COLOUR'. 'Ah,' said the presenter. 'Well why don't I cover off colour first. As you can see, forty-two per cent of the sample thought the colour was just right. Twenty-one per cent thought it was too blue, but seventeen found it not blue enough.'

'What about the other – er – twenty percent?' said Jerry.

'They had no opinion.'

'Really?' Jerry looked astonished. Imagine all those people not having an opinion! However he didn't seem to have an opinion on them not having an opinion, so Miles stepped in and said, 'That's consistent for a household category such as this – especially in the C2D social range. It isn't a problem.'

'That seventeen per cent's a problem,' said Scott. 'Colour equates with efficacy in the consumer's mind. A weak colour equals a weak product.'

Miles shrugged. 'So make it bluer.'

'But twenty-one per cent think it's too blue already,' said Jerry.

'It can't be too blue,' said Scott.

I was sitting in this meeting at AKL's offices in Bristol. I call it a meeting, in fact it was more of a rally. A whole tribe of technical, production and sales people had tagged along besides the marketing team, and there we all were stacked round a grotty little table in some airless hole watching the research company making a hash of their presentation.

The presentation was on *Consonance Testing*. What this means, as far as I can gather, is that you get a bunch of consumers together and tell them that you're thinking of launching a lavatory cleaner shaped like an elephant. They express varying amounts of interest in the notion (unless of course they don't have an opinion). Then you show them the product. They take a look at it, sniff it, turn it upside down, go off with it, squirt it up their lavatories... For all you know they spread it on toast and eat it. They do what they like with it. Then you check the *consonance* between their opinions before (if they had any), and their opinions after. As far as I can tell if there's a lot of consonance, you're onto a good thing. If there isn't, you're not.

The presenter was getting into a terrible tangle. Every time he put up a slide it would say something different to what he wanted it to say. When he talked about cleaning power the slide said odour. When he talked about directionality the slide said cleaning power. And when he talked about odour the slide, for some reason, said: 'PRESENTATION TO JAY'S POTTED MEATS AND POULTRY (Jan 1996)'.

Jerry, needless to say, kept piping up with questions, all of which Scott or Miles would brutally squash, usually before the presenter could open his mouth. After a while in fact the presenter more or less shut up while Scott and Miles swapped assertions. Scott had himself all set up at the end of the table like some kind of stipendiary magistrate. There's another one that's into power seating. When we came in he made straight for the chair and got out his little organiser. By way of contrast, Jerry came in loaded to the eyebrows with files and reports and crap of all sorts, which he set out in great slabs all over the table. Every chart sent him flapping through some document so he could verify it against his own data and ask more questions.

Me, I kept mum. I think it's a good policy. In my experience most of the people in meetings don't say anything, except the hotshots and the idiots. Nobody said anything in this one except Miles and Scott and Jerry. Occasionally a poker-faced production man would pull his chin and say he doubted if he could do whatever it was that needed doing. The sales guys sat in a huddle, gawping uncomprehendingly at the charts. Katherine Napier stared brazenly out of the window.

'Finally, attitudes to the elephant-trunk spigot nozzle,' said the presenter. The screen flashed up 'PROPENSITY TO PURCHASE AT 75P', and he gave a little moan.

'The sample was, statistically speaking, unanimous in their dislike of the ribbed trunk-nozzle. Sixty-two per cent said it looked "Silly" or agreed with the statement 'I don't like it.' Seventeen per cent thought it looked 'unnatural'. Although it must be added that all those who expressed an opinion commended its directional effectiveness.'

A hot silence followed the pronouncement. The presenter sat down. The sales people looked at each other uneasily. Somebody coughed.

'What about the moulded ears?' said Jerry.

'Never mind the ears,' said Scott. 'The ears are secondary to the trunk.'

'They quite liked the ears,' said the presenter.

'Was it the trunk *per se*,' demanded Miles, 'or was it the ribbing?'

'Well...both, really. They just didn't like it.'

'But on balance, trunk or ribbing?'

'On balance, the ribbing,' said the presenter hopelessly.

'No problem,' said Miles, 'Lose the ribbing.'

'That okay, Brian?' demanded Scott of the production manager.

'Well...' began Brian.

'Course it's okay,' said Scott. 'It's got to be easier to make it without ribbing than with ribbing.'

'Depends,' said Brian.

'Depends on what?'

'The machine. The *tooling*.'

'Get rid of it. I'll clear it with the MD.'

All the eyes on the table swivelled backwards and forwards like spectators at a tennis match every time Scott had a conversation with anyone.

Brian shrugged and returned to his doodle.

'That's that, then,' said Scott decisively. 'Thank you, gentlemen.'

We went for lunch at the staff canteen. On the way over I fell into step with Miles.

'Was that all right? Will they go ahead?'

'Naturally.'

'It's just, I mean, they seemed to chuck out the whole concept. They didn't like the trunk.'

'Bollocks to that. They're just a load of half-wit housewives. We're not going to listen to anything *they* say.'

'Oh.' I walked on for a bit. 'Why do we do the research then?'

'To justify the launch to the board.'

'You mean we don't pay any attention to it at all?'

'Of course we don't. What do you think this is? If the research throws up a problem, fire the researcher. Scott's going to launch this. It's why he's here.'

For lunch I ate a leathery looking salad and a piece of cold pie, followed by tinned fruit and ice-cream. Jerry sat next to me and ate steak and potatoes and pudding and custard and cheese and biscuits. Scott parked himself opposite and talked briskly to Miles about top-end distribution. Everyone seemed to have forgotten about or be ignoring the research presentation and its findings.

'Lovely weather,' somebody said to Jerry.

'Bad for sales,' said Jerry.

'Why's that, Jerry?' I asked.

Jerry turned to me with his cheeks bulging.

'Water conservation,' he said. 'People don't flush the loo as much in hot weather. Frequency of cleaning goes down. Besides, we know from research that people use the lavatory less in summer than in winter. So a summer like this will lose us five, ten per cent on flush colorants and pan treats.'

There didn't seem any way of taking the conversation much further, but I gave it a go. Jerry started eating his biscuits and cheese. He'd get a little biscuit then pack on a wad of butter and drape a big slobbery wedge of Camembert on the top. The biscuit was about five per cent of the final construction.

'Doesn't the hot weather stimulate soft drinks usage?' I asked. 'And so, in due course, er, lavatory usage? If you see what I mean.'

Jerry looked nonplussed. 'Hadn't occurred to me. Maybe you could do a paper on it and fax it down.'

'Ex-factories are down on blocks and colorants,' said Scott suddenly.

It obviously wasn't good news so I shook my head sympathetically.

'Although they're up year on year,' said Scott.

'Good.'

'But we're behind the market as a whole.'

'Ah.'

'We're ahead of target, though.'

'Right.'

'But nowhere near by prediction.'

'No?'

He returned to his plate.

'Anyone for coffee?' said a female voice. Katherine Napier had got up and was jotting down orders on a napkin. I asked for tea.

'I wouldn't. It's powdered. Actually it tastes of coffee. You're better to have coffee. The coffee tastes more like coffee than the tea does.'

'All right.'

She went off to the machine and Jerry gave me a prod.

'Good girl, that,' he said.

'Yes?'

He winked porkily and was on the point of amplifying, but at that moment a change of expression spread across his features and he sneezed explosively. With surprising agility he whipped a little bottle of nasal spray from an inside pocket and rammed it up one nostril. Then he followed up with a great, gross bubbling nose blow.

'Hay fever,' he gasped.

The moment had passed, thankfully; I went to the machine to give Katherine a hand with the coffee.

'Well?' she said, tapping in the orders. 'What do you think?'

'What about? The research?'

'Not the research. All this.'

'It's...well, it's okay. Do you mean the canteen or the whole thing?'

'The whole thing.'

'Interesting,' I said warily.

'Here,' she said. 'That's Mike Scott's, that's Miles', that's Jerry's. Got them?'

'Got them.'

Two seconds after grasping the bendy plastic beakers the heat transmitted roastingly to my finger tips. I made a heroic plunge to the table, practically throwing the lot into Scott's face when I got there. It was terrible coffee. I looked round at the other tables. What a dump. Was that what Katherine Napier was getting at? All around AKL employees sat slumped over plates and cups, smoking listlessly and looking at the clock. Another thing about the place – the company obviously has a policy of active discrimination in favour of the handicapped and disadvantaged. Everywhere you looked there'd be somebody with a hair lip or a fucked up spine, or no ears, or something. As I sat a dwarf came stumping by with a tray... Admirable, of course, but faintly unsettling with it: like being in a mixture between a clinic, an asylum and a school refectory.

People began to shamble off. Jerry took me off for a factory visit. On the way he stopped off at his office. I'm sure he didn't need to stop off at his office. I think he wanted to demonstrate what an in-demand guy he was.

'Any messages, Jean?' he enquired of the huge exhausted secretary by the door. 'No.'

He made some calls just the same. I know mine is nothing to write home about, but his office was absolutely, definitively the most dispiriting and crappiest I'd ever been in. For a start it was about the size of a smallish airing cupboard. Secondly, it was entirely full of rubbish. Thirdly, with Jerry in there, it was entirely full of Jerry. I practically had to sit on his knee.

Over his buckled and loaded desk was a poster of a rhinoceros saying, 'I may have my faults, but being wrong isn't one of them.'

Outside was much the same. Far too many people and desks and machines and waste-paper baskets in far too small an area, with photographs all over the place of dogs and kittens and cartoon koala bears, and gags about not having to be crazy to work here but it helps. Next to Jean's desk, sagging over a brimming ashtray, was stuck a woolly mammoth with 'I need a hug' embroidered on its bottom. All the sadness of every office in all the universe seemed collected in that woolly mammoth.

Eventually Jerry got off the phone and marched me through miles more corridor until we reached the entrance to the factory, where we put on overalls. 'Don't touch anything,' he said. 'And don't breathe in by the acids. Come on.'

I worked in a factory once, in Acton. Holiday job. It was a blotting paper factory. I was a quality inspector. People would wheel pallets full of blotting paper up to me and I'd say, 'That looks fine.' This was the extent of my responsibilities. I quit after two weeks.

This one was a lot bigger. This one was huge. Thousands of pipes and bits and pieces ran hither and thither connecting up a line of gratifyingly large cauldrons full of witches' brew. Jerry rattled off a string of chemical names as we passed them, becoming inaudible as we approached a thumping generator in the centre powering a host of satellite machines. Blokes in overalls prodded things with spanners. One was stirring a big vat full of slime with a long wooden spoon. I half expected him to take a mouthful.

'What's that?' I bellowed, pointing to a particularly rowdy machine.

'Bottling,' yelled Jerry. 'Hundred a minute.'

The noise abated a little on the other side, where a line of Asian women slapped labels onto plastic bottles. They eyed us torpidly, and one of them stuck a label on upside down.

'Is that all they do?' I asked Jerry.

'Yes of course it is,' he said, affrontedly.

He took me into a new building.

'This is where we'll be producing Camel,' he said. 'We'll source the fluid from existing capacity, then perfume it here. All the packaging machinery's brand new. From Denmark. You should mention that in the advertising.'

I nodded. I couldn't think of anything sillier. *New Toilet Elephant! The revolutionary lavatory cleaner that's bottled by a new machine that comes from Denmark...*

'Right,' said Jerry. 'Time I was off. I'll get Katherine to run you to the station.'

I thanked him for everything and he disappeared back into the factory. I ambled about a bit in the sun. Katherine didn't show. Behind me the factory gave off muffled throbs and a deafening siren went off. I was struck by the workers coming off shift, their cheerfulness as they emerged into the light, shouting taunts and cheerios at co-workers, lighting up and unrolling newspapers. They looked jolly enough.

'They'll all be out of work next month. Poor bastards.'

It was Katherine. She was standing behind me, watching the exodus. The keys to Jerry's Mondeo jinked from her finger.

'I'm sorry to hear that. Why?'

She shrugged. 'Scottie's been having a go at the factory manager to cut costs. Part of the rationalisation.'

She didn't seem inclined to go anywhere, but sat down on a drum arranging her legs in the sun. We talked on for a little while, about AKL and the newly imposed rationalisation. She made it abundantly clear she wasn't into her work; she seemed to take it for granted that I wasn't either.

'So tell me,' I said eventually. 'What was that funny face all about? In London the other day?'

'That meeting. Wasn't it priceless? All that stuff Miles came out with about The Toilet in The Nineties, with nobody allowed to say Elephant and you falling asleep in the corner.'

'It's got its comic side,' I admitted.

'Every side's got its comic side. The whole thing's one big comic side. Blimey,' she said, looking at her watch. 'We'd better get going.'

She drove haphazardly through the rush-hour traffic, almost exclusively in third gear, dropping me at the station in time for the four fifteen.

I caught the Paddington train, availing myself of the full afternoon tea service in first class, complete with crumpets and raisin bread. It wasn't half bad. I still can't get over travelling first class. I start up guiltily when the inspector appears before remembering I'm not a student any more. Though travelling first class isn't all roses. Loud conversations break out between boring reps on their way back from ghastly appointments. The man sitting opposite me, making no small display of the facility, called his office repeatedly on a portable phone. The one next to him muttered darkly about two-year projections into a dictaphone... Why don't they take it easy and look out the window? Not that all of my co-passengers were business-minded. There was a brisk two-way traffic to the buffet. By four twenty every other table was kitted out with cans and miniatures; by five twenty-five half the carriage was pie-eyed. I sipped my tea primly as a group to my right got noisier. One of them, 'Dave', had managed to get hold of a guard's cap and went lurching down the carriage calling for tickets. His air of paunchy dishevelment carried enough BR authenticity to fool a couple of passengers into groping for their wallets. How his mates roared! There they sat, lager lords of the carriage, cans hoisted for Dave's triumphant return. Later they all got off at Reading and Dave reverted abruptly to being a sad, fat, lonely little drunk.

I didn't bother going back to the agency. I hopped in a cab and went home. The flat greeted me in dusty stillness; the strains of Connie's radio sending up fruity voices from below. I wound the clock in the sitting room, which had been cheerfully reading ten to eleven for the past three weeks, watered my limp and runtish pot plants, and gave the old place a bit of a clean round. It gets amazingly grubby considering how tiny it is. Dirt multiplies in the air. Keeping yourself clean in London's quite an undertaking too, I find, demanding a shower either end of the day as well as a regular ear, fingernail and nostril valeting service. If you want to keep reasonably fit into the bargain, why, that's a whole new set of disciplines. Just keeping the whole show on the road, it takes up so much *time*. Don't you find? I had intended, for example, to make myself a proper meal with what was left of the nosh I bought at the weekend. But by the time I'd cleaned the place, and cleaned myself, and got changed, and ironed a shirt, I simply couldn't be doing with it. I despatched half a loaf of white sliced bread standing by the sink till I stopped feeling hungry, then drank some mineral water.

I took a final pull on the bottle and burped prodigiously. By the way, I know what you're thinking. Forget it. She isn't my type. Anyway, she'll be going out with someone. Mind you, there's no denying she's attractive. What was Jerry getting at, do you think, with all that winking and nudging? She can't be having it away with *him*. Who else is there?

I had an affair last Christmas with a girl at work. Carina, her name was. (For some reason all the women at SSA have names ending in 'a': I think it must be a condition of employment.) Carina was a temp. She was breathtakingly beautiful. It was an unmitigated disaster. It's difficult going out with people at work. It's difficult enough *working* with people at work. After a spell she shacked up with Tod from accounts. Then she left.

Edward phoned and we went out for a Tandoori. I wasn't hungry but I shovelled it down companionably. He wanted to take me on to a club to meet this Lucy of his, but I gave it a miss. He tried to persuade me, telling me I was boring and never did anything after half past nine any more (he's right, I don't) – which I resisted. I watched the tail light of his bike dwindling away down Holborn towards Oxford Street. I wasn't sorry. I didn't feel like standing in a nightclub trying to make myself heard by a strange girl. And Edward's girlfriends tend to be strange girls.

I had other reasons too. To tell you the truth, I was beginning to regret the chicken korma. Or could it have been the mushroom lohbi? I lay on my hot sheets one hour later listening to the goings on in my insides, and I mean listening; Connie could probably hear it too, the popping and fizzing, the slurping and gurgling, the frankly astonishing flatulence. Oof...It's just as well I don't have anything in the girlfriend department myself at the present. You'd have to be a saint in heaven above to put up with this. Perhaps that's what I should give up. Perhaps I should give up *curry*. Perhaps I should give up curry and start dating girls again. Resolutions swam before me... Perhaps I should start jogging again. Perhaps I should give up drinking (again)... Perhaps I should phone my father more often...

Perhaps I should, perhaps I should, said my head as my guts rearranged, drifting in and out of unconsciousness.

CHAPTER FIVE

I woke with a jolt at quarter to nine in an uncontrollably smelly bedroom with an overpowering need to go to the lavatory *right now*. You couldn't call that indigestion last night. That was insurrection. That was my stomach saying: look – enough is enough... It wasn't simply over-eating either. The korma, I decided, was at the root of the problem. The korma was *dodgy*. I perched gingerly on the seat with the hole, calculating how late in I'd be. One thing was clear: I was in here for a good half-hour to forty-five minutes... I wonder how much time is lost to industry this way? You often see the figures for alcohol. Never for Curry. They should sub-list it: *Curry – 12,049 working days...* I hate being late in to work. I don't have the excuse of distance. The impression most people have formed is that I live practically next door; which, of course, relatively speaking, I do. Just there's this obstacle course in between called central London. I got on a bus at nine thirty-five, getting off again at nine forty-five having proceeded forty yards. The road was being taken up opposite the Russell Hotel. New phone lines. For a spell I walked backwards, barging into tourists and traffic cones, scanning for taxis. Then I gave up and set off through the constipated traffic at a shuffling jog trot.

It's incredible, isn't it? You can jet halfway across the planet in practically the time it takes to order a gin and tonic, but can you get across London on a Friday morning? Can you *bollocks*.

It was the same in every side street and hidey-hole I cut down. Illegally parked cars blended indistinguishably with legitimate ones in one great hot huddle. The only way of telling the difference was that half of them were clamped. STOP! DO

NOT ATTEMPT TO MOVE THIS VEHICLE... Move it? Don't make me laugh. Clamping, now there's a bright idea. Clamping – nice one. An ingenious solution to inner city traffic congestion. Most of these had probably been clamped with the driver in there and the engine running. But I'm driving! I'm on my way to so-and-so! You're not on your way nowhere, matey boy. Only the despatch riders, cocked on their over-glanded mounts, nudged spasmodically through the crush. I watched one accelerate away from a light, then concertina terrifyingly to a halt in front of a pushchair shoved into its path. Deafeningly it throttled up and burned off again. I sometimes envy Edward his lifestyle but I don't envy the bike work. It can't be that enjoyable, all front brake and first gear, and dangerous with it. The life-expectancy of the full-timers must be broadly on a par with infantry officers in 1917. Ay! The things you do to pay the bills... The things you keep doing, day in, day out, for ever – until you die, or retire, or go mad; or all three, one after the other.

I eventually found a cab on Regent's Street, which put me out by the agency just before eleven. Ken the doorman gave me a knowing leer and looked pantomimically at his watch. I rode the lift in sweaty anticipation with my stomach lending a light musical commentary. Bio-chemical experiments were taking place in the echo chamber beneath my solar plexus... And then the lift ushered me out with a particularly strident *bing bong*, just as a bubble of wind the size of a party balloon welled up imperiously next to my colon.

Miles and Mike Sharp were standing talking in the lobby.

Immediately I improvised. There's no point in half measures if you're going to bullshit. I told them my flat had been broken into. I painted pictures of scattered clothing and frowning forensics. Up the fire escape, yeah. Never heard a thing, no. Professional job. Lost much? Oh, stereo, TV, a bit of cash... It seemed to go okay. I think they bought it. At least, Mike said 'Too bad', and lit a cigarette, and Miles said, 'Right.' When Mike had gone on he said,

'I've had Jerry on the phone. He wants you to fax over the paper you promised him on soft drinks consumption and its effect on lavatory usage.'

'Does he? We only talked about it yesterday. Anyway, I wasn't really being serious.'

'Jerry's serious. You'd better get him something.'

'Carpet Mania have been on the phone since nine,' said Vanessa, when I got to my desk. 'And your father called, and your brother.'

Well, first things first, I thought, and phoned my brother. There was a pause while the girl at the other end tried to find him, during which a telephonic rendering of the Mozart horn concerto came on the line. My brother works at this swanky computer outfit in the Docklands, where he also lives, in a hideous and costly new development on the Isle of Dogs. He's nine years older than me, married with a kid (my niece, Rebecca – a sweetheart), and a dog, and cat, and a car with spoilers the size of bunk beds. All the trimmings. To all intents and purposes he's an uncle rather than a brother, but we meet up every couple of months or so, and I give bears to Rebecca.

'Stephen? It's William.'

'Hi, William. Listen, I can't stay. Dad's been on the phone. He'd forgotten where he was meeting you, so he said he'd be at your flat at quarter to one. All right?'

'What? Oh, the silly old sod.'

'It's pretty close to where you work, isn't it?'

'Well yes, theoretically. But the traffic's terrible just now. Took me over an hour to get in this morning.'

'Yes?' said my brother disinterestedly. I don't think they have traffic in Docklands. 'Well, look...see you soon, all right?'

'Hold on. Can I reach him somewhere?'

'Don't think so. Take care.'

As soon as I put the phone down it went off again.

'Brodie. Oh, hi Jerry. Yes, Miles said. I'll get it off to you as soon as I...by two o'clock. I see. Well could you tell him I'm just tracking down the data? Thanks then...yup...cheers.'

The phone went again.

'Brodie? Vivienne here. Where have you been? Have you got the artwork for tomorrow's insertions? Where is it?'

'I'll fax it down. Yes, I'm sorry it's late. Right, right...yes, we're taking steps to ensure they appear tomorrow...sure, sure...right, right...I'll get onto it.'

And again.

'Yes? I mean, Brodie speaking.'

'Hello? Hello?'

'Oh. Hi, dad. I'm glad you called. I've just been talking to Stephen.'

'Hello?' The line crackled. 'William? I'm afraid it's rather a poor line. I can't hear you.'

I raised my voice. 'Dad, listen. Don't go to the flat. Meet me outside The Ritz at one. Okay? Outside The Ritz.'

'I'll meet you at your flat,' bellowed my father.

'No! Outside the Ritz!' I shouted.

'*What?*'

'Out-Side-The-RITZ!' I howled, despairingly.

'Oh, The Ritz,' said my father, suddenly normal. 'All right then. How nice. I'd better go now – my ten pee's run out.'

I sank back exhausted into my chair and the phone went again.

'WHAT? Oh, hello, Miles. Yeah, sorry about that, the bloody phone's been going ever since I... Yes, he called me a second ago... Well yes, for Christ's sake, I'll do it... Okay, I'll do that too... Right then. Bye.'

Scott had been on to Jerry again. Jerry had been on to Miles again. They seemed to have a major bee in their bonnets about this soft drinks thing. Jerry kept telling me, and clearly Miles too, that he felt we could be *missing a trick*. What kind of trick? In what way missing it? I dug out an ancient chart from an old presentation I found in a drawer and cobbled together some balls about relative soft drink consumption patterns across the past few years matched against average June/July temperatures. Actually the June/July temperatures bit was interesting. Summers definitely are hotting up, you know. Did you know that the ten warmest summers on record all occurred over the last fifteen years? According to the met office, if the trend carries on, the average July temperature in London in the year 2050 will be the same as it is now in Florida. Florida? That's in the tropics, isn't it? Blimey. Does that mean the North Pole will defrost? I absent-mindedly turned the fridge off in my flat a month ago and the results were indescribable. Connie can supply you with the details. I imagine things would be broadly comparable if the ice caps went. Everybody with a suntan, and Essex a jacuzzi.

I couldn't pursue the train of thought. The phone trilled at thirty-second intervals. Taking a break at twelve thirty I paid an experimental pre-lunch visit to the toilet, which passed off reasonably successfully, all things considering. The tum appeared to be subsiding. Mind you, I was still a little doubtful about the concept of lunch. It might be all right. On the other hand, it might not be all right. I mean, who could say? Next door to me in the adjoining cubicle came the sounds of opening tabloid and lowering trousers, followed by a satisfied little grunt and a series of unspeakable ploppings. I made a move. I sneaked down the stairs to avoid being spotted by the lift, and headed out for Piccadilly.

My father wasn't outside The Ritz. I loitered about with gradually mounting impatience until I realised why. He wasn't outside The Ritz because he was inside The Ritz. I could make out the dome of his bald pate and a raised newspaper in a high-backed chair in reception.

'William!' he beamed, rising. 'It *is* good of you to take me here. The last time I came was in 1944, after I came out of the army. Stephen must have told you the news.'

'No?'

'Why, about the new job.'

'No, really, he hasn't said a thing.'

'My dear boy! Come and have a drink and let me fill you in.'

He set off for the bar. Or rather he set off for the ladies' lavatory until a uniformed flunky realigned him. The next thing I knew we were in a cool, leathery suite in front of a little trough of cocktail olives with the flunky taking down the order. And not just any old order: Champagne.

You can imagine all this was taking me somewhat by surprise. My idea had been to wheel him into the Italian off New Bond Street that does three courses and half a litre for six pounds fifty. I don't imagine places like this do anything for six pounds fifty. Cocktail olives, possibly. My father was in extraordinarily high spirits. He gave the order for the champagne with an expectant beam, as if expecting the waiter to say 'Ooh, how nice!' I'd never seen him so elated. When it came some of the bubbles went up his nose and he sneezed with a report like a small bomb. He eyed me with sudden, watery solemnity.

'I've got a fellowship,' he said; and his face re-wreathed itself in grins.

'Dad, that's fantastic! Congratulations.'

'I could have told you last week, but I preferred to see you. I wanted someone to celebrate with.'

We clinked glasses ceremonially. It didn't surprise me to learn he'd already had a couple at the pub round the corner. I wouldn't call my father a serious drinker, but when he does push the boat out he tends to do so in spectacular fashion, usually at plummy college shindigs, with hundred-year-old clarets and thousand-year-old ports and things. Plus I think he gets through a fair amount of malt by himself in the flat. And he goes to the pub quite a bit... Maybe I would call my father a serious drinker.

'There's just one thing, though.'

'What's that?'

'It's in California.'

'California!'

'Yes. Los Angeles. What do you think? It looked rather nice in the photographs. Sunny.'

'Well, I...yeah, it's lovely. I'm just a bit surprised. I mean, you haven't been out of England for, what, ten years? You've hardly been out of Cambridge.'

'That's right. I gave it a lot of thought and, you know, I decided I fancied the idea. It's an excellent post – first rate research facilities. Good salary. I'll be a professor – although practically everyone over there's a professor,' he added, dipping into his glass.

'Dad, don't get me wrong. I'm delighted. When would you go out?'

'The term begins in September. I thought I would fly some time in August. Have a drop more champagne? Perhaps it would be best to get another bottle.'

We had lunch. My father, as is his custom, stopped talking as soon as the food arrived and ate with popeyed concentration. I diverted him with an account of the last week at work, the world of lavatory cleaner and discount carpets, and he nodded and ate, ate and nodded, smiling absently from time to time. He's always been too locked into his own arcane pursuits to spare much interest for my or Stephen's goings on. For a brief period after I fluked my first, when it looked like I might pursue an academic career, he perked up and introduced me to a series of dithery old colleagues; but he subsided happily enough when I opted for advertising instead. The elephant idea appealed to his sense of whimsy, but that was about as far as it went. He couldn't really get to grips with the idea of getting under the rim. My father's line is that life generally, and advertising in particular, is far too complicated these days and he doesn't understand any of it. As far as advertising's concerned he's got a point. I don't understand a lot of it, and I'm on the inside. I saw a poster the other day that just said 'Message Understood', next to a black and white picture of a dalmatian in training shoes. What you make of that? 'We make excellent sandwiches': that's what I call good advertising. You know what's going on. Also, unusually for the medium, it's true.

I didn't eat a great deal. My interior was coming to terms with the champagne and not giving it the best of receptions. By the end of the first course I was volcanic with suppressed wind. I was also uneasily calculating the cost of the meal, which my father clearly regarded as my toot. He shares a common misconception that ad people earn colossal salaries. Some of them do. Not me.

Not the nippers. He also credits me with an expense account covering everything short of the mortgage. In all this, it has to be said, I haven't troubled to put him right: partly because he wouldn't really believe me; but partly because I quite enjoy the spurious sense of affluence it confers.

The coffee arrived and my father lit one of his filterless fags. Unearthly rumblings were by this time coming from my waistband. Funny how some people seem to thrive on cigarettes. Dad's been smoking these things, the highest tar the law allows, for thirty-five years, and never so much as clears his throat. While Jerry, for instance, with his extra milds, looks a complete wreck all the time. He has this way of sucking the smoke down, holding his breath till he goes red, then exhaling with a whoosh, like somebody blowing out candles on a birthday cake. It's worse than Mike Sharp. Each time he does it you think, this is it – this is the cardiac. One day it will be.

'Let me get this,' said my father when the bill arrived.

'Nonsense. It's not every day your dad's made a professor.'

It was farcically expensive. I went to the gents to get over it, and ease the pressure on my warring interior. On return I found my father with the coy look on his face that presaged the asking of a favour.

'William – I was wondering. Would you be able to do something very kind for me? You must say if you can't, though.'

'Sure.'

'It's Toby. I can't take him with me when I go. And it's a four-year tenure.'

'You want me to look after him?'

'I'd ask Stephen, but you know he's got that cat of his, and the last time they came to Cambridge Toby spent a penny in his car... He wasn't very keen.'

I thought about my shoe box flat, the bus to work, my erratic personal life. I thought of Tobes, short of leg and short of breath, needing feeding, walking... It wasn't on. It just wasn't possible.

'Of course I'll have him,' I found myself saying. 'It'd be a pleasure.'

'Bless you,' said my father. 'Bless you.'

We stood outside pumping hands in the blinding sunlight.

'Come to Cambridge soon,' said my father. He gave me an envelope before he got in the cab.

'What's this?'

'Open it,' he said. The door slammed shut and he pulled away with a wave.

I opened it. Inside was a cheque for one thousand pounds. With it was a note saying, '*For dog biscuits*'.

I stood for a few seconds, holding the scraps of paper stupidly in front of me. My first reaction was an absurd sense that I had somehow engineered a swap: my father, for a dog and a thousand pounds. But the main effect was to hit home to me that this was for real, that my father really was upping sticks and taking off to the other side of the world. I suddenly felt forlorn, and faintly jealous.

A bell tolled, breaking into my reverie and prompting an exaggerated double take at my watch. Four o'clock! Four o'clock's pushing it even by Friday lunchtime standards. I cantered headlong into the traffic, provoking a squall of hoots and squawks from outraged cars and taxis, and a great klaxon blast from a coach full of Japanese. Two minutes later I was in the lift, heaving for breath.

The doors parted with a mighty *bing bong*.

Miles and Mike Sharp were standing talking in the lobby.

This time I just had to butch it out. Miles turned his head, but Sharpy barely seemed to see me as I marched bluffly past. He was talking, if I remember correctly, about the explosion of choice facing the housewife as she walks down the aisle. Miles was looking fed up. He's heard it before too.

A good thing about getting back late from lunch: the afternoon goes quickly. By the time I'd taken my coat off it was practically time to go home. I sat in a mildly fuddled state, pondering my father's bombshell and my thousand pounds, absently crumpling up the phone messages stuck to my desk. Nobody else seemed to be doing any work, and the phones were strangely silent, so I just dossed and yawned and fingered my cheque till six o'clock. Excepting a brief attack of wind at five forty-five my insides seemed reasonably settled again. I began to wish I'd eaten more of my lunch.

At six thirty, retrospectively, I realise I made a fundamental mistake. What I ought to have done was go home. What I did was go on a Guinness frenzy with Hippo and some of the lads. And after that – and I know this is straining credibility – after that what I did was, I went for a Tandoori. It made sense at the time. We came out of the last and seediest of the pubs along our route, and there it was, smack in front of us, a purple aquarium full of the shadowy forms of people eating, giving out deeply moving curry smells.

'Anyone on for a ruby?' I remember somebody saying, and the next thing we were parked in front of a deck of popadoms with Hippo hollering for pints.

The next thing I remember is being explicitly ill in the tiny loo next to the bar. I couldn't believe the noises I was managing to make in there – great protracted shouts of nausea, magnified to appalling volume by the geometry of the room and the acoustics of the bowl. How my fellow-diners must have enjoyed it. I remember looking up at the wall in a moment of respite and staring straight at a cardboard picture of some Eastern god or guru in the form of a highly decorated bull elephant with dozens of coiled and writhing limbs... It struck me drunkenly as apt that I should be observed, at this point in time, here, at my lowest ebb, in the toilet...*by an elephant.*

I eventually banked the cheque a week later, following a panic-stricken period when I couldn't find it anywhere (the kindly old Greek at the dry cleaners handed it to me with a wink when I collected my suit, consigned for fumigation after Friday). I had an urge to blow the lot on something deeply frivolous, like cakes, or lavatory paper – anything that would return a tangibly large quantity of goods for the cash outlay. In the end I bought two pairs of insanely expensive shoes at McAffee's on Bond Street and stashed the rest on deposit. I have a fetish for McAffee shoes. They're handmade and weigh about a stone each. You get the best part of a whole cow on each foot. It gives me a kick buying shoes like that. It gives me a psychological lift. I sit at my phone in the office, listening to Vivienne or Jerry going on and on, yes-ing, no-ing, demurring, disagreeing, with one foot hitched up on the bin, admiring the reflections in the mirrored toecap, thrilling at the regularity and intricacy of the double row of stitching sloping down the outside seam, revelling in the knowledge that it will cost at least fifty quid to get them re-soled (fifty quid!)... And Jerry wheedles and exhales and expostulates, making those little grunty noises, trying to get me to do things for him; and I think, you may be the client, but I bet you don't own a pair of McAffee's costing a ton and a half a shot – let alone *two.*

I tackled Miles on the subject of coming off Carpet Mania. He told me to talk to Mike. I went to Mike, who looked blank, and advised me to have a word with Miles. I had another word with Miles, who said he'd have a word with Mike. Since then I haven't heard anything. I hope I come off soon. It takes up too much of my time. Also, I discover, chatting to the finance director in the lift, it isn't making us any money. Quite the reverse, in fact. I wonder if anybody else realises? I wonder if anybody cares?

I went home for my father's birthday-cum-new-job party. He invited along some of his students, confident, voluble types in blazers and pratty little neckties, and we all got drunk at my father's flat and a series of Cambridge pubs. At one point a curry even seemed on the cards, but the danger passed... He flies in six weeks. In six weeks my flat for one becomes a flat for one plus a pug. Toby was in good fettle. Dad and I walked him by the river on the Sunday morning, with the eights cutting past in close succession like great wooden insects. When Toby got hot – immediately, in other words – my father dunked him in the water, whence he sneezingly emerged like a latter-day canine Venus, and trundled on refreshed.

That evening a massive storm broke. I caught the train back through the pyrotechnics, watching the rain washing the glass on the window of my carriage as it homed in on the city.

CHAPTER SIX

I don't believe this is happening to me.

'Our objective,' Jerry was saying, 'is to locate and capture the enemy flag. Their objective is to locate and capture our flag. If we capture their flag before they capture our flag, we win. If they capture ours before we capture theirs, they do. Any questions?'

Jerry was wearing full combat gear, toting an automatic pistol. He looked like a khaki sumo wrestler, Rambo on a doughnut diet.

'What happens if you get shot?'

'Well you try not to, of course. But according to the manual – '

'Surely you're dead if you get shot?' said Katherine Napier.

'Not necessarily,' said Jerry. 'It could be a flesh wound.'

'Well how can you tell? Whether you're dead or not?'

'I think you just use your discretion.'

'Unless you get shot in the head,' said Katherine Napier.

'Unless you get shot in the head,' said Jerry.

Jerry, having inadvertently shot himself in the head when handed his paintgun, was technically speaking already dead. A mauve smear on his forehead, now obscured by a beret, testified to his marksmanship. Jerry had been designated 'team leader'. We'd convened on some godforsaken patch of shrub in Hertfordshire for the weekend to play an Elimination Wargame, organised for executive diversion by some mad marine or psychotic ex-para. '*The Weekend with a Difference*', said the literature. It was Scott's idea. He said it would foster team spirit and competitive attitude. Miles went along with it, and Mike Sharp footed the bill. So here we all were in our two teams, dressed like extras from a Vietnam movie (or possibly a *Carry On* film), being briefed on how to achieve the objective with a difference: killing each other.

I hate this stuff. As a kid I was never into guns or James Bond films. Even when I was six it all struck me as incredibly stupid. And the last way I want to spend a weekend is horsing around with Miles and Scott and Jerry in some bog shooting one another with little balls of paint and capturing flags.

It was all being taken highly seriously. The ex-para gave us a long lecture on Survival, extending to techniques for killing and eating sheep, badgers, voles – anything that moved – if we happened to get lost in the wild and feel peckish. Wild, my bum. Two sides of the game area were golf course, and you could hear the rumble of a motorway the other side of the ridge. Plus we'd been kitted out with enough processed meals and glucose tablets to last a fortnight, on top of all the guns and bombs and incendiary devices that made up our personal armouries (Mike having paid extra for the deluxe option, where they tog you up to the nines with crap of all kinds). Our opposing team – a firm of accountants from Manchester – had clanked off into the bushes fifteen minutes back. Presumably they too had bought all that horse shit about team spirit and the will to win.

Jerry and Scott began a protracted wrangle about the strategy for the morning. It was obvious who was going to be the real team leader. Not that I had any more confidence in Scott than Jerry. He seemed to approach the exercise in the same way he approached packaged goods marketing, talking at length about objectives and phases and key action plans, without really committing himself to anything by way of what to do. He even had a little management handbook with him, 'MANAGEMENT NOW', by some granite-jawed corporate he-man from Harvard Business School... I had other preoccupations, besides. For a start I needed pretty imperatively to go to the lavatory. Ever since that double Tandoori fiasco my bowels have developed a tyrannical grip on my bodily timetable. It's no longer a case of ah, I need to go to the lavatory, I'll bear it in mind and go when I have a moment... now it's *I need to go to the lavatory*, like a panicking three-year-old. (Sorry to dwell on the subject. Ever since I was put on this project my world has steadily come to be dominated by the lavatory. It just has.)

It had started to drizzle and a wind was getting up. Whatever happened to that roasting summer, that blistering June and microwave May? You know what happened at the start of last week? It snowed. I couldn't believe it. It fucking snowed. I went out for my sandwich and, lo, it was snowing. Beginning of August, central London, snow. What's going on? Everyone stopped talking about global warming and started talking about the new ice age. The next day the temperature reached a hundred and five. Everyone started talking about global warming again. It can't be both (can it?). I wish...I wish it would just *settle down*. It's unsettling, this weather, that's what it is. Unsettling. Perhaps it's got a bearing on my bowel movements?

'Right,' said Scott. 'We proceed in V formation due west for half a mile, keeping watch for the enemy. Upon sight of the enemy, report directly to the team leader. Nobody is to open fire without the prior approval of myself. Or Jerry,' he added a second later.

Off we trooped. Almost immediately there was a loud *phut* and Katherine Napier said, 'Oops – sorry everyone.' A large purple blob materialised on Jerry's posterior; he craned round and said, 'Fuck.'

'Time out,' said Scott. 'Jerry – where are you hit?'

'On my bottom,' said Jerry.

'Right. Stretcher party. William Brodie, Miles Fraser. Come along.'

'Is that strictly necessary?' said Miles. 'It was an accident, like last time.'

'We're going to do this for real or not at all,' said Scott. 'Katherine Napier – take more care with that weapon in future.'

'Right you are.'

'Fetch the stretcher, Brodie. Double time. There's one in the team shed.'

I double-timed to the team shed, gratefully pausing to utilise the team lavatory (at double time), and returned with the team stretcher. By this time Miles had persuaded Scott to give the stretcher a miss, so I was sent back again.

'We've lost sixteen minutes,' frowned Scott. 'Sharpen up, everyone. Move out.'

After that nothing happened for quarter of an hour. We tramped along in some kind of formation, sweeping the horizon, but not an accountant in sight. Then we came across a patch of wood and split up to patrol individually, watching out for ambushes.

It was quite eerie once the others melted away into cover. The wood was very silent and you felt your footfalls resounding crunchily for hundreds of yards. I lost my bearings almost immediately and blundered cautiously in the direction I thought I ought to be heading. At any moment I expected an accountant to rear up out of a thicket and plug me. So when, in due course, I heard a rustle in the brush to my right I instantly loosed off a half magazine in the direction of the noise without pausing to make enquiries.

'Ow,' said a voice. 'Stop it!'

'Katherine?'

'I'm in here. Stop shooting me.'

'Sorry. I thought you were an accountant.'

I clubbed through a tangle of branches and came across Katherine kneeling by her discarded pack, dabbing at a pair of purple splats on her torso.

'Sorry,' I said again, internally congratulating myself on the accuracy of my fire.

'That's okay. I couldn't find any accountants, so I thought I'd have a rest.'

'Seen the others at all?'

'No.' She stopped tending her wounds and wrestled a packet of fags from her kit bag.

'Cigarette?'

'I don't smoke.'

'Fair enough.' She lit one and sat back against a tree stump, pushing the hair out of her eyes. I sat down next to her.

'Isn't this ridiculous?'

'Excruciating,' I agreed.

'Tell me,' she said, 'were you ever a boy scout?'

'Certainly not.'

'I was a brownie for a while. We did camping and adventures and first aid and stuff. I hated it. After a while I got thrown out.'

'Yes? What for?'

'Fighting.'

'Did you shoot Jerry on purpose?' I asked.

'Yes. I couldn't stop myself. He's got such an inviting back end.'

'Poor Jerry.'

'Yeah, right.'

We sat on for a while. Katherine smoked another cigarette, and then another, frowning up at the leaves.

'Why don't you leave AKL?' I said. 'You obviously don't like it.'

'Oh, it's all right I guess. This elephant thing's a bit of a laugh.'

'Your degree's in Chemistry, isn't it? Surely with a Chemistry degree there are tons of other things you could do. Better things.'

'Such as?'

'I don't know. Invent miracle drugs, or...cream toppings.'

'It doesn't really take my fancy. I don't know what I want to do. What about you? Have you always wanted to work in advertising?'

'Oh no. I just applied on spec in my final year at college and got the job. I think that's how a lot of people do it.'

'Hmm. Bit worrying, isn't it? I mean, you wander into something for want of anything better to do. Next thing you know you're retiring. Mind you,' she added enigmatically, 'It keeps you from worrying about other things.'

We were interrupted before I had time to respond.

'You are completely surrounded,' said a voice. 'Come out with your hands raised.'

'Scott!' breathed Katherine, wide-eyed.

We'd both instinctively squatted down low.

'What shall we do?' she whispered.

'Stop giggling. He takes this seriously.'

'You have five seconds before we open fire,' said Scott's voice.

'It's all right!' I said, standing up. 'It's me and Katherine.'

Scott had his gun levelled at me at full arm's length, TV-cop style. He lowered it reluctantly to this side. Jerry and Miles were nowhere in sight.

'What the hell are you doing in there?' he demanded.

'I found Katherine – she'd been hit.'

'I'd been hit,' echoed Katherine, indicating her splodges.

Scott looked pissed off, but couldn't argue with the splodges. Clearly his warlike instincts had been thwarted. He asked for a situation report on the ambush, which Katherine gave plausibly enough.

'Right,' said Scott. 'We'd better rendezvous with Jerry and Miles. Come with me.'

We moved out. Almost immediately the wood petered out and we came to a little bunker affair with our flag on it and Miles on guard. We fanned out and squatted round it, like Custer's last stand.

Jerry didn't show. I studied the insect community going about its unfathomable business an inch below my nose. It was like Piccadilly Circus down there: ants in all directions, beetles, grubs, crickets... And everyone with plenty to do, plenty on his mind, a clear purpose in life. No career anxieties there.

After what seemed like about an hour and a half Scott crawled over to me.

'I want you to scout for Jerry. Miles and I need to stay with the flag, and

Katherine's non-combatant. Come back within fifteen minutes whether or not you find him.'

I went back into the wood again. There was no sign of Jerry anywhere. I was just on the point of returning when a loud boom sounded, followed by the noise of shouting and firing. A second later Jerry came crashing into the clearing, running like an escaped rhinoceros. In his fist he clutched a blue chequered flag.

'Cover me!' he bawled, and plunged on past through the trees.

I barely had time to raise my paintgun when two men, both wearing protective glasses and headbands, came surging out in pursuit. When they saw me they started shooting at me as they ran. I shot back. We all missed one another and I went clumping after them.

I reached the edge of the wood just in time to see Jerry nose-dive into our bunker with a triumphant bellow. His pursuers slowed up, then doubled over with stitches; I came puffing up behind.

'I've got it!' Jerry was yelling, brandishing the flag. 'I've got it! We've won!'

Scott, unequivocally upstaged, grunted approval, and Miles shook Jerry by the hand.

'Well done, lads,' gasped one of the accountants. 'You win the first phase.'

'Yeah,' gurgled the other. 'Nice one.'

Jerry began an excitable account of how he had stalked up upon the unguarded foe and wrested the flag away single-handedly, to be apprehended by a returning posse and chased back in a hail of fire.

'Hang on a minute,' said one of the accountants suddenly. He seemed transfixed by Jerry's ample backside.

'What is it?'

'This man's been shot. He's been shot in the rear.' He pointed to the purple patch on Jerry's right buttock.

There was a dreadful silence.

'That happened before we began,' said Jerry. 'One of the guns went off by mistake.'

'Doesn't make any difference. The rules state that once injured a player is out of the contest.' The accountant produced a little booklet from the interior of his costume and brandished it firmly.

Jerry subsided like a burst tyre.

Scott gave Miles a terrible look.

'Your round then, gentlemen,' he said.

*

From then on things went inexorably downhill. Scott was shirty with Miles over that stretcher business. Miles was shirty because Scott was shirty. Jerry was shirty because he wasn't a hero after all. Everyone was shirty with Katherine for plugging Jerry in the backside. Scott spent a good fifteen minutes laying down the law all over again about codes of command and decision making. It had begun to rain quite hard. We squelched off grimly for phase two.

By the end of the afternoon everyone was fed up. Even Scott, who had fallen into a pond, seemed to be losing his team spirit, to say nothing of his competitive attitude. It's difficult to keep a competitive attitude when you keep sneezing all the time. Jerry shot himself again – twice – thus invalidating himself from phases two and three (both of which we lost). The final straw was when Katherine twisted her ankle, and it was mercifully agreed to pack it in and go home early.

I caught the train back to London with Miles, who sneeringly dismissed the whole exercise and flattened the business section of the paper in front of him on the table. After that we didn't exchange a word till King's Cross.

On the Tuesday following we had another meeting at the agency. Katherine was absent, due to her ankle; but Jerry and Scott were there, the latter with, it grieves me to report, a real lulu of a cold. Nobody talked about the weekend. Jerry made a tentatively jocular reference at the kick-off, which Scott killed with a watery glare. He sat with a bale of Kleenex, groggily directing matters. The meeting proceeded frostily. Scott and Miles have fallen out. It's rather comical to witness their icy exchanges, like two old ladies at odds after a contretemps at the church fete. I kept my head down.

'Tosser,' said Miles, after they'd left.

'By the way,' he said, as we turned into the corridor. 'I spoke to Mike again. He'll take you off the carpet business, just he can't yet. He's got to get a replacement.'

'Thanks, Miles. I appreciate it.'

He paused by the stairs and studied his cuffs for a moment.

'How are you getting on with Jerry?' he said.

'Okay. He's a bit of an old woman.'

'And Scott?'

'I can't bear him.'

'He's a difficult bastard. You've got to stand up to him.'

'Sure.'

'You meet a lot of Scotts in this profession, Brodie. Not just at the client end, either. Don't let them get on top of you.'

You know what I think? *I think he likes me*. Miles. You see, I don't think he has any friends. Scott was his friend. He isn't now. What do you know? Even Miles has needs, emotions.

He moved away.

'Miles...' I said. He turned. 'I think you're doing a brilliant job on this project... I've really learnt a lot in the last few weeks.'

He smiled thinly. 'Thanks, Brodie,' he said. 'I appreciate it.'

CHAPTER SEVEN

Predictably, I have fallen morbidly in love with Katherine Napier. Yeah yeah. I know what I said. I said she wasn't my type. She *isn't* my type. Am I hers? I doubt it.

This is the last thing I need. I should imagine it's a good rule of thumb not to fall in love with your clients. I should imagine it isn't the done thing. Compromising professional relationships, and all that. But Katherine and I don't have a professional relationship. To date, she's behaved like an errant schoolgirl and I like her elder brother.

It's hopeless. I rehearse conversations, encounters. I sit in the flat making eyes at the wall like a fifteen-year-old. I conjure her image: in meetings, a little island of female presence amongst the jackets and ties and moustaches; on that daft wargame, got up like a squaddy, impish, sexy – yes, beguiling, boyish...

Maybe that's it. Maybe I'm a latent homosexual.

Get a grip, Brodie, you haven't got time for all this.

It's true – I haven't. My days are filling up. Since the wargame weekend the workload's doubled, tripled. I get up earlier and earlier to make extra hours to get it all in. Ken the doorman sets his watch by my seven a.m. entrances, my six forty-five specials... But it's going all right. I don't want to speak too soon, but it isn't going at all badly, despite the fact I'm *still* on Carpet Mania (can you believe that?), Mike Sharp having elected in the end to hire a trainee to work under me, rather than a properly trained executive to take it over. Probably couldn't find anyone willing to take it on. So I now have the responsibility of minding this unfortunate waif on top of everything else. Ah, me.

It must be – what? – three weeks ago I took my father to the airport. I drove us down in his ancient orange Beetle, Toby in the back with the suitcases. We hung about awkwardly in departures, waiting for the flight to be called.

'You'll visit me?' he said for the twentieth time.

'I'd love to,' I replied.

They called the flight at last. Lingeringly, we shook hands. I wanted to give him a hug, but I couldn't. We're out of the hugging habit, dad and me. So much unspoken affection compressed into a handshake.

'Goodbye, Dad.'

'Goodbye, William. Take care of Toby.'

To intense mutual embarrassment each of us was blinking away tears. 'Come here,' said my father, unexpectedly, and we embraced in the thronging crowd of Americans converging for the flight.

As soon as he'd gone I did cry briefly. But I felt substantially less desolate than five minutes previously.

And so my flat has its own personal guard dog, or guard pug. Toby hangs out there for the long hours I'm at the office. I try and make it back in reasonable time to give him a walk, but it isn't easy. Poor Toby. It can't be much of a life. I guess that's part of the deal of being a dog: accepting, adapting, taking life as it comes.

Connie, for one, is delighted by his arrival and keeps making excuses to come and drink him in. Toby responds by snuffling deeply in the sheet-like folds of her skirts. I assume they contain interesting scents. Toby certainly can't get enough. After a while I haul him off and she goes away saying 'Sweet' or 'Poppet'. Other interests of Toby's include sleeping, moulting, eating his breakfast (a favourite), taking the air with me round the squares, and going to the lavatory. This he does with astonishing frequency in the course of a walk, up to twenty or thirty times, carefully measured, always with the last pee – like the first – on the front doorstep. I've tried taking him into work occasionally, but it doesn't go down very well. The secretaries goo and cuddle him, but he draws reactions ranging from quiet censure to frank incredulity from the executive quarter. And it is a bit of a performance getting him on and off the bus.

I kept the Beetle, but haven't used it yet. It sits smugly on its Residents Only parking space, waiting to get broken into.

*

Scott has taken to fixing savagely early meetings in Bristol, doubtless in a move to reassert his authority after the paintball debacle. This week he set a record by phoning up to diary in a meeting for eight thirty on Friday morning. I acceded, grimly calculating what time I'd need to get up in order to get there on time. If it takes just on two hours, and twenty minutes in the cab, plus the twenty minutes Scott keeps you dangling in reception (Chapter 12: *Keeping Them Dangling In Reception*)... But even as I fished for the timetable Scott pre-empted me.

'Will you be coming by car?'

'Train, I thought.'

'Come by car,' he said. 'I'd like you to do some store checks round town later that day. Jerry was going to do it, but he's leaving early that afternoon for his holiday.' His tone indicated that he regarded holiday taking as a criminally frivolous indulgence.

'All right,' I said. I didn't mind. Store checking isn't such a chore. My only reservation was the Beetle. Going downhill it can sometimes get up to about fifty-five, sixty... So here to Bristol – let's see now – should take between three and four hours. Allowing time to get lost finding AKL in the one-way system, I'll be okay if I leave no later than...four thirty.

In fact it took me close on five hours. I had to change a tyre a mile after chugging onto the M4, which set me back nearly an hour. I eventually burst past the catatonic security man and through the revolving doors at eleven minutes past nine.

'I think they've started without you,' said the receptionist. 'Go straight on in.'

I didn't go straight on in. I went to the lavatory for a panicky but nevertheless prolonged crap, delivered in a series of inconclusive instalments. God knows how long I was in there. The receptionist must have thought I was giving birth. This bum disorder or botty malfunction I've been suffering from – it has to be stress-related. It hits me every time I need to be somewhere in a hurry. No longer is the lavatory my haven of rest in the executive world. Now it's as if I'm in some ghastly confessional as I quack away in there, atoning for sins too dire to put a name to. Also, why – and this needn't detain us too long – why does my shit smell *so awful*?

Not that it's ever smelled exactly wonderful, but recently...oy! It has this kind of *oak-smoked* aroma, like it's been maturing in casks for years... It must be my diet. It must be what I eat. Food, after all, turns into shit. So if the food you eat isn't really food, but *shit*, what you end up with is Supershit, Shit Plus, Shit 3 – The Motion Picture (in 3-D)... Fifteen minutes later a thoroughly chastened William Brodie stood in front of the mirror drying his hands on a paper towel marked '*AKL: The Professionals*'... Considering they're supposed to be a lavatory hygiene company, the AKL loo was in a disgraceful state. A solitary, grit-studded sliver of soap skulked on the floor amongst soiled tissues and discarded sticking plasters. Above the basin was stuck a sign: 'NOW WASH YOUR HANDS', with another next to it reading: 'WARNING: WATER UNSAFE TO DRINK', beside which an unknown hand had stencilled: 'BOLLOCKS'. A selection of jottings on a gynaecological theme adorned the wall inside the loo itself, and someone had written: '*Why not have a wank?*' at knee height. Why not? No time, no time.

I strode out and into the meeting.

They were talking about the range of odours with which Elephant might be endowed. Pine Fresh was the research favourite, but Lemon Tang ran a strong second.

'Lemon's a major housewife attractant when it comes to fruit-influenced aromas for consumer goods,' said Scott.

An uncertain silence followed this pronouncement. A couple of heads nodded slowly, and Jerry said, 'Right.' Such as it was, Scott developed his line of argument. Scott's view was that lemon, as a smell, was more dynamic than pine, and would project the brand into a new dimension. I looked round furtively, half expecting some form of spontaneous protest at this rubbish, but further sage nodding ensued. Jerry, for one, agreed: lemon *was* more dynamic than pine. The next two hours were spent discussing a further research project to ratify the decision. After that we talked budgets. Scott, while indicating that the launch budget for Elephant would not be insubstantial, sounded off at length about the iniquitous expense of advertising, casting accusatory looks down the table in my direction. What could I say? Advertising is expensive, no two ways about it. I solemnly promised to effect savings wherever possible. Jerry nodded like a toy cow in the back of a car: we *must* effect savings wherever possible... Scott's already been effecting savings. Boy, has he been effecting those savings. True to Katherine's prophecy half the work force at the bottling plant were made redundant the week before last. And that's just for starters. You got the impression he'd happily fire himself to effect a few more savings. You certainly got the impression he'd happily fire Jerry. I wonder if Jerry got that impression? It can only be a matter of time.

Curried chicken (with rice) was prominent on the canteen board, when we went for a late bite in the canteen at five to two. Curried chicken, in fact, was all there was on the canteen board. Everything else had been eaten. My stomach gave an anticipatory heave at the aroma. I had no option to decline, ravenous though I was. It would have been digestive suicide. I secured a plateful of plain rice, which I laced with brown sauce from an encrusted bottle.

'That doesn't look very appetising,' said Katherine when, following extensive manoeuvring with tray aloft, I contrived to sit down beside her.

'I'm going vegetarian,' I lied.

'Oh.' She eyed my plate doubtfully. 'Hitler was a vegetarian – did you know that?'

'Yeah yeah.'

'He was. And he loved animals.'

'No, I meant I knew that.'

'Vegetarians tend not to.'

Jerry parked himself opposite with a heaped and smouldering plate, which he commenced to despatch with open-mouthed gusto.

'This is *good*,' he said.

It was more than could be said for my rice with brown sauce, but I soldiered gamely through it, washing it down with a cup of coffee-flavoured tea. Jerry was off in an hour, and in high spirits. He started briefing us on his holiday itinerary – a series of stop-overs at campsites and caravan pits across Brittany, complete with wife, neighbour, neighbour's wife, kids, neighbour's kids, friends of neighbour's kid's (they had his last year), old uncle Tom Cobbly et al. It sounded ghastly. Disinclined to separate the actions of talking and feeding, Katherine and I were further treated to a churning visual accompaniment. I wasn't feeling so hot, to tell you the truth. The rice sat like lead in my stomach and the chemicals in the tea were bringing on a headache. And the stuffiness of the refectory, my early start and Jerry's narrative were combining to render me hallucinatory with sleepiness. It felt like about eight in the evening.

'Are you okay?' said Katherine, when Jerry rolled off to the coffee machine.

'I feel a bit shattered. I had to get up at four.'

'*Four?*'

Ashamed of the antimachismo surrounding the reason (a joke car), I developed the Toby angle, explaining I was looking after my dad's dog, which needed a minimum one hour's exercise morning and night. The problem with this however, it occurred to me even as I said it, is the antimachismo surrounding the dog.

'What kind of dog is it?' asked Katherine.

'A pug,' I admitted. Joke car, joke dog.

'Why don't I do the store checks? If you're feeling tired?'

'I really ought to...'

'Then I'll come too – if you like.'

'Would you?'

'Of course. I'll tell Jerry.'

Fifteen minutes later Katherine was crouched over the wheel of the Beetle with her nose practically touching the windscreen, gunning it chaotically round Bristol. I sat bolt upright and wide awake with apprehension in the passenger seat. We did some stores – a line of grimy eight-till-lates, a couple of mini marts, a co-op, jotting down details of competitive presence; then Katherine said, 'I'm bored with this.'

'Yes.'

'Shall we pack it in?'

'Let's.'

We got back in the Beetle.

'Why don't we go to the seaside?' said Katherine. 'It's only four thirty.'

'Is there any? Near here?'

'The Gower peninsula is an hour away. You could crash out for a bit.'

It was a ripe suggestion, and far too sensible to resist.

'Okay,' I said. 'I'd like that.'

Katherine drove fast, with all the windows down, creating a roar that precluded conversation. Presently I fell asleep. When I woke up again we were bowling down between hedges on a narrow lane studded with cowpats and ex-rabbits. Katherine was still driving with an air of exaggerated concentration, peering intently through the bugs' graveyard on the windscreen. A cigarette burnt between the fingers of her left hand, peppering me with fine ash. The sky was clear, the sun low on the horizon. I felt disorientated by sleep.

'Where are we?' I asked.

'Gower,' said Katherine. She took her eyes alarmingly off the road and gave me a grin. 'You were out of it.'

'What time is it? It feels about midnight.'

'About nine.'

'Nine!... I thought you said this was an hour away?'

'I called in on my mother. She has a cottage here. You didn't wake up.'

'So where are we going now?'

'To the seaside,' said Katherine, as if to a child.

'Don't worry,' she added. 'We can stop over at mum's.'

The lane began to give out, and we pulled over on a verge. I could see sand dunes and scrub up ahead.

'Seaside,' announced Katherine. 'Isn't it gorgeous?'

'Fabulous,' I said.

'Fancy a swim? It's still warm.'

'I don't have any things.'

'Never mind. There's a towel on the back seat – we can share it.'

She got out, and I followed with the towel, eyeing it dubiously. I'd put it there for Toby, who luckily hadn't moulted on it that much. We walked along a little defile through the dunes towards the gradually increasing noise of waves.

'This cottage,' I said. 'Does your mother live there by herself?'

'Yes.'

'I take it your parents are divorced?'

'That's right. Mummy got this cottage a couple of months ago. She was brought up round here.'

'There – look at that,' she said, suddenly.

We'd crested a dune and stood all of a sudden facing a broad expanse of beach, bordered on both sides by cliffs. The sun was lowering orangely over the sea, due west ahead of us. It was quite implausibly beautiful.

'Low tide!' said Katherine. 'Come on.'

In any other circumstances – with anybody else, any other girl – the whole scene would have been pure cinema: sunset skinnydipping with the object of desire...and pretty corny cinema at that. But the difference, as Katherine matter-of-factly began to undress, and I shyly turned away to do the same, was that it didn't feel sexy, or set up, or even particularly *romantic*. It had pretty much the same quality as the Brighton jaunt with Edward earlier in the summer – a couple of overgrown kids out for the hell of it, going for a swim. Even when she straightened up in her underwear (shallow bra, tennis-player pants), I didn't feel anything like desire, but rather a kind of avuncular concern: the child would catch her death, for heaven's sake – what did she think she was doing? She was thin. You never really realise these things until you see people undressed. Without waiting for me, she set off at a patter across the sand towards the water a hundred yards distant. Gingerly lowering my suit trousers, but opting very firmly to retain the boxers, I headed after her.

We hit the water at roughly the same time in a scampering dash across the final twenty yards, whooping with bravado, then gasping at the cold. I tripped on a wave, getting up again just in time to be biffed over by another, bigger one; then I plunged in head first and swam blindly.

I caught sight of the dark tangle of Katherine's hair at one point to my right, immediately losing it again as another wave rolled over me. The surf was pretty high, and I had to swim hard to get past the line of breakers to gain the relative calm of the deeper water. Here I trod water and got my breath back, looking about for Katherine. I couldn't believe I was doing this... A few hours earlier I'd been talking lavatory cleaner in Bristol, and now... Where was Katherine? I circled, then called her name: nothing. The light seemed to have ebbed away significantly over the last few minutes, and the water was dark, like oil. Exhilaration gave way to dread. Katherine was dead. She'd drowned, got smashed into a boulder, engulfed by a jellyfish, bisected by a shark... I called again: 'Katherine? Katherine!...'

Out of nowhere a hand appeared and, with remarkable force, pushed my head under the water. I thrashed to the surface and found myself looking straight into her face.

'You silly cow!' I spluttered. She laughed and slapped a splash at me. I retaliated. Without thinking I made a lunge and dragged us both underwater.

The bodily contact brought me back to an acute sense of the present. We surfaced, still interlocked, and bobbed gasping on the swell. Well, here we go, I thought; but it was Katherine who took the initiative. Still panting, she landed a salty kiss on my mouth. And then she was gone, wriggling out of my grip and striking back towards the shore.

I couldn't catch up with her. I was, for one thing, incommoded by a wanging erection all of a sudden. And she was a strong swimmer, seemingly unaffected by lack of size, or the cigarette diet. By the time I reached her she was back at the clothes pile, clutching the towel and shivering in the breeze.

I think it was the erection that decided things at this point. I am not unnaturally well-endowed, but it was difficult to overlook the transformation of my boxer shorts into a marquee. Not that I came over all cave man or anything. Sex in the sand is fine in films, but impractical in the everyday. Too gritty. Besides, and more concerningly, Katherine was by now shaking uncontrollably with cold. I held her, towel between us (discreetly thwarting my upright member), and tried to warm her up. After a bit I gave her a kiss, which went okay, considering the trembling lips and chattering teeth. Continuing in captain sensible mode I proceeded to help her bundle into her clothes before drying off and dressing myself. For the first time I felt vaguely in command of affairs.

Back in the car I switched on the engine and turned the archaic heating mechanism up to full blast. To the sound of a hundred hair-dryers the interior began to warm up.

'Better?' I asked, after some minutes. We were snuggled cutely on the back seat, feeding warmth through one another's limbs. 'Mmm. . .' went Katherine, eyes closed. She didn't seem inclined to kiss, or, for that matter, make passionate love on the upholstery. So we stayed put until the heating got too much, whereupon I gently disengaged myself to turn it off.

When I returned she was fast asleep. I looked at her closely for the first time, noting the texture of her skin, minor blemishes, a rather appealing mole on her neck; then, for an hour or so, I caressed her damp hair.

I felt extraordinary: very definitely in love, and also slightly ill. Or is that how it feels to be very definitely in love? I'm not certain. It wasn't disagreeable. It was just...*odd*.

At midnight I decided I ought to get us back to the cottage.

'Katherine,' I whispered. 'Katherine.'

'What is it?' She woke up with a little start, relaxing when she saw me.

'I think we ought to get back. Don't you?'

'...mm.'

'Incidentaly – I'm crazy about you.'

She smiled faintly, and fell asleep again. I woke her with a kiss – well, more of a snog really – and we spent the next fifteen minutes or so necking agreeably, until I got cramp in my supporting arm and had to call a halt. We drove back up the lane.

Katherine said 'right' or 'left', sleepily, until we got to the outline of a pale stone building, when she said, 'Here we are.'

Inside a fire was still alight in the kitchen grate. There was a mug and a paper on the table, and a pair of spectacles.

'Mummy must be asleep,' breathed Katherine. I agreed, hoarsely. 'Want some tea?'

'You bet.'

We had some tea, sitting in front of the fire. Now that *was* romantic. Sexy too, right enough. Something about the way coal fires throw light and shadow on a darkened room. I was all for making it there and then, which Katherine must have realised, because after a few fumblings she said, 'Not here. Upstairs.'

In the bedroom the moon cast a faint light through curtainless windows. There was no furniture in the room apart from the bed. We undressed for a second time.

I got onto the bed first. It gave a premonitory twang. When Katherine got on it gave a second. The moment we both moved it made the sound of blackboards scraping. We froze, farcically, in mid grab.

'I'd forgotten,' said Katherine, wide-eyed.

'Forgotten what?'

'How ancient this bed is. It belonged to my grandmother.'

At the mention of her grandmother, the bed twanged again, spookily, from deep in its innards.

'Is there another bed?' I whispered. 'One that post-dates your grandmother?'

'No. We'll just have to ignore it.'

Ignoring it proved totally out of the question. Any time either of us shifted our weight the devil's own orchestra sent a chorus of creaking and groaning round the bedroom. After a bit Katherine said, 'We'll have to stop. It'll wake my mother.'

Unfortunately I was unable to contradict this. The noises we were producing would have woken Cardiff. Katherine began to shake with giggles, setting the bed off into new refrains.

'I'm sorry,' she said. 'You look so crestfallen. And it is rather funny.'

It was. The trouble was, I was rather horny.

'Go to sleep. There'll be time.'

'I know. Kath…?'

'Yes?'

'I really am crazy about you, you know. I have been for the longest time. I think I love you.'

She gave me a kiss. 'Go to sleep,' she said, and went to sleep.

I lay awake much of the night, listening to the blood-thump of my heart and the tick of an old clock on the landing.

*

'Hello,' said a voice.

I opened my eyes. A woman I'd never set eyes on before was standing in front of the bed with a tray.

'Hello,' I said.

'You must be exhausted,' she said. 'Here's some tea.'

Katherine was still asleep beside me. It's her mother, said my head. Introduce yourself.

'Er – I'm William,' I said, ridiculously.

'Susan Napier,' said Susan Napier. 'Nice to meet you.'

I struggled to a sitting position and accepted the cup, while my mind backtracked blearily over the exchange. I must be exhausted... What, from spending a night with Katherine? That was a bit... No, no, no, she...

Katherine's mother was standing by the window looking out. 'You went bathing last night,' she said.

'We did, yes.'

'It's nice, isn't it?'

'It is.'

'We haven't had this house very long. You must excuse it all being a bit spartan. I hope you slept all right?'

'Fine...thank you.'

'Well I'll leave you both to come to,' she said. 'Come and have some breakfast when you want to.'

As soon as she'd gone I noticed to my horror a priapic pyramid in the bedding by my lap. Old Colonel Cock was still standing to attention. Oh well, I thought, nestling back into the sheets; it could hardly be more embarrassing than it already had been.

Katherine's mother must have been – forty-five? fifty? She was pretty, obviously one of the age gracefully contingent. She resembled Katherine physically. But how she most reminded me of Katherine was in her handling of the situation. Here was a bloke she'd never met, in bed, in the nude, with a hard-on, with her daughter. Fair enough. Give him a cup of tea and say hello.

Katherine shifted, turned over, opened her eyes.

'Good morning,' I said.

'Hiya.'

'Like some tea?' She took some. 'I've just met your mum,' I said.

'Isn't she beautiful?' said Katherine.

'Very. Tell me,' I said, 'Did you warn her I'd be here when you saw her last night?'

'I said you might be, yes. Why?'

'It's just…I didn't expect her to come in like that.'

'Oh don't worry about that. She's brought back strange men from time to time as well.'

'Really?' I reviewed the information. Then I said: 'So what other strange men have you brought in?'

'None, silly. She has. Well, once.'

'One all,' I said.

'One all,' agreed Katherine.

We breakfasted *à trois* round the table in the kitchen. I was fantastically hungry and had to resist the urge to eat toast two-handed. Katherine chomped down some ghastly-looking bowl of muck from an organic cereal bag. Katherine's mum sipped tea. She talked about the house, the area, how she'd gone to the school up the road and so on. We established the fact that she used to be a teacher, but had packed it in to work as press officer for an environmental agency. Under polite prompting she amplified on the depredations of the power stations up the coast, the threat to wildlife, the over-development of the area. I sympathised.

'Don't worry,' she laughed. 'I won't ask you for any money.'

We went for a walk together by the shore. A strong wind blew in from the sea, sending the breakers up to prodigious heights before smacking them down on the rocks. Here and there intrepid surfers in wet suits fought against the swell.

It was getting on for mid day when I remembered Toby.

'Oh, Christ,' I said, stopping in mid stride.

'What's the matter?'

'I've just remembered – I left my father's dog in the flat in London yesterday morning. I should have gone back.'

I felt furious. With myself, for neglecting Toby for over a day and a half; with Toby – unreasonably – for breaking up the weekend.

'I'll have to go,' I said. 'I'm sorry about this. It's entirely my fault.'

'Have some lunch before you leave,' said Susan.

'It's kind of you. I really must get back.'

'Don't fret,' said Katherine. 'I'm sure he'll be okay. It's probably very good for animals to fast – like humans. I'll come with you.'

'Will you?'

'Certainly. If you'd like that.'

'Of course I would.'

'Then I will.'

She did. We set off with sandwiches and thermos at five to twelve, waving out the window until the cottage and Susan Napier disappeared round the bend.

'Don't worry,' Katherine said again.

'I do though. Poor little dog. He has a bad enough time of it anyway without me neglecting him more than I'm forced to.'

'He'll be all right,' said Katherine. 'Really he will.'

But I could not be mollified. I kept imagining the passing of time, with old Tobes sitting it out in that beastly little kitchen. He'd probably be barking the block down.

The drive took four hours, flat out all the way. Katherine took my gear hand for a spell on the motorway, then relinquished it and stared out the window.

'Where do you live?' she said, as we came into London.

'Near Euston.'

'Whereabouts?'

'Just near there.'

She turned back to the window.

'Kath, I'm sorry. I'm angry with myself. I really appreciate you coming back with me.'

'It's okay. Tell me about your flat.'

I told her. Presently we were pulling up at Regent's Square. I took the stairs three at a time, then stood fumbling with the keys. The third lock stuck, as it sometimes does. I swore horribly. Why wasn't Toby barking? Usually he barks his face off when he hears me coming in. Sick with foreboding, I wrenched open the door and blundered through to the kitchen...

Toby was dead. He lay without a shadow of movement next to his basket.

Katherine framed herself in the doorway behind me as I crumpled onto one knee in front of him.

Then Toby opened both eyes and sneezed in my face, following up with a line of delighted yowls. He bounced up and pranced skittishly round the room. He made a bee line for Katherine, woofing.

'See?' she said, grappling with him.

'I thought he was dead.'

'Doesn't look it, does he? Why don't I take him for a pee while you fix some food for him?'

They clattered off down the stairs. I stood for a few moments, dopily rearranging my emotions. Then I got to work. I scoured the floor for misadventures, found two, and did a bit of mop and bucket. I swept up enough pug hair to stuff a small sofa. I conducted a quick spot-check on the rest of the flat. Dusty, but it would do. Lastly, I stuffed all the bed linen into a cupboard and changed the sheets. By the time Toby's panting announced the rearrival of Katherine I had the old place looking reasonably ship-shape.

'I've never seen a dog pee as much,' said Katherine.

'He's a champion pee-er,' I agreed.

I gave Toby a loaded bowl of dog food, which he began to gollop down at speed. Katherine admired the flat. The grand tour lasted as long as it took Toby to eat his meal. As soon as he had finished we took him out again.

He seemed quite unaffected by his spell in solitary, trundling along with a definite perkiness. Katherine, I was pleased to see, viewed him with affection. She commented on his walk – a rolling, corky gait – and the bunnyhop action with which he mounted the stairs. I took her hand, teenage-style grip (severely interlocked), and we wandered happily through the busy streets heading towards Regent's Park, where I let Toby off the lead and we jogged with him until all three of us simultaneously conked out and sat down on the grass.

'Is that the zoo?' asked Katherine, pointing at the fenced up structures by the north perimeter.

'Yup.'

'Ever been there?'

'As a kid, I think.'

'Have they got elephants, do you know?'

'Bound to.'

'We should go and see them.'

'I suppose we should,' I said. 'But later. It'll be too busy now. Let's take back Tobes – I think he'd like a drink of water.'

'I think you're right,' said Katherine. Toby was panting lavishly. I carried him part of the way home, setting him down experimentally from time to time to see if he fancied footing it, whereupon he would lie histrionically on his side with his paws in the air. At one point a rangy old alsatian with mad yellow eyes came loping round a corner and stopped dead in front of the supine Tobes, reviewing his options. Fuck it or eat it? But even as I moved to intervene Toby bounced to his feet, woofing fearsomely, and the alsatian took himself off with elastic-band bounds.

That evening, finally, we made love.

I fell asleep afterwards. When I woke up again it was dark. Katherine was awake beside me, staring at the stars on the other side of the skylight.

'I like it here,' she said. 'You're very lucky.'

'I know. Now I'm luckier.'

'Look at that sky.'

'I often do.'

We lay on for a bit. Toby wuffed in his sleep, next door. The sound of a car alarm whining away in the square was briefly overlaid by a cacophony of police sirens. Gradually the noise faded back to the usual city noises.

'I love you,' I said, for the first time that hour.

'Brodie...we barely know each other.'

'It makes no difference.'

'Maybe.'

'Do you? Love me?'

'I think about you quite a lot.'

'That isn't quite the same, is it?'

'Is there somebody else?' I asked. 'Just tell me if there is. I'd rather know.'

'There was,' said Katherine. 'I don't think there is now.'

'You look cheerful,' said Hippo, on the Monday. 'Get laid at the weekend, or what?'

'Mind your own business.'

'You *did* get laid! Hey, everyone – Brodie finally got his end away!' A couple of heads looked up from calculators and VDUs, smirking.

'For fuck's sake, Hippo. No I didn't.'

'Oh.' He looked genuinely disappointed. A phone went off and he answered it. 'Yeah? Yeah, he's here. It's for you-hoo.'

'Hello?'

'Brodie?' Miles' voice. 'Would you come up?'

'Certainly.'

Miles was standing by the window of his office, looking out over the view of other windows of other offices.

'Take a seat.' I squelched into the yielding leather. Miles sat on his desk and looked down at me. 'I've resigned,' he said. 'It's over to you now, Brodie.'

'Oh... Why?'

'Scott wanted me off the account. Don't worry, I've got another job to go to.'

'Jesus. I'm sorry, Miles.'

'Don't be. It's all part of the business. Look at it this way – it's an unbeatable opportunity for you.'

'I suppose so.'

'What do you mean, you suppose so? It is. Take it. Pull this off and you could be sitting in this office in six months' time on four times what you're earning now.' He stood up again. Evidently he still had things to do. I fought my way upright and held out a hand. The end of a beautiful partnership.

'Take it easy, Brodie. See you around.'

'Bye, Miles. Good luck.'

Back at my desk I picked up the prototype Elephant pack and turned it slowly in my hand. Who'd have thought a toilet cleaner would shape lives like this?

The telephone exploded in front of me.

'Brodie?' said Vanessa. 'Mike Scott on the line for you.'

I paused a second, then gripped the phone by the neck. It's over to you now, Brodie.

'Put him through,' I said.

PART TWO

NATURE'S GREAT MASTERPIECE

CHAPTER EIGHT

Somewhere in my father's study in Cambridge is an elephant's foot. It's full of string, playing cards, odds and ends. Funny, really. The number of times I must have opened it up as a kid to fish out some sellotape or a pencil sharpener, knowing I was putting my hand into an elephant's foot, but never really making any connection between the foot and an elephant.

Thinking about it, there's actually quite a number of miscellaneous bits of elephant distributed round the Cambridge flat – the chess pieces are ivory; so are the handles of the cheese knives... If you put it all together you'd go some way to reassembling a complete elephant.

I went to the zoo a couple of weeks back to check out the elephants. In office hours, what's more – a legitimate exercise in self-instruction to assist the briefing of Toilet Elephant. I think I know everything there is to know about toilets, but I'm sketchy on elephants. Except for knowing that they're big, and have trunks and tusks, and from time to time donate their feet to ornament studies and sitting rooms.

Actually it was their feet that struck me first of all when I saw them. They have these lovely chunky little legs with pneumatic ankles to cradle the impact of walking. On the hard concrete of the elephant pen the noise of them ambling about was little more than a carpet-slipper shuffle. Very soothing to witness. I could have stayed and watched for ages.

It was a grey, blustery day. Autumn happened with great suddenness over the first weekend in October, heralded by tearing winds that stripped the leaves from the branches with brutal efficiency. The wind's quite something. Whenever you venture outdoors it turns you inside out, snatching your tie and sticking it up your nose, flipping up skirts, inflating nuns, buffeting over drunks and old folks to little yelps and yodels of panic. Litter and leaves dance in the air in great columns. For a spell I found it quite refreshing; now it's getting on my nerves.

Inside the zoo I consulted a map while a flailing copy of *The Sun* wrapped itself around my ankles. I had no intention of stopping to gawk at every cage, no sir. Straight elephants for me. This was *business*. But I did detour through the aquarium on the way, to get out of the wind. Inside it was dark and, apart from a few kids, peaceful. I walked briskly past electric eels, moustachioed chubb, and a lugubrious-looking giant humphead that closely resembled Jerry. Come to that the moustachioed chubb looked not unlike Scott. I have a theory that Scott grew his moustache (on the advice of his management handbook) to gain psychological authority over his peers. Possibly the chubb did the same. Why else would a chubb want a moustache?

There was a straggling crowd outside the elephant and rhino pavilion. Rosie the rhinoceros, on one side, stood in armour-plated indifference. There were four elephants, a Jerry-esque whopper and three smaller relations. The crowd looked on fondly as they walked ponderously round the pen, like four podgy schoolboys. A list of elephant hobbies and activities was tacked to the railing. Abetted by jolly cartoons it spelled out how the elephants spend their days at the zoo, a combination of feeding, bathing, going for walks, 'playing' and meeting people. Not such a bad lifestyle. After a bit some keepers arrived with brooms and bullhooks. One spoke sternly in the ear of the Jerry elephant, who listened like a doleful Billy Bunter before kneeling down and rolling massively onto one side. The crowd tittered appreciatively. Then the keeper brushed her leathery old tummy with the broom. The same process was repeated for the others in turn, then they were given some hay with carrots mixed in, which they ate in large, ruminative mouthfuls. After they'd finished, and rounded off proceedings with a crap apiece the size of a football, they plodded noiselessly through a door and disappeared into some internal quarter. The crowd dispersed. I hung about, reluctant to leave, until I spotted a keeper emerging from the pen with a bucket in his hand.

'Can I ask you a couple of questions?' I said. 'About the elephants?'

He eyed me for a moment. 'What can I tell you?' he said.

'How long have they been here?'

'Varies. Between seven and twelve years.'

'Before that?'

'They came from Sri Lanka.'

'Are they quite domesticated?'

'Just like a dog, or a working animal, yes. You have to take care, naturally, with their size and power... But these four are quite docile. Used to give rides to the kids.'

'Used to?'

'People don't like seeing them doing it, what with all the publicity about ivory and that. Silly really,' he added. 'The elephants loved it.'

He gave me a leaflet, which I stuffed into my jacket. I think he was relieved I wasn't some kind of agitator. Leaning into the wind, I trudged back towards the gates.

On an impulse I diverted near the exit and followed directions to the Giant Panda. There's something about pandas that just makes you want to go and take a look at them. But he wasn't there. A notice on the bars said he'd been flown to Mexico on mating loan. Mexico! What a life. Pandas are the rock stars of the animal kingdom: indolent, adored, plied with mating opportunities. Also, a thing I've thought in the past, and I guess this applies to elephants too – they seem quite relaxed about living in the zoo. You can't say that of all the animals. Try getting the sprawling orang-utans or Rosie the rhino to look cheerful about life. But pandas, elephants, I don't know... they *look* mellow about the whole thing. Okay, so the living quarters are nothing to write home about. Space is a bit short, but then this is London. My flat's hardly what you'd describe as capacious. And they get plenty of grub and attention. Who's complaining?

As a matter of fact some people were complaining, by the gorillas. A posse of campaigners had set up stall there with a banner and some gruesome photographs of monkeys in laboratories. Parents ferried curious children by as fast as possible, and a zoo official in a suit tried to make himself heard above the chanting. I detoured to avoid it and immediately got lost in a small maze of birdwalks full of parrots and birds of prey under wire. Now that *was* depressing. Imagine being a bird and not being able to fly. I blundered on and found myself, incongruously, surrounded by sheep. 'SHEEP,' said the notice on the gate. What's going on? I don't pay to see *sheep*. The sheep didn't appear too thrilled to see me, either. Or are the sheep laid on for deprived city kids who never go into the country? If so, that's the most depressing thought of all.

I got out eventually. The wind was shifting direction, and a tangle of brown clouds was brewing up for a downpour. I got in a taxi as the first fat drops darkened the pavement.

CHAPTER NINE

Good *afternoon, AKL, The Professionals, how can I help you?'* said a sing-song voice.
'Katherine Napier, please.'
'Putting you through.'
There was a pause. The danger at this point is that Katherine won't be there and the secretary, with pea-brained initiative, will put me straight through to Jerry, or Scott.
'Katherine.'
'Hi, it's me. Listen – am I coming down this weekend?'
'I don't think it's possible. Mummy's got people at the cottage.'
'Well, why not come here?'
'...Can I call you back? Jerry's waving at me.'
I'm slightly concerned, Katherine-wise. We don't get to see each other anything like enough. True, we've spent every weekend together since that first one, either in London or Wales. But it isn't anything like enough. You can't count meetings in Bristol, or the office. We managed once to escape back to the flat at lunchtime for an amorous half an hour, but I don't think we'll be repeating the exercise. Toby got wildly excited at our return. He managed to free himself from the kitchen after fifteen minutes of throttled yowling and crashing about, and bounced onto the duvet, thrusting his whiskery face between ours – Hello! Can I play too?...I've been extra-considerate towards Tobes since the incident when he got left. I genuinely do take him for an hour's walk both ends of the day, getting up impossibly early to fit it in. Consequently Toby is in tremendous fettle and I'm in a state of chronic collapse.

After my visit to the zoo I put pen to paper to write the definitive creative brief for Paul Short. The creative brief should, ideally, be exactly that: brief. Mine certainly was. I had it down to less than half a side. If there was one *key* thought, I decided, Miles-like, that the advertising should concentrate on, it had to be -

'Directionality,' I said. '*Getting under the rim.*'

I was sitting in Paul Short's office, justifying my Key Communication: 'ONLY AN ELEPHANT CLEANS RIGHT UNDER THE RIM.' I was rather proud of it.

Paul glanced at the brief when I handed it to him, then tossed it aside. 'It's about elephants, yeah?' he said.

'Well...'

'I mean, never mind all this rim business.'

'The thing is, it's shaped *like* an elephant so that it...'

'I'll need six weeks,' said Paul Short, by way of terminating the discussion.

'Ah. The client really needs it in two... '

He looked at me with lethargic disdain.

'Tell the client,' he said, with the air of a poet or painter, 'we'll show him his advertising...*when it's great.*'

'That's all right,' said Mike Sharp, when I told him. 'He'll get it done on time. I'll have a word with him.'

That was two weeks ago.

Sure enough, Scott got on the phone. I fobbed him off with a variety of lies, then trotted round to ask Mike Sharp if he knew how Shortie was coming along with the ad. He gave me a blank look.

'Coming along with what ad?'

'The Elephant ad.'

'Haven't a fucking clue. I don't think he's looked at it yet.'

'Oh... It's just, if you recall, Scott wanted it inside two weeks, and you –'

'Two weeks! Tell him to fuck off.'

'But...'

'Tell him he can have it in...ten days. And, all right, I'll speak to Paul for you.'

'Ten days is unacceptable,' said Scott, when I told him.

'I'm sorry. We just need the extra time.'

'Well it's unacceptable. In the final analysis.'

I wheedled, cajoled, apologised. Eventually he phoned off, having insisted on diarying a meeting for the presentation of creative ideas in precisely ten days time.

I wonder if we'll have any creative ideas in precisely ten days time?

'Paul will crack it,' said Mike later. 'Relax.'

In the end Katherine did come down at the weekend. We went to the zoo together and took a look at the elephants. The Giant Panda was still on mating loan. We watched the elephants' antics as they bathed in a small concrete tank. The Jerry elephant hosed down the others, who trumpeted comically, wallowing in the shallow water.

'Nature's great masterpiece,' I said.

'Who said that?'

'John Donne. Look at that one – what a comedian.' One of the minor elephants was vainly attempting to clamber over one of the others, which had keeled over on its side and was puffing spray in the air. A ripple of laughter went through the crowd. After a bit they were coralled back into the pen and fed.

'Do you suppose there'll be elephants in the advertising?' said Katherine.

'Probably.'

'Where will you get them from?'

'I hadn't thought. The zoo, I suppose. Perhaps a circus.'

'Pity it isn't Toilet Dog. You could have cast Toby.'

We took Toby out for a walk when we got back. On our way we encountered Connie with a small, slothful black poodle. She was eying it fondly as it waddled round the railings.

'Jamie,' she said, in response to our enquiry. 'Looking after him for me sister.'

Jamie and Toby engaged in a prolonged and pop-eyed bum-sniffing exercise, circling one another on tiptoe.

'Making friends,' said Connie, indulgently.

As if on cue Jamie mounted Toby's rear end. Toby stood stock still looking mildly surprised, as if a small bomb had gone off just out of earshot. I hauled them apart, the poodle essaying to bite me with small, pointy teeth.

'He's a little imp,' crooned Connie at the snarling Jamie.

'He's a little pervert,' said Katherine, as soon as we were inside. 'Toby didn't look too put out, though, did he? I wonder if he's gay?'

'You don't get gay dogs.'

'No? I wonder.'

I took Katherine to Paddington on the Sunday evening. We embraced lingeringly on the platform, getting jostled by men and women with suitcases.

'I wish I could take tomorrow off,' she said.

'Why don't you?'

'They'll get suspicious.'

'Then why don't you leave, pack it all in, move down here with me? Get a proper job.'

'Like yours?'

'Well...'

'It's funny, Brodie. I have a kind of compulsion to see through this Elephant thing. I want to see it in the shops.'

'I know what you mean.'

'And it isn't long now, when you think about it. It'll be out in December.'

'Don't remind me. I have to get an ad approved first.'

'How's that coming along?'

'Hard to say. I've briefed it in. I've no idea what'll come out the other end.'

The Tannoy announced the imminent departure of the Bristol Temple Meads train. Katherine said, 'I think I'd better get on.'

She leant out of the carriage window and we kissed. The train began to move, and I walked down the platform with it until, with a little jolt of acceleration, it pulled ahead of me. Katherine's hair blew over her face as she waved. It made me ache with tenderness.

'I love you!' I bellowed, into the ear of a passing Arab. He shot me a quizzical glance.

'Your girl?'

'Yes.'

'Nice.'

'Thanks very much.'

He moved away, a little troop of family following in his wake. The train disappeared. I followed on, slowly, digging my hands into the pockets of my jeans, relishing the clip of my heels on the echoing concrete. Goddammit I'm nuts about that girl. Amazing the difference it makes to your life. Your whole outlook changes. I looked beamingly at the people about me. All of life was there, and I loved it indiscriminately. People were giving me a wide berth. Probably thought I was mad, or evangelical – Colonel Smiley from the planet Happy... I gave twenty pee to a busker kicking up a din by the ticket barrier, then bought a burger at a burger nook manned by seven-foot Ethiopians in cardboard hats. But I was too happy to eat it. I proffered it to a suspicious old bag lady, who grasped it and backed off rapidly, denouncing me with her mouth full as soon as I was at a safe distance. A bit of bun fell on the floor and was savaged by pigeons. I loved them all: bun, bag lady, pigeons.

Outside a traffic warden was standing next to the Beetle. He eyed me censoriously as I approached, stiffening with hostility when I gave him a grin and said hello. Don't fuck with me, hippie... He was one of the new breed of traffic warden, the privatised ones. Have you seen them? They have different uniforms and get paid by the scalp rather than the hour. But I loved him too. Greater love hath no man than to love a traffic warden.

'I don't want to argue about this,' he said, and stuck a ticket on the windscreen.

'How much am I in for?'

'Seventeen pounds.'

'Sure you don't want to argue about it?'

He gave me a look and moved on to the next car. Scott would make a good traffic warden. He never wants to argue about it either. He wants to give you a ticket.

I drove back and took Toby for his midnight stretch. He peed twenty-seven times.

CHAPTER TEN

*W*e *open on rolling African countryside. A vast herd of elephants sweeps majestically into view across the pampa. Music by Mahler throughout. A mighty bull elephant breaks away from the herd and stops beside Victoria Falls. He trumpets dramatically. Cut away to reaction shots from grazing antelope, gnu, and lions. The bull elephant sucks water through his trunk and blows it mightily in the air in a great arc. Cut away to exotic birds, in slow motion rocketing up out of the spray from the falls.Cut to silhouette of elephant framed against the sun setting over Mount Kenya. Dramatic music.*

Super: Put an Elephant in your Toilet – Toilet Elephant, from AKL.

SFX: Elephant trumpeting.

'Well?' said Mike Sharp. 'What do you think?'

'It's...striking,' I said.

'Isn't it? This is going to sweep the awards.'

'...It's just, I don't think it's what the client will have in mind.'

'What do you mean?'

'Well, for one thing, it doesn't actually show the product.'

'Exactly. It *challenges*...this is the kind of work that dictates consumer throughput.'

'Ye-es...'

'Paul wants to use David Attenborough for the shoot. You'll need to get onto his agent.'

The phone went, and Mike began another conversation. While he spoke I looked uneasily at the fax that had arrived the previous afternoon, from Scott. I read again:

PROJECT CAMEL: ADVERTISING DEVELOPMENT

The following points are mandatory in all advertising communication:
1. Highlight unique directionality benefit
2. Emphasise thick, clinging germicide power
3. Flag introductory offer price – 89 pence
4. Refer to attractive lemon-tang perfume
5. Demonstrate child-safe cap
6. Communicate environmental benefits
7. Reinforce consumer perception of AKL as manufacturer of a range of quality washroom and lavatory products (feature range)
8. Incorporate mission statement: 'AKL: The Professionals in the Lavatory'
9. Underline company reputation for customer service
10. All communication to be imbued with company heritage
(signed) Mike Scott.

Mike was still talking on the phone. I reread the script pensively. If I presented this Victoria Falls stuff to Scott after receiving his little list he would unquestionably go off his rocker. On the other hand, if I showed anything other than enthusiasm for Paul's script, Mike would unquestionably go off his... When he came off the phone I showed him Scottie's list. He didn't seem perturbed in the least.

'This isn't a problem. Just tell him he can't have it every way. Anyway, the ad meets most of these criteria.'

'It does?'

'Certainly. The environmental side; directionality; cleaning power...'

'Cleaning power?'

'The elephant is the most powerful creature on earth.'

'Ah.'

'Just *sell* it, Brodie. It'll do the business for Scott and it'll make us famous. You want that, don't you? Good. I tell you what – I'll come to the presentation on Thursday. What time is it?'

'Eight thirty.'

'Eight what? Why's it so fucking early?'

'Scott insisted.'

'Hmm. All right then. I can see I need to speak to Scott.'

I went away feeling a good deal perkier. If Mike could sell that script, fine. We're off to Africa. If not at least it wouldn't be my fault.

Back at my desk I ignored the telephone and concentrated instead on a little stack of literature about the African elephant. After all, if Kenya it is to be, then I need to have the low-down on the Kenyan variety. After an hour of frequently interrupted reading I had established that Asian and African elephants differ in as far as their ears are not the same shape. That, as far as I can gather, is about the extent of it. Asian elephants are a tad smaller. Although – did you know this? – there used to be several different types of elephant, not just two, and as recently as the time of Christ. Endangering species isn't a purely modern activity. We've been at it for ages. Thousands of elephants were wiped out in the ancient world, in wars and Roman games. And the ivory trade obviously hasn't done them any favours over subsequent centuries. In fact, the impression I get from most of the reports is that we'll have to get a move on to film a vast herd of elephants anywhere... I read on grimly. All the elephant population charts go into nose-dive around 1980. Fifteen years ago there were twice as many in Africa as there are now. *Twice as many...* Other dire predictions crossed the pages: not just about elephants, but all kinds of other species too. You name it, it's endangered. And not just through human beastliness and stupidity. The key thing seems to be that *habitats* are disappearing. They're disappearing because we need the space for us. There's only so much space on the globe. That's what it is: elephants are too *big*. They take up too much room. Who's it going to be – us, or the ones with the long noses?

'We'll shoot in two African states,' said Paul. 'The one the wossname waterfall's in, and Kenya for Mount Kenya. What's the production budget?'

'I don't know. Scott's already been having a go about cost, though.'

'Tell him to fuck off. Shoot it cheap and it'll look cheap. Another thing – can't shoot till the spring. The light won't be right.'

'But Scott needs the ad for his sales conference – they're launching in six weeks.'

'Six weeks! Tell him to fuck off.'

You've got to admit, the tell-him-to-fuck-off school of life is a clean and simple one. Consider the advantages...Paul – the gas man's here with a gas bill. Tell him to fuck off. Time to get up and go to work, Paul! Fuck off. Just tell everyone who gets up your nose to fuck off! Feeling low? Go out in the street and tell the first person you see to fuck off. Oy, you – *fuck* off.

'Can you come to the presentation on Thursday morning?' I asked. 'Mike would like you to be there.'

'What time is it?'

'Eight thirty.'

'Eight thirty! *Fuck off!*'

I fucked off. It's sometimes the best option with Paul.

Thursday a.m. Let's go.

The alarm goes at a quarter to six, fifteen minutes ahead of my usual reveille. I'm taking no chances on my big day here. Springing lightly out of bed I assume mugger's gear – dark tracksuit, gloves, extra woolly balaclava – and bundle downstairs with Toby in hot pursuit. Toby loves these early starts. In his book it's never too early to be up and doing. We hit the street and head off round the squares, a lamplit tour of literary London. Charles Dickens lived here. Evelyn Waugh had a flat there. T.S. Eliot drank at that pub. Virginia Woolf used that laundrette. This is a pretty historic area, you know. Every other building has its blue plaque and preservation order. Toby pauses to dump effortfully in the gutter outside the Soane Museum, while I jog up and down to keep warm, rehearsing my speech to Scott and Jerry (and Katherine – she'll be there). What we *have* here, Mike, is...The *key* thought of this commercial, Jerry, is...Who knows? Maybe they'll buy it.

Playing safe, I cut a corner and haul Toby back towards Regent's Square ten minutes ahead of schedule. I plonk down his breakfast and make the tea as he gulps it down. Then it's all the way down again for another crap and supplementary peeing (I really don't know how he does it. His bladder must be like the Tardis.) And up we go again to get dressed and out of here.

So far, the saying has it, so good. But what's this? Why, of all mornings, do I manage to sever my jugular vein (or so it would appear) when shaving? There is blood in pints. And wherefore the surprise zit on the tip of the nose? Furiously, I swab and plaster. Unaccountably, all my underwear is missing. I hoist a fetid pair from the laundry box, grimacing as I clamber within. Next, the freshly ironed shirt laid out in preparation the night before dispenses with its buttons: they come off in my hand, neatly, one by one, as I thumb them through the holes. Son of a bitch! The only other clean one lies crumpled in the laundry basket. Cursing horribly, I wrench open the door to the kitchen cupboard and reach inside for the iron. But today is not my day. Today was scheduled fuck-up-Brodie day way on back before the dawn of time. The cupboard, normally well behaved and unassuming, springs into action. A broom topples down to chin me. The hoover loafs me in the knee. The ironing board exercises a scissors attack. A heavy French casserole feels the call of gravity. What's going on? Why me? Why now?

I shovel the frolicsome contents back within and set up the iron and ironing board. The shirt's as dry as cardboard. The wrinkles lie like ancient contour lines, implacably resisting the heat. I discover the right sleeve has been hanging in Toby's water bowl the while, operating a blotting paper effect...Tetchily I wring it out and plank the metal on it with a hiss... Finishing off I pull for the other sleeve. Mysterious resistance: Toby is sitting on it. He looks up at me trustfully. I yank it out, to his evident surprise (you can see him thinking: Fuck me!) and unpick the matting of dog hair overlaying the cuff.

Eventually, at seven fifteen, I burst onto the pavement and sprint for the bus stop. I spot the 189's red behind trundling off down Southampton Way and chase along in its sooty wake for two hundred yards, feet slapping on the pavement, to overtake it at the next bus stop and fling myself within. No worries. Work in half an hour, this time in the morning...

Recovering my breath, I stare out the window. Traffic's heavy. Wonder why? Check the watch – seven twenty. Surreptitiously check neighbour's watch – also seven twenty. A police car shouts its way past, then another, then a van, then a pair of shiny fire engines. Now what?

'Bomb scare, mate,' says my neighbour. 'Fucking IRA, innit.'

'Where?'

'Inna Strand. Bastards.'

Bomb scare. Uh huh. Off we get again...

But even as I rise the bus gains the bus lane, unaffected by the chaos, and goes plunging off in the wake of the sirens, plummeting towards Aldwych. Ah well, I reckon, hop off at the Strand – but the fucker diverts! Of course it diverts! There's a bomb in the fucking Strand! It diverts over Waterloo Bridge. That's quite a diversion if you're heading for Haymarket...And Waterloo Bridge, naturally, is a solid line of patient metal, like a production line at a car factory, fixed, unmoving, there for ever. London – don't you love it?

'Can I get off? I've got to be somewhere.'

'Sorry, mate. 'Gainst regulations before the stop.'

'Well where's the stop?'

'Waterloo Station.'

'But it could take hours to get to Waterloo Station! Look at the state of the traffic.'

Shrug. So be it. These are the quantum physics of bus travel. Ninety yards in nine seconds. Ninety yards in ninety minutes. Something you live with, innit.

To an enraged shout I bludgeon open the retracting door, yanking hard on the emergency handles. And then I'm off and running back towards the city...

'Can't come through here.' A police palm, turned flat towards me.

'I have to get to Piccadilly – what's the best bet?'

'Tube from Waterloo.'

Ten minutes later I'm pausing for breath on the down escalator at Waterloo. Naturally, the tube is exceptionally late and crowded. I join the scrimmage at the sliding doors, cramming myself within at the last possible moment, face packed up against the glass. The tube starts. It goes into a tunnel. The tube stops. It appears to be suffering from wind. Several belchy shudderings later it starts again. It stops again. It starts again. It has a rest then gives it another go. An irate voice comes over the intercom telling us to stop pressing up against the doors – the tube doesn't like it. Well I'm not nuts about it either, pal... It is unbearably hot. To my right an elbow is jabbing hard into my kidneys. The bloke behind me, who I can only surmise lives on a diet of raw onions and Camp Coffee, exhales powerfully at five-second intervals... *How does anyone stand this stuff?* To think that some people put up with it every day! What for? Wouldn't they rather be buried in a shallow grave and covered in earth?

I alight at Green Park Station at 8.29.

The lift puts me out at 8.33.

'Oh, there you are,' says Mike Sharp. 'They've just arrived. I can't be there after all, I'm afraid – something's come up. Sock it to them, yeah?'

Nine fifty three.

'It's unacceptable,' says Scott. 'In the final analysis.'

'What is it that you aren't happy with?'

'Everything. It isn't where we want the brand to be.'

'I see. Where would you like the brand to be?'

'I indicated in my note.'

'Yes, I saw that... But there were quite a number of different elements there if you recall. I'm sure you would agree that the television advertising can only communicate so much really effectively.'

'No, I wouldn't agree with that. In the final analysis. Your job is to communicate what I want communicated. This isn't where we want the brand to be.'

'Hear, hear.' Jerry.

'Fine, but can I just say...'

Scott holds up a palm. 'I don't want to argue about this,' he says.

'Well?'

'He hated it.'

'What? What do you mean, he hated it?'

'I mean he hated it. It wasn't where he wanted the brand to be.'

'For fuck's sake.' Mike strode powerfully round the room. 'What did he say about the location?'

'It wasn't where he wanted the brand to be.'

'What about the herd of elephants – he must have gone for that.'

'They weren't where he wanted the brand to be either.'

'Where does he want his fucking brand to be?'

'There.' I gave him the fax.

'What's this?'

'His notes on the advertising. You remember I showed it to you a fortnight ago.'

'No you didn't. I've never seen this before. When did you get this?'

'He faxed it over at the start of last week. I showed it to you when we were looking at the script.'

'Out of the question. I'd have remembered *this*. Jesus.' He sat heavily in a thick leather chair. For a few seconds he glowered at the fax. Then he glowered at me. Then he reached for his intercom.

'Cressida? Get Paul up here, now.'

'Well?' said Paul, presently.

'He didn't buy it.'

'You mean you didn't sell it?'

'I wasn't there. He didn't like it.'

'What about it didn't he like?'

'The lot.'

'Ah, tell him to fuck off,' said Paul. 'Why wasn't I diaried for this? I'd have sold it.'

'I told you,' I said. 'You decided not to come.'

'When did you tell me? You never told me. Nobody told me.'

'Tuesday.'

'Tuesday? Fuck off. No way. I wasn't even *in* on Tuesday. '

'We had lunch on Tuesday,' said Mike. 'You must have been in.'

'Well I was here for lunch,' said Paul, with the air of one conceding a minor point.

There was a pause.

'I've got to go to the opera,' said Mike heavily, as if it were a funeral. 'We'll talk about this later.'

'Well?'

'I got my head kicked in. What do you think?'

'I'm sorry, Brodie.'

'Ah, stuff it. Who gives a shit? Thanks for asking. What did you think of the script?'

'Expensive.'

'Not half.'

'And pretty silly.'

'Yes.'

'When do you think you'll have another to present?'

'Dunno. Next week?'

'Scott's furious about it.'

'Good, good.'

'Brodie?'

'Hello?'

'Listen, I can't come down at the weekend after all – I'm sorry...hello?'

'Yeah, yeah – I'm here. Can I ask why?'

'It's kind of personal. I'll see you next weekend instead okay? Okay?'

'Okay.'

'Don't let it bother you. It isn't a big deal. Look, I have to go now.'

'See you at the next presentation then.'

'I guess. Bye, Brodes.'

'Carpet Mania for you,' said Vanessa, holding up her phone as I put down mine. 'Something about the wrong headlines appearing on yesterday's ads.'

That evening, for reasons best known to myself, I got steamingly drunk with Hippo and the lads.

CHAPTER ELEVEN

It never really seemed to get light on Saturday. I went out to get a paper under a grid of troubled rain clouds, the kind that try to dump their load but never manage more than the occasional wheezy sputter, while the wind gusted and changed direction, bullying the trees. Pensioners plodded along like the survivors of some totalitarian cleanout, hunched, defeated, gripping their plastic bags like talismen. When I got home I went straight back to bed again. Toby catapulted onto my lap and began a thorough and noisy overhaul of his personal hygiene. I looked through the news section. Random disaster jumped off the pages. Irritably I flapped past the quakes and crashes, and found myself reading an article about the polar bears in Bristol Zoo, Misha and Nina, aged twenty-five and thirty-one respectively. Observers had come to the conclusion that Misha and Nina were none too thrilled by the lifestyle on offer in the zoo's polar bear department. They would spend hours pacing backwards and forwards, making repetitive movements. So they got a psychiatrist on the case. The psychiatrist spent time studying Misha and Nina's behaviour before diagnosing them as – wait for it – depressed. They were depressed. Under the weather. What to do? You can't have depressed polar bears moping about the place. Bad for morale. It upsets the public. It makes the public *depressed*. So a programme of 'enrichment' was initiated, to cheer them up. Traffic cones, plastic barrels and footballs were introduced for recreation. Their food was scattered round the pit so that the bears would have to forage for it. And they were given logs flavoured with garlic and beef extract to chew on like lollies. The article concluded that the bears now lead 'richer, busier lives'.

I saw a film once about a man (played by Ben Kingsley), and a woman (played by Glenda Jackson) who hit upon the idea of setting free the giant turtles at London Zoo (played, presumably, by the giant turtles at London Zoo.) It was a beautiful film – humane, life-affirming, romantic. With the co-operation of the turtle-keeper (Michael Gambon), they put the turtles into crates and drove them off to Polperro in Cornwall, where they released them back into the sea. Everyone lived happily ever after. Especially Glenda Jackson and Michael Gambon, who had become lovers.

I lay in the crumpled debris of my Guardian, brooding on the story of Misha and Nina. I wish someone could drive them to Scotland, put them on an iceberg and float them back to the Arctic. Plastic balls and garlic-flavoured logs – give me a break. You change something fundamental in an animal when you give it a garlic-flavoured log. Misha and Nina aren't polar bears any more. Polar bears hunt seals under twenty feet of ice. These two are a sideshow, a couple of Mongol children in a concrete playpen.

The thing is, you *couldn't* return Misha and Nina to the wild, just like you couldn't return the elephants at London Zoo to the wild. For one thing the animals themselves aren't wild any more. For another – there isn't much wild worth speaking of to return them to.

Toby was licking his genitals with bottle-eyed concentration. Wonder if I could return him to the wild? Pugs aren't really dogs. They're toy dogs, cross-bred for a laugh by some joker in ancient China. Toby's dog characteristics are not pronounced. He is, for example, the only dog I know to have been chased by a rabbit. Honest to God. Dad took Tobes out in the fens when he was small, and they encountered some rabbits. Toby took one look and backed off. I'm not tangling with no rabbits... Although, curiously, he's quite bold with other dogs. It takes all sorts.

After lunch I caught a bus down to the South Bank and walked for a bit by the river. The water was thick and brown and swirly, like freshly stirred tea, coiling in weird configurations. I had a browse amongst the windswept second-hand bookstalls and picked up a book by a nineteenth-century botanist and explorer. There was lots about elephants in it. It was nice to discover that even in those high-hunting days there were a handful of gentle and enlightened characters who could take delight in elephants for their own sake, not as game trophies or raw material for billiard balls. I paid a quid for it and tucked it under my jacket.

When I got back I took Toby out for a trot, then sat down with my book and a pint of tea in front of the gas fire. Toby jockeyed for position in front of the heat, grunting contentedly. I thought for a while about the elephants at the zoo, getting a fix on them in my head. Then I opened the book at random and started to read. The prose was richly archaic and, in its cumbersome way, deeply affecting.

Like immortal flowers they have drifted down to us on the ocean of time, and their strangeness and beauty bring to our imaginations a dream and a picture of that unknown world, immeasurably far removed, where man was not: and when they perish, something of the gladness goes out from nature, and the sunshine loses something of its brightness.

It's true. It does. Strangeness and beauty...I felt a twinge of guilt. It's all very well moralising about elephants and polar bears – the day before yesterday I was doing my utmost to get Scott to approve a television commercial explicitly linking these immortal flowers with a revolutionary new kind of lavatory cleaner that cleans right under the rim. Toilet Elephant: now there's a concept for you; Toilet Elephant, there's a funny old juxtaposition... Ah, stuff it. I doubt the elephants would really care. They've got enough on their minds.

I called Katherine, but she wasn't there. I called Edward instead, but he was out too. Feeling suddenly depressed, I poured myself an inch of whisky from a dusty bottle in the kitchen. I'd bought it ages ago for the time my father came to see the flat after I first moved in. It tasted filthy – I hate whisky – but I swallowed it down like medicine and poured another. I sat with the bottle in front of me in the kitchen, drinking and staring aimlessly at the cooker. The whisky didn't make me feel more cheerful. It made me feel fucked up and lonely. I wished I could talk to Katherine, and tried her number again.

About half past ten I got hungry and made myself some soup and toast. At least, soup and toast was the theory. A good deal of both seemed to end up on the floor, much to the approval of the foraging Toby. It wasn't till I caught sight of myself in the reflection of the darkened window, cheeks abulge, slapping margarine on a slice of toast, that I appalled myself sufficiently to pour the whisky down the sink and go to bed. Toby paddled after me expectantly. Shit – I'd forgotten his walk. Another reason not to get smashed by yourself. I clambered back into my half-discarded clothes and wrestled him into his lead.

Outside the fresh air made me feel slightly giddy all of a sudden. I slipped Toby's leash and leant against the railings as he trotted off to make a round of the trees. The wind had eased, but it was cold. I followed his fawn behind with my eyes, breathing deeply.

'You arright, son?'

I half turned and found myself looking at a vagrant – not one of the regulars. He can't have been that much older than me. He was carrying a tin of Superstrong and having some difficulty focussing.

'I'm pissed.'

'Fair enough, aye. No bad way to be. That your dog?'

'Yes.'

'Funny wee bugger, eh?'

'Mm.'

'Cigarette?'

'No, thanks.'

'You fancy a drop o' this?'

I eyed the can torpidly. I'd no idea whisky did this to you. 'It's very kind,' I said, '...but I think I'm going to be sick.'

He came closer and laid an arm on my shoulder. The pong coming off him was unreal. *'It's okay, son,'* he said, kindly, speaking with the air of an expert, a professional man in such matters: *'You're okay.'*

In this way I brought my Saturday night to a close, throwing up by my front door, consoled by a tramp. Luckily, even at the time, it struck me as faintly comic, and I was able to go to bed much cheered. 'See you around, then,' called my friend, as I regained the stairs with Toby at my heels. I didn't doubt it.

The telephone traumatised me awake at nine fifteen on Sunday morning. Did I mention I bought an answer machine? I didn't want to miss calls from Kath while I was out with Toby. But I didn't miss calls from Kath. I missed calls for Kev, the plumber. Every time I played back the tape I'd hear a detailed account of some plumbing problem and a brusque demand for services. Perhaps I should sell the contacts to a real plumber?

And another thing, on the subject of telephones. My fucking bank's been calling me up at home. Can you believe that? It's my own fault. I decided to switch accounts to one of these trendy new banks where you can phone them up any time and get them to do things. What the ads omit to mention is that there's a corollary to being able to phone them up any time. They can phone you up any time. And they do. It started when my cheque card never arrived. I phoned up to kick some ass and discovered some comedy character had got hold of it and gone off on a spree. A couple of weeks back, for example, he spent a hundred and fifty pounds at a service station on the M6. *How?* It can't be easy spending that kind of money at a service station. What did he buy – a year's supply of souvenir shortbread? Egg and chips times fifty?

I fumbled for the receiver, knocked it off onto the floor, groped it to my ear. 'Yeah?'

'Get up, Brodie, you lazy fuck. We're going for a ride.'

'Edward...now is not the optimum moment.'

'Yes it is. It's a brilliant day and there's nothing on the roads. I've already been to Reading and back. Come *on*. I'll be over in ten minutes.'

'Give me an hour.'

'Hour, bollocks. We'll be in Newcastle in an hour. Get dressed.'

I clambered heavily out of bed. Toby was woofing peremptorily next door. Out in the square the sunlight blinded me, sending great shockwaves through my skull, already fully occupied with a mother and father of a hangover, a hangover from the vintage school of hangovers. But it was a beautiful morning, still and crisp, with a low sun and mist smoking off the grass. My friend from the night before was sitting on a bench on the other side of the square, drinking a carton of tea. We waved at one another. Toby went chugging over to him and started inhaling his trousers.

Twenty minutes later I was crouched on the back of Edward's bike, letting the noise and the acceleration and the cold air blast the gooks out of my system. We hammered off up the M11, ripping past the occasional car tootling up the inside lane. In no time at all we were slowing down into the outskirts of Cambridge.

'What you reckon?' shouted Edward over his shoulder.

'Fucking marvellous!'

'Breakfast?'

'Do it.'

We dismounted on King's Parade and entered a quiet little tea room serving breakfast to dozy undergraduates. The matron in command looked meaningfully at Edward's leathers for a second, but took the order.

'So?' said Edward, pouring tea into dainty little cups. 'What you been up to?'

'Well. Last night I got drunk by myself in the flat and threw up. Ask me why.'

'Why?'

'I got depressed.'

'Why?'

'Various things. I think Katherine may be seeing someone else.'

'Why do you think that?'

'She wouldn't come over this weekend.'

'What else?'

'That's it.'

'There must be more than that.'

'I don't know, Edward. I'm crazy about her, but I just kind of get the feeling she's not so keen any more.'

'Go on.'

The plates arrived and we waded in with our elbows sticking out at right angles. I went on. I developed my theory. When I was finished Edward lit a cigarette and pushed his plate away.

'I honestly think you're worrying for no reason.'

'It gives me something to do.'

'Relax, B. Everything's cool.'

'What about you? Still seeing Lucy?'

'Lucy?'

'That girl from Saatchis.'

'Oh right. Yes, we still see a bit of each other. I've been busy, though. I'm getting some cash together to go abroad. I've been doing some long-distance work. Know where I went the day before yesterday? Stirling. I went and took a look at the dear old school while I was up there.'

'Still standing?'

'Yup. Looks smaller, though. I remember it about the size of Windsor Castle.'

'Seems like a lifetime ago, doesn't it?'

'Thank Christ.'

'You know, I envy you, Edward. You don't seem to have a care in the world.'

'Oh, I don't know. I think my hair may be starting to fall out.'

'What's the secret?'

'Rub onions into your scalp?'

'No...you know what I mean.'

'Easy. Find something you care about and pursue it.'

'What do you care about? Motorbikes?'

'Freedom. What do you care about? Lavatory cleaner?'

'I don't know what I care about. Actually, that isn't true. I care about a lot of things. It's just...oh, I don't know.'

'Will there be anything else?' said the matron, looming beside us.

'Just the bill, thanks.'

'That was a really wonderful breakfast,' said Edward. He gave her one of his rare smiles.

'Thank you – thank you very much.' She smiled back.

'See how easy it is to make people happy? Think I should take her for a ride? What were you saying?'

'It's nothing. Let's go.'

'Where to?'

'Come and take a look at my father's place. There's something I want to pick up.'

A bell bonged twelve as we turned into Portugal Place. Two clergymen came ticking past us on their boneshakers, trousers stuffed into their socks. A cat was sunning itself picturesquely on the doorstep to number 25. 'Nice place,' said Edward. 'You should flog it to a property developer.'

'It belongs to the college.'

'Too bad.'

The door yielded slowly, obstructed by junk mail. Inside the familiar smell lingered potently, a musky bachelor smell of tobacco and books and shoe polish, as tangible as the heavy furnishings.

'What are you after?'

'I'll show you. Come through here.'

I went through to the study. Over by the window, its wooden lid furry with dust, stood the elephant's foot.

'What the hell is that?'

'Used to belong to an elephant.'

'Crumbs.' Edward took it from me carefully. 'Big toenails.'

I took it back and opened it: a ball of string, bulldog clips, pencils. Junk.

'You taking it with you?' said Edward doubtfully.

'Would it fit on the bike?'

'I don't know. Possibly.'

'Okay, I've a better idea.'

We left the flat and walked to Jesus bridge. The Cam glittered dazzlingly in the light. A couple of punts floundered past in zig zags, piloted by a wobbly tourists with chilly and apprehensive passengers. I waited till the coast was clear, then tipped the foot over the parapet like a cannon ball. There was a cavernous plop. Edward looked at me enquiringly.

'I'll explain another time,' I said. 'Let's get going now.'

I got back at five after a whirlwind tour of East Anglia, feeling generally pepped up. A couple of pangs of conscience about the foot, but nothing serious. I can't believe dad will notice its absence. I'd better think twice before I chuck the cutlery and the chess pieces into the drink, mind you. You can take these impulses too far.

I picked up the phone and dialled Katherine's number. There was a pause, followed by a loud screech. Then I got an interminable conversation between two Welshmen talking about vegetables. Then I got the dialling tone. I dialled again and got a tweedy, pre-recorded voice telling me to try later. A call to the telephone engineer confirmed the verdict: the phone was fucked. One fucked phone.

Determined to brook no obstacle, I rooted around the bedroom collecting loose change and headed out to find a phone box. But the local phone boxes weren't in such great condition either. I think there must have been a match earlier that day, or possibly a riot, or an earthquake. I crunched through broken glass, peering into evil-smelling booths where the receivers swung at the end of their wires like hanged men. Eventually, on Tottenham Court Road, I located an operational machine. Unusually, none of previous callers had vomited, defecated or given birth during the course of their calls. The walls were stuck around with prostitutes' cards, bluntly advertising the age and chest size of the girls in question, with suggestive little illustrations and line drawings. I made a cursory survey while I fumbled out the change. Youth, blondeness, and a willingness to undergo corporal punishment seems to be what the market dictates. *Cane me*, suggested one. *Cum in my face*, enjoined a second. I have to tell you, I wouldn't fancy this line of work... Bad enough taking endless calls for Kev the plumber – imagine being on the end of the line for some of this stuff. Good afternoon – I'm interested in cumming in your face... Sick, sick. Sick, and not all that sexy.

I posted my coins and dialled. Two rings. Three rings.

'Hello?' said a voice. A mature, male voice.

For a second I studied the panel displaying the number I'd dialled: it was Katherine's. But Katherine lives alone, don't you see, in a studio flat. Ergo, Katherine it should be who answers the telephone.

'Is...Katherine there?' The words dropped slowly into the greasy receiver.

'She's taking a shower. Who's calling?'

'A friend of hers.'

'Would you like her to call you back?...Hello?'

'No. No thanks.'

I returned the receiver to its clip and leant back against the glass, thinking, thinking. There could be a simple explanation. Or there could be another. Gradually, the pornography on the wall formed a blurred collage in front of my eyes, blending with the welt of obscene imagery taking shape in my head.

'Shit,' I said out loud, after a while, and thumped the box with the meat of my hand. '*Shit*.'

Have you ever tried beating up a phone box? It's a doddle. What you do is, basically, you give it a *really good kicking*. It's pretty one-sided. The phone box doesn't get a look-in.

A word of advice, however, for anyone thinking of giving it a go. Be selective about your phone box. Select your phone box selectively. Why do you think that phone box, of all phone boxes, was un-pissed-in, pristine, operational? Any ideas?

It's opposite Tottenham Court Road Police Station: that's why.

I spent the next five hours in a cell. Quite an experience, and one which I shall be making efforts not to repeat. The police were quite chummy, all things considered. I think they spotted I wasn't a particularly talented vandal. Indeed, there was considerable ribaldry at my expense. Probably no bad thing. It took my mind away from the imaginations that clustered whenever I replayed the phone call. At two in the morning my brother bailed me and drove me back to the flat.

'What you do it for?' he asked, legitimately enough.

'Don't ask.'

'I am asking. I think the least you can do if you drag me all the way out here at this time of night to get you out of a cell is to to tell me what it's all about. You weren't drunk? Have you been taking drugs?'

'No.'

'Was it a bet? A dare?'

'I'd had some bad news. I was upset. Okay?'

Stephen looked at me narrowly. 'A girl?'

'Well done.'

He grunted. 'Pretty stupid way to behave, even so.'

'I know. Can we leave it at that and go to bed?'

We left it at that. I went to bed, but I didn't sleep. I wasn't feeling too clever. What's happening to me? Tell me something – give me your frank opinion. Am I losing my marbles? Am I going patso? And if so, why? Stress? Booze? Elephants?

Katherine called me next morning at the office. The explanation was, of course, fabulously straightforward.

'Your *father*?'

'Yes – he's just got back from abroad. Why, who did you think it was?'

'I...why didn't you say?'

'Oh, Brodie.' There was a giggle. 'You didn't think...'

'I did.'

'An older man, eh?'

'And wiser.'

'I don't know what to make of this jealousy bit. You obviously don't trust me one iota.'

'It isn't that, Kath, I swear. I'm just – I don't know...the truth is I haven't really been myself the last couple of days.' And I told her about the tramp, the elephant's foot, the phone box, the police cell. When she'd finished laughing she said, 'Brodie, Brodie, Brodie...You're cracking up! I can't believe you got arrested for smashing in a phone box.'

'Neither can I. I have to go to court in a fortnight. I'll probably wind up in Strangeways.'

There was further merriment from the end of the line.

'Look,' she said. 'I'll tell you what. Put your tiny mind at rest. Come to the Gower next weekend. It's my mother's birthday. Dad'll be there – you can meet him.'

'I thought your parents were divorced?'

'They are.'

'Oh. Don't divorced couples throw plates at each other?'

'Not always. As a matter of fact Mum and Dad hit it off much better now than they did when they were married.'

'What does he do?'

'He's a pilot.'

'Rich?'

'I don't know. Quite, I think. Why?'

'Maybe that's something I could do instead of advertising. It's beginning to get me down.'

'Hang in there, Brodie. You're doing fine. Even Scottie quite likes you.'

'Really?'

'No of course he doesn't. I just said that to cheer you up. Better go now. Behave yourself, okay?'

'Okay. Bye, Kath.'

'Bye, crazy. Keep smiling.'

I put the phone down. I still didn't feel too clever, but I felt a lot happier.

We open on an attractive young housewife, fully kitted out with household cleaning equipment: dusters, aerosols, loo brush etc. She speaks to camera:

'Housework's a chore! Luckily my cleaning lady's up to the job — aren't you Flo?' Flo appears. She is an elephant dressed in a chequered pinny and four gigantic fluffy pink carpet slippers. She takes up a duster with her trunk and cleans along the picture rail.

'My neighbours asked me, why an elephant? I told them, have a look at my loo!'

Cut away to close-up of lavatory.

'It looks clean…but germs can lurk under the rim, escaping even the toughest cleaner. But Flo puts paid to that! With new Toilet Elephant, from AKL.'

Flo picks up product and squirts it round the bowl. Close-up of under-the-rim action.

'The unique trunk nozzle shoots thick, lemon-perfumed cleaner into every recess of the toilet…the kind of thoroughness you've come to expect from AKL — The Professionals in The Lavatory.'

Cut away to pack shot. Dissolve into range shot of all AKL washroom products.

Male voice over: 'New Toilet Elephant — for total under-the-rim freshness. From AKL.'

Subtitle: AKL: The Professionals in The Lavatory.

Starburst 1: Only 89p!

Starburst 2: Environmentally friendly!

Sound Effects: Elephant trumpeting.

'Well?' said Mike Sharp. 'What do you think?'

'Better,' said Scott, after a little pause.

'Much better!' said Jerry.

'But it's still unsatisfactory,' said Scott.

'In what way?'

'It doesn't refer to the child-safe cap.'

'We can illustrate it.'

'I want it highlighted.'

'Okay, we'll see what we can do. What else?'

'I still don't like the trumpeting at the end.'

'I'll talk to Paul about it. Anything else?'

'It's too long.'

'It's only thirty seconds.'

'That's too long. You know my views on this. I wanted a twenty.'

'But there's a lot to say – I'm sure you'd agree.'

'You're the creative people. You need to make it work more efficiently.'

Mike Sharp paused to light a cigarette, puffing and billowing in grand style. 'Listen,' he said, 'Michael...You know how accommodating Paul's been...He was more than happy to put in the starbursts. He's welcomed and gone along with all your suggestions. But I just don't think it's *possible* to shoot this ad in under thirty seconds.'

There was a silence.

'Could you do it twenty-five?' suggested Jerry.

'You can't buy 25-second slots,' I said. 'The contractors don't deal in them.'

'Oh? Why not?'

'Never mind why not,' said Scott. 'They just don't. Very well...I *might* consider a thirty if you can do me a ten-second cut-down in addition. And at no extra cost.'

'Of course,' said Mike. 'So we have a script?'

The meeting held its breath.

'We have a script,' said Scott.

And everybody shook hands.

'I disown it,' said Paul.

'Nonsense, nonsense. It's *fine*. The client's nuts about it.'

Paul snorted. 'So he should be. He fucking wrote it. The only thing it's got in common with the ad we started off with is the trumpeting at the end.'

'Brilliant touch that. Brilliant. Client loves it.'

Mike was in tremendous spirits. He'd had a fair amount to drink on the train on the way back. So had I, but not for the same reason. It makes me nervous sitting for three hours opposite Mike Sharp.

'Oh,' he added, 'there is just *one* more little thing...'

Paul eyed him malevolently.

'...the child-safe cap.'

'What about the child-safe cap?'

'Scott wants it highlighted a *teeny weeny* bit more than it is at the moment.'

'Tell him to –'

'But other than that he loves it. *Loves* it. All we need now,' he said, swivelling towards me, '...is an elephant.'

An elephant, eh?

Jerry called the next day, just as I was getting my mouth round a mid-morning bacon roll. 'Found one yet?' he asked.

'We're looking,' I said. 'It isn't that easy, as a matter of fact. Zoos don't lend them out, and none of the other sources we've tried have been very keen.'

'What do you mean?'

'Well, on letting us film their animals.'

'Really?' As usual, Jerry sounded amazed, astonished. 'Well what about the production estimate? Have you got any costs in yet?'

'Right. I've got an initial quote from Silverstone Redwing. Paul wants to use Carl Redwing for the shoot. He's a very highly regarded director.'

'How much?' said Jerry.

I told him. There was a stunned silence.

'*How much?*'

'I know it's a lot, Jerry, but the thing is, it *is* a three-day shoot, and –'

'Three days!'

'...and there'll be the set build –'

'What set build?'

'In the studio.'

'What studio? What do you need a *studio* for? Why can't you just film it in a house?'

'Jerry, believe me, this film demands a studio shoot. In any case, it'd probably cost more to film on location.'

'Who's talking about a location? What do you think this is – *Gone With the Wind*? Just shoot it in someone's house.'

'I'm afraid it isn't as simple as that.'

There was a snort. 'How much of that cost is the director's fee?' I told him. It did sound a lot of money. It *was* a lot of money – but that's the way it goes. Good directors cost a lot of money. And boy do we need a good director on this script. You see, a crappy script (like this one), shot by a good director, ends up as a marginally less crappy film. But a crappy script shot by a *crappy* director ends up a substantially *more* crappy film. Its crappiness increases. It suffers incremental crappiness. But try explaining that to Jerry. Try telling a bear to shit in a toilet.

He exhaled noisily. 'Well I can tell you now, Brodie, this quote is quite unacceptable. Quite unacceptable.'

I looked dully at the reflections in my shoes. For once the magic didn't work. I don't need this shit. I don't *need* it... Why can't they just accept it? We're going to make the ad whatever happens, so can't we just get on with it? Please? Have we really got to go through all this grief? Have we *got* to haggle? An incident from the summer flashed into my mind... An elderly Afghan in a dirty robe had picked up a 20p banana at a fruit stall on Charing Cross road, and was offering 15p for it to the bored cockney behind the barrow. 'Look, mate,' said the cockney. 'This isn't Baghdad – just buy it or fuck off, will ya?'

'Look, Jerry,' I said. 'Just buy it or fuck off, will you?'

Actually I didn't say that. I explained the money to him while he made a noise like a cow swallowing a beetroot. Eventually he got bored.

'We'll see what *Mike* has to say about this,' he said, and hung up. I'm sure we will.

And in the meantime, no elephant. A complete absence of elephants. To tell you the truth, I hadn't been trying all that hard. You've seen that script. Fluffy slippers and a chequered pinny...I'm ashamed to be associated with it. Really, I am. But what to do? Resign? I've got a mortgage to pay. I've got debts to service, a dog to support. I can't afford to. Tell me – what would *you* do? How would you handle it? I'd really like to know. I called up Katherine and talked to her about it. Hang in there, she said. Just hang on in there.

'But it's *horrible*, Kath. I can't think of anything more shitty and demeaning.'

'It's not that bad – '

'Yes it is. Absolutely it is.'

'Listen. It does you credit, but you've got to ignore it. It won't make any difference if you make a stand about this anyway. You'll just end up in the shit and somebody else will do it instead.'

'I know,' I said. 'I know.'

As a matter of fact, somebody else did do it instead. I got a phone call later in the morning from Caroline Silverstone, the producer.

'Brodie? I think I may have found one.'

'Yes? Where?'

'There's a Ukranian circus visiting the week we need to shoot. They've got a performing elephant called Monica they're willing to hire out during the day. They're asking quite a bit, but it's worth it.'

'Good. Fine. Great.'

'I've biked over some literature with photographs in it for you to show to your client. We are going to need an animatronic elephant as well, though.'

'A what?'

'Computerised model. For the tricky bits – in case Monica doesn't play ball on the set.'

'Is that extra money?'

'Yes.' She gave me the cost. An astonishingly large amount of money.

'Okay,' I said heavily. 'Let me get on to the client. I'll call you back.'

I went out for a sandwich to cheer myself up. The shops were full of Christmas decorations, but there wasn't much gaiety on the streets. Everyone looked harassed and fucked-about, slogging along with their heads down under a sky the colour of the pavement. Even Mario looked under the weather. I ate a roll and an apple hunched on a bench in Green Park, importuned by beggars and pigeons, then headed back to the office.

When I returned I found a package on my desk. Inside was a highly coloured brochure promoting the circus. A yellow sticky marked the elephant page. There was Monica, standing on hind legs, trunk curled in the air. There she was again, playing the piano. 'Monica plays Tchaikovsky!' said the caption. There was one broadly sensible photograph of Monica eating a banana. I cut it out and faxed it down to Jerry with a note explaining matters.

'How's it going?' asked Mike Sharp, appearing suddenly out of nowhere. He smelled strongly of claret.

'Fine. We've got an elephant.' I showed him the brochure.

'All right! Well done, Brodes. Keep at it.'

'I've talked to Jerry about costs. He kicked up a fuss.'

'Of course he did. They always do. Just agree with everything and then charge it later.'

'Oh...All right.' He wandered off and I turned back to my desk.

At four o'clock Scott called to reject the elephant.

'It's unacceptable,' he said.

'Ah. In what way?'

'It isn't how we see the elephant. It's too brown and wrinkly.'

'It's just an elephant, Mike. That's how elephants are.'

'Well it won't do. It needs to be big, and grey. With tusks.'

'The thing is, the supply of elephants for commercial use in this country is extremely limited. There simply aren't any big African tuskers available – and certainly none that could perform in front of a camera.'

'Well this one is unacceptable.'

I exhaled gently through the nostrils.

'Well, have you got any suggestions in that case? Because I don't think it's going to be possible to get another one.'

'That's for you to sort out.'

'But there's nothing further we can do – short of dropping the elephant altogether and starting all over again.'

'We must have the elephant. It's central to the brand.'

'Then we must have this one.'

'I'm not approving this elephant. I want a bigger, greyer elephant. With tusks.'

'What's the problem?' demanded Mike Sharp, appearing instantly when I came off the phone. He looked tired, and his good humour seemed to have ebbed. One of the buttons had come off his shirt, and I could see the dark whorl of his navel set in the straining curve of his gut.

'Scott doesn't like the elephant.'

'What's wrong with the fucking elephant?'

'He says it's too small. And wrinkly. And brown. Overall, too brown, wrinkly and small.'

'For fuck's *sake*.' He lit a cigarette and sucked on it fiercely. 'Just tell him that's what elephants look like. *Tell* him.'

He stalked off. Almost immediately the phone went again. I let it ring four times, then picked it up like a lead weight.

'Brodie? It's me. Listen, I overheard your conversation with Scott. I'll have a go at persuading him about the elephant. Just give him twenty-four hours, okay.'

'Katherine...you're a superstar.'

'I think if you can arrange to get it for the Sales Conference as well as the shoot it could tip the balance. Scott's setting a lot of store by the conference: it's his big day. Just a tip. Got to go – see you Saturday.'

'See you then. You're an angel.'

'Who's an angel?' said Vanessa, peering over my partition wall. There's no privacy in this place.

'Nobody you know.'

'Is this the elephant?' She picked up the pictures.

'That's her.'

'Sweet.'

'Yeah.'

'Can it really play the piano?'

'Apparently. They're very intelligent animals. More so than most human beings as a matter of fact.'

'I used to play the piano,' she said, wistfully. 'When I was a girl. Gave it up, though.' She drifted off to the coffee machine.

Gradually the office emptied. I stuck around for no reason in particular, watching it get dark and flipping through the leaves of the circus brochure. As well as Monica there were performing dogs, dromedaries, tigers, horses and chimpanzees. There was a jolly ensemble shot of all the animals together, flanked by beefy cossacks with whips. I stared at it for several minutes. A telephone bleated away in a far corner, tripping periodically from desk to desk. Whoever it was obviously wasn't taking no for an answer. I picked it up after five minutes or so and softly replaced it again. Silence fell – or the closest you get to silence in an office building, a medley of small electrical hums and distant street noises, and I became aware it was raining hard outside. Suddenly I wanted to be out there feeling the rain on my face, and I stood up to leave.

By the lift I met Mike Sharp struggling his way into an expensive raincoat. He glanced at the clock – eight twenty – and gave me an approving look.

'How did you get on with Scott?' he said.

'I talked to him again,' I lied. 'He's okay.'

'Well done. You're doing a good job, Brodie.'

We rode the lift together. 'No coat?' said Mike.

'No.'

'Want my umbrella?'

'It's okay thanks. I'll bus it.'

But I didn't bus it. I walked, getting very wet indeed in the process. I sometimes think that London is at its most beautiful when it's wet, after dark, with everything spangling blackly in the streetlight. The rain hosed down, drumming on the roofs of the cars and taxis edging down Piccadilly, the drivers peering out like ghosts. There were hardly any pedestrians around, just the odd couple scuttling for cover, the occasional drunk too far gone to care, or notice. By the time I got back I was completely sodden. I didn't bother to change, taking Toby out for a trot round the deserted squares just as I was. I towelled him down afterwards, leaving his coat in punky spikes, and lit the gas fire. Toby sat and steamed in front of it, and soon the flat was filled with the rich aroma of wet pug.

It was a stupid thing to do, of course. I'm not that sure why I did it. I woke the next morning with a feverish cold, runny schnoz and all, and had to detour via the chemist to pick up a brick of tissues and some aspirin. I honked and trumpeted my way in on the bus, eating aspirins like smarties. By the time I arrived I was already feeling like death.

'You should take the day off,' said Vanessa.

'I can't. Too much to do.' By way of corroboration the phone went off. 'Brodie,' I said, thickly.

'Morning, Brodie. Jerry here. I'm calling to say the elephant is acceptable – as long as we are able to use it at the conference in addition to the shoot – for the unveil at the launch. I assume that will be possible?'

'I'll enquire. Leave it with me.'

'I think we may have royalty there,' added Jerry, impressively.

'Oh – great.'

'Not, you know, the main ones. One of the outer lot, but still bloody good.'

'Absolutely.'

'Mum's the word, though.'

'Right.'

'Got that quote down yet?'

'We're looking at it.'

'Hmm. All right then. Speak to you later.'

I called Caroline Silverstone and told her the news. She clicked her tongue over the request and said she'd see what she could do.

The rest of the day went by in a blur. Unwisely I accompanied Hippo down the pub at lunch time, thinking a swift one might make me feel better. But it didn't make me feel better. It made me feel worse. Eventually, at four fifteen, I conceded defeat and went home to bed. Toby was chuffed by my early return, though plainly puzzled at my lassitude. Baulked of his usual exercise, he passed the time instead by dragging himself round and round the flat on his stomach, panting lasciviously and rolling his eyes. After half an hour or so I got fed up with this and locked him in the kitchen again, whereupon he set up a regular woof at ten-second intervals... Jesus – can't a man have a couple of hours to be ill around here? *'Shut up!'* I bellowed, with superhuman ferocity. There was an abrupt silence. I fell asleep.

At around nine I woke up and immediately felt guilty. I let Toby out of the kitchen. He slunk into the sitting room and sat at the far end, looking at me apprehensively with big gooseberry eyes. 'I'm sorry, old son,' I said, kneeling beside him and patting his old suede head. 'I'm sorry.'

We spent the night together with him on the other half of the bed, snoring and smelling fit to bust. It made a change from Katherine.

In my dreams, which were prolonged and anarchic, I was chased round and round Regent's Square by Scott and Jerry, mounted on elephants. Big, grey elephants, with tusks.

CHAPTER THIRTEEN

I wasn't well enough to drive to Wales on Saturday morning, but I went anyway, swathed in blankets, with all the heating on. Toby sat on the passenger seat and looked out of the window. His fourth trip. We stopped at a service station and I bought him a sandwich. I hadn't eaten anything myself for a day and a half, just tea, plenty of it, and pills. Being ill isn't that unpleasant, actually, as long as it's nothing too serious. I felt permanently high, as if the drugs I was popping were hallucinogenic rather than analgesic. Maybe they were. I know Edward, in the days when he went in for that kind of thing, said that paracetomol and Diet Coke took a lot of beating.

'You poor thing,' said Susan Napier, when I arrived. 'You shouldn't have come.'

'Happy birthday,' I said. I gave her some roses.

'Thank you – they're beautiful. Come on in and sit by the fire. Katherine and John are out taking a walk. They should be back soon. Tell me all about this commercial you're making for Katherine's company.'

'You don't want to hear about that.'

'But I do. It sounds most exciting. I gather you've been negotiating for an elephant?'

'Yes,' I admitted.

'Where's it coming from?'

'A visiting Russian circus. We're borrowing her.'

'Does it bother you?'

'Yes. I don't think elephants should be used in circuses. Let alone in lavatory cleaner commercials.'

'You've got a point. It isn't very nice.'

'Katherine thinks I'm taking it too far. I think she thinks I'm a bit of a crank. I am a bit of a crank, I suppose.'

'I don't think so. Your heart's in the right place. It's difficult to change some things, that's all.'

'How's your work going?'

'Slowly. There are plans to redevelop an area up the coast, which we're trying to oppose. I don't think we'll be successful, though.'

'Difficult to change some things, isn't it?'

'Yes.' She laughed ruefully.

Katherine and her father pitched up a few minutes later. Kath offered me a cold, pink cheek to kiss and berated me for coming in my condition. John Napier shook my hand. He was nothing like I had been expecting – older and tireder-looking, with soft bags under his eyes and thinning grey hair. His manner was very much that of Katherine and Susan, though, vivacious and informal, and I found myself taking to him as we talked over lunch. He spoke animatedly about the countries he flew to and between, a life of air security and hotel bedrooms, snapshot glimpses and stopovers. He talked warmly of South Africa, his current home. I, who had never thought of that land in anything other than newsreel footage, found myself picturing the lushness and heat with something approaching longing. You can get enough of the English climate.

'What about your parents?' he enquired.

'My mother died when I was small. My father teaches in California.'

'I wish I'd met him,' said Katherine. 'He sounds a sweety.'

'He is. You must.'

'Maybe I could fix cheap tickets?' suggested John.

'That would be marvellous.'

'I think William should get some rest,' said Susan, after the meal. 'You don't look at all well.'

I slept all afternoon in the creaky bed upstairs. When I woke up again it was dark. Somebody had lit the fire in the grate and shadows leapt around the walls. Katherine was sitting on a stool beside me. She leant over and stroked my arm.

'I like your dad,' I said.

'He's nice, isn't he?'

'Why did they get divorced?'

'He was away all the time. It didn't work.'

'But they loved each other?'

'They still do.'

'That's really sad.'

'It's sad, but it's one of those things. Sometimes loving someone doesn't make any difference – it just doesn't work out.'

'How old were you when it happened?'

'Nine.'

'Why didn't you tell me, Kath – last weekend?'

'I wanted to have some time by myself, with him, that was all.'

'But you could have explained.'

'Brodie...I shouldn't *have* to explain. I shouldn't have to be accountable. Nor should you.'

'Okay.' I let it go. 'But what's going to happen to us, Kath? Are we just going to carry on like this? Or what?'

She looked away. 'I don't know. Neither of us is in a position to do much about it. Anyway, what's the big deal? Chill out.'

'I'll leave the agency. I'm not enjoying it any more anyway.'

'What would you do – come and work at AKL?'

I laughed, although the idea of working under Scott was far from humorous. 'Oh, I don't know. What about you – how long are you going to stick it out?'

'I don't know either. Don't *hassle* me, Brodie. Let it be, can you?'

'Okay,' I said, and took her hand. She kissed my fingers. 'How are you feeling now?'

'Druggy. Not bad.'

'Happy?'

'Yeah, I'm happy. Are you happy?'

'I'm happy. Get some more rest now. I'll take Toby out.'

When I woke again I could hear the sounds of steps on the wooden staircase, and whispered goodnights. I wondered sleepily where everyone would be bedding down. There's only two bedrooms, and I'd turned one of them into an infirmary. But Kath came in anyway, softly closing the door behind her. I didn't alert her to my wakefulness, but watched instead as she stirred up the embers of the fire, then undressed methodically in front of the glow, neatly folding her things away. The flickering orange light and the effects of my fever made the scene eerily erotic. For several minutes she sat naked on the stool in front of the hearth, combing her brown hair out and sideways. Then she slipped a loose white T shirt over her head and stood up, letting it shimmer down to the tops of her thighs. She stretched, gathering her hair in her hands and holding it above her head, then froze suddenly, listening. I listened too... Softly, but unmistakably, the sounds of love-making filtered through from the landing, a rhythmic, urgent noise. Katherine frowned, then smiled softly. She sat pensively on the edge of the bed, her back to me.

The sound went on, and on. I was pretty impressed, to tell you the truth. Impressed, and oddly comforted. Impressed, oddly comforted, and – let's be honest – deeply aroused.

I laid a finger on Katherine's spine and traced her vertebrae under the soft cotton. She shuddered, arching her back, and then in a single motion turned and we embraced. Both our bodies seemed about two hundred degrees hotter than usual. Katherine raised herself above me and knelt, pulling the shirt over her head in a movement, and the next thing we were whaling away to a full philharmonic accompaniment from the bedsprings. It was a quite extraordinary bout of love-making, far noisier, fiercer and more passionate than any previously. Katherine seemed possessed, crazy – almost in pain, while I felt, well – surreal's about the closest I can come to it. It was the first time I'd had intercourse with a temperature of a hundred and two.

The row was indescribable. Eventually Katherine climaxed with a great panting shout, like a tennis player just making the point at a tiebreak, and we subsided sweatily into the tormented mattress. The silence that followed was absolute and profound.

'Katherine,' I heard myself saying. 'Will you marry me?'

CHAPTER FOURTEEN

Elephants fall in love. They do. At least, that's what I've read. It's one of their many so-called human characteristics, like living to eighty, given the chance, and weeping salt tears in distress. Put another way, falling in love is one of our elephant characteristics. The differences are merely those of proportion. Elephants don't do things in half measures. Foreplay between elephants, for instance, can go on for up to three days. They use their trunks to caress one another's bodies and faces; they interlock the tips gently, like lovers holding hands. And they stay loyal after mating. That's more than you can say for most of us and all.

'Give me six months,' Katherine kept saying. 'You don't know me still, Brodie. We need time.'

'I love you,' I kept saying. 'It's totally straightforward. If you love me, say yes. That's all there is to it.'

'But it isn't. You're...you're too *romantic*, Brodie. You expect the world to shape itself around your dreams. It isn't like that. Neither of us knows what the hell we're doing, where we're going.'

'Do you love me, Katherine? Yes or no?'

She looked straight into my eyes. Hers were dark and troubled. 'I love you terribly,' she said. 'But it's the wrong time for both of us. Six months. Ask me in six months.'

There was nothing I could say to persuade her. I kissed her eyebrows, left one, right one. 'May eleven,' I said. 'I'll put it in the diary.' And we made love again, gently this time, tenderly.

*

The next morning my fever had dropped and I felt a million times better. We got up late and drank tea with John and Susan, perching in a row on the bench by the front door. John looked better too: younger, more relaxed.

'Know what I want to do?' he said, finishing off his mug and standing up.

'What do you want to do?'

'Chop some wood. Anybody object?'

'Of course not, darling. Chop away.'

'Can I chop too?' I asked.

'Why not?'

We went round to the back. John gave me a vast axe, and took up a lump hammer and wedge. He didn't say anything, but gave me a grin and set up a big hunk of log. I attacked it inexpertly, shaving a small slice off the side. He corrected my stance, and I had another go. Before long we had a production line going, and a satisfying pile of cut wood building up against the outhouse wall. Despite the cold I was perspiring freely, feeling the crap in my system force its way out through the pores. I remember thinking as I swung the axe and it bit into the grain – this, this is the happiest I have ever been: perhaps the happiest I'll ever know.

After half an hour or so we had a breather, contemplating our pile.

'When did you meet Katherine?' John asked.

'In July. She's my client, you know.'

'Must be funny.'

'Yes.'

'Do your colleagues know about it?'

'God no. That would be dreadful.'

'Would it? Why?'

'It would...I don't know...it would change things. I think it would be seen as unprofessional.'

'How is Katherine? I so rarely see her. She's awfully thin. Does she like her work, do you think?'

'No. That's something we have in common.'

He looked up at the sky, at the gulls scudding about in the wind. 'I think you'll find ninety per cent of all employed people have that in common,' he said.

'What about you? You seem to like your work.'

'As a matter of fact I love it. I'm terribly lucky. But there is a downside, of course.'

'You mean – Susan?'

'And Katherine. I made a choice, you see. I chose my job. Times like now I sometimes feel I made the wrong decision.' He smiled at me broadly. 'Shouldn't really tell you all this. I like your face.'

'Thank you! Yours isn't so bad either.'

Hopped up on all this man-to-man stuff I practically decapitated myself on the upswing, then whacked a log so hard that one half shot sideways and went through a window.

At six o'clock I shovelled Toby into the Beetle and said my goodbyes.

'Thanks again for the flowers,' said Susan.

'Thanks again for having me over.'

'Glad you're feeling fitter.'

'Never better. This place is good for me.'

John shook hands and I kissed Susan. They turned away tactfully and walked back up the path.

'Well?'

'We're getting good at goodbyes, aren't we?'

'Katherine – I meant everything. Everything.'

'I know you did.' She squeezed my hand. Toby barked impatiently from inside the car.

'May eleven,' I said.

She waved until I was out of sight, a diminutive, dwindling figure in the rear mirror.

CHAPTER FIFTEEN

I didn't go to prison in the end. I got fined three hundred notes and a wigging from the magistrate. Plus I had to pay costs, a not inconsiderable sum. Taken all in all it pretty much wiped out the remains of the money my father gave me. What a pisser.

Talking of money, I got the quote through eventually. Scott blew his lid when he heard the estimate and called up Paul direct to give him what for. The upshot was that Paul talked to Carl Redwing, who halved his rate on the spot. Mysteriously, he's keen to shoot it. Jerry dribbled on about it for a bit longer, but Scott bought it. He needs the film for this conference of his.

I met Monica the day before the shoot. I'd been despatched with the apron and giant slippers to check out the fit and make arrangements for transportation the following day. The circus was pitched in Battersea Park. I picked my way through a platoon of caravans towards the big tent, where Ivan the elephant man was enjoying a cigarette and a mug of tea. I'd met Ivan already at the pre-production meeting in the agency, and taken to him in a big way. He was large and swarthy, with broken teeth and a boozer's nose, and plainly found the advertising world to his liking. He ogled the mini-skirted secretaries shamelessly and sucked down the complimentary Chardonnay like orange squash. He biffed Paul on the back and prodded Mike in the stomach. His English was good, with every word delivered in a tone of resolute and noisy cheerfulness, irrespective of content or context.

'Ah! You have the carpet slippers,' he bellowed. 'Good, good. Monica will look very pretty in these.'

'Will she be able to walk in them?' I asked doubtfully.

'Monica is a very talented elephant,' said Ivan. 'Come and meet her now.' Monica was enjoying a light lunch out the back. A thin chain attached her left hind leg to a post, which jingled lightly as she shifted her weight. She looked up with her mouth full, chewing lazily, and extended her trunk towards Ivan. He stroked it affectionately. 'Hello, old lady,' he said. 'Meet Mr Brodie, advertising man. You're going to be a star! How about that, huh?' Monica rolled an eye at me, a small, expressive eye in a large old head. It looked remarkably human.

'How long have you known her, Ivan?'

'Nineteen years now. We work together all that time.'

'She likes you.'

'We like each other – eh, Monica?' Monica tumbled her head up and down, flapping her parchment ears. It really was uncanny the way she seemed to understand him.

'Pity about the chain,' I said.

'The law,' said Ivan dismissively. 'She wouldn't go out walking. She likes it too much here – don't you girl?' I couldn't help but agree with him. I'd been all set to disapprove, but she looked so patently contented – and clearly delighted by Ivan's attention – that I had to put my anthropomorphic feelings back in their box. I'd never seen a happier elephant.

'You want to come to the show?' asked Ivan as we headed back.

'No thanks. Too much to do.'

'Of course.' He clamped my hand and shook it up and down. 'I see you six o'clock tomorrow, yes? We take the van, you show the way.'

'Six o'clock. See you, Ivan. Love to Monica.'

Know who Monica reminds me of? Toby, in a curious kind of way. They have the same affable manner, the same delight in human society. True, there are differences in scale: Monica is eight feet high and weighs four and a half tons; Toby is one foot high and, despite a degree of stoutness, some way short of four and a half tons. I took Toby with me the next morning, unwilling to leave him on his own for such a long day. We set an all time record with our morning walk at quarter to five. By half past the two of us were chuntering along the south bank in the Beetle towards Battersea.

Ivan was waiting as arranged, leaning against the elephant truck. 'Good morning!' he shouted. 'How are you this morning?'

'I'm good, thanks. I've brought my dog along – I hope that's okay.'

'For sure. Let me meet him.'

Toby emerged from the passenger side and peed lengthily against a guy-rope. Ivan gazed at him in frank amazement.

'This is a *dog*?' he said.

'Certainly it's a dog. Don't you have pugs in Russia?'

'*Pugs*? No. No pugs.' He stated this firmly, shaking his head, as if Stalin had rounded up all pugs in 1946 and had them deported to the Gulag. He stooped to inspect. Toby looked up at him ingratiatingly, puffing out small clouds of frosty air in the blackness.

'Very ugly,' announced Ivan at length. 'But very interesting. Name?'

'Toby.'

'We will be friends, yes, Toby?' He patted him heftily and Toby did another pee. 'Very interesting,' repeated Ivan.

I peeked in the back of the truck. Monica's vast bottom loomed out at me, the little Eeyore tail swishing gently. 'Does she mind travelling?' I asked.

'She's used to it. Go now, no?'

'Yes, let's go.'

He started the engine and we pulled away. I spread the A to Z on my lap, finger on the section of docklands where the studio was located. Ivan discoursed volubly as we drove along, asking questions about London, the Queen, Manchester United, Radio One. His appetite for detail was insatiable.

'You have a wife?'

'No.'

'A girl some place?'

'Yes.'

He nodded sagely. 'I have a wife for many years. Last year she leave me for an office-worker.'

'I'm sorry.'

He gave a great bark of a laugh. 'Why sorry? To live alone is good. Have you read Dhammapada?'

'I don't believe so.'

'Very wise book. Very great.' He quoted boomingly: 'With a fool there is no companionship. With few desires, live alone and do no evil – like an elephant in the forest, roaming at will' – and grinned at me.

'Is that what it says?'

He nodded emphatically. 'Like an elephant, Mr Brodie! Like an elephant!' and chuckled hugely, slapping the wheel. I laughed too.

We stopped in Bermondsey and had some breakfast at a café. 'Woss in the van?' asked a passing navvy. 'An elephant,' I said. I'd been longing for someone to give me the chance to say that.

At seven fifty, ten minutes ahead of itinerary, we arrive at the studio, a great hulk of a warehouse surrounded by security fencing. A fat old porter in a peaked hat was yawning by the barrier to the empty car park.

'From Short Sharp Advertising,' I explained. I showed him a card. 'We're here for the shoot.'

The porter frowned. 'Shoot?' he said, as if this kind of activity was unknown in a film studio. 'What shoot?'

'AKL – codename Camel.'

'Camel?'

'Yes.'

He checked a little pad then looked up again. 'What's in the van?'

'An elephant,' I said. 'For the shoot.'

'You what?'

'An elephant – we're shooting an elephant. Here, today. Can we park, please?'

'You can't bring an elephant in here,' said the porter firmly, sure of his ground.

'Look, it's for the *shoot*. Caroline Silverstone arranged everything.'

'Caroline who?'

'Caroline Silverstone.'

He consulted his pad again. 'You can't park that in here,' he announced.

'What do you mean we can't park here? Where are we supposed to park? We're here *for the shoot*. What's so bloody difficult?'

He eyed me with all the assurance of somebody with a small but absolute power of veto. 'You can't park that in here,' was all he'd say. I tried other tactics: I threatened, pleaded, cajoled. 'You can't park that in here.' The single-mindedness of it! I suppose if your sole professional responsibility is stopping people parking in car parks and nothing else, you get good at it. You get better at it than the next guy. And this one was an expert. He should have gone on *Mastermind*: occupation – Car Park Attendant; specialist subject – Stopping people parking in car parks... He really had a talent for it. After a while Ivan leant over. 'Listen,' he said. 'You let us in. Or I break your arms – yes?'

Naturally that did it. The porter beat a retreat to inside his little cabin and sat talking into a walkie-talkie. We got out of the truck just as Caroline Silverstone appeared in a spiffy little Mercedes Sports.

'What's the problem here?'

'This old fool won't let us in.'

'Jack? Let them in, will you, darling? They're with me.'

Jack looked out suspiciously, like a tortoise. 'They've got an elephant in there,' he said.

'I know. It's all right, it's for the shoot.'

He grunted and pushed a button. 'Thanks, darling,' said Caroline, flashing him a smile. We pulled in.

'You should have slipped him a couple of quid,' she said when we climbed out for a second time.

'*Why*? Why should I slip the old turd anything? It's his fucking job, isn't it?'

'Well...he's been with them a long time,' she said, vaguely.

She went inside and started opening doors, while Ivan disembarked Monica. She backed massively down the ramp and stood obediently on the tarmac. Toby, who was truffling around in some litter, stopped dead in front of her. Clearly an elephant was a wholly, radically new concept for him. He wagged his tail experimentally. He sat down. He put his ears back and sneezed a couple of times. Monica pondered Toby for a second; clearly a pug was something of a new concept for her as well. Then she stretched her trunk slowly towards him, straight out, and pointed it like a gun at his head. Toby retreated hastily underneath the Beetle. I fished him out and left him inside on his blanket, peering out at the immobile Monica with an expression of squashy outrage on his face. He looked even more put out than the porter.

Nothing really happened after that for three or four hours. Gradually, in dribs and drabs, a few people in T-shirts arrived and started dismantling some scaffolding. Then some more people in T-shirts arrived and stood about drinking coffee out of styrofoam cups, smoking cigarettes and breaking wind. There was no sign of Carl Redwing or Paul Short. Jerry pitched up at eleven thirty in his Mondeo, which he parked, after a short wrangle with the porter, next to the Beetle. 'Morning all!' he called, fighting his way out of the door. 'Stone me! Is that the elephant?'

Ivan, standing next to me, stared at the space-hopper of Jerry's tummy with much the same awe that Jerry was staring at Monica. 'Who is the very fat man?' he asked.

'*Shh*. That's the client. Come and be introduced.'

'Got started yet?' demanded Jerry when we'd all shook hands. He looked about him expectantly, as if waiting for someone to shout 'Action!'

'Not really. We're waiting for Paul and the director.'

'Really? I thought the itinerary said commence eight o'clock.'

'Yes, well...they've probably got stuck in traffic.'

Jerry grunted. You could see him thinking: we pay for a three-day shoot and what do we get...'They've been setting up the set,' I offered.

'Hmm. I'd have thought they'd have done that yesterday. So who are all these people?' He waved a hand at the gaggle of blokes in T-shirts, who were noisily despatching some doughnuts and arguing about football.

'Er, technicians. Why not have a cup of coffee, Jerry? Something to eat?'

One thing you can say about shoots – at least the grub's good. At half past ten a mobile catering unit had arrived, staffed by a squad of horsy girls in pearls and aprons, and a supply of cakes and sandwiches had been set up. In my experience, such as it is (a couple of noisy Carpet Mania commercials consisting of a man shouting to camera for ten seconds about Axminsters) absolutely bugger all happens at shoots almost all the time. Everyone stands about eating and drinking and smoking while lighting people scratch their bums and say they don't think it can be done from that angle. 'Is Mike coming along at any stage?' I asked.

'Tomorrow,' said Jerry, through a scrambled egg and smoked salmon roll.

'And Katherine?'

'Katherine? Oh, she's not coming,' he said, as if the notion were an outlandish one. 'Pass one of those bagels, would you.'

At midday Carl and Paul arrived and things finally started to happen. The simpler cuts were shot – the packshot, the under-the-rim stuff, and everyone broke for lunch.

Monica went in front of the camera at three. There was a delay while she was manoeuvred into the carpet slippers, then another while the apron was wound about her midriff. Ivan spoke to her quietly in Russian the while, patting her flank. I didn't like to watch, so I took off for a spell and walked Toby round the perimeter. When I returned they were shooting. The actress playing the housewife would say her line, turning brightly to Monica, and the director would call out: '*Cut...and one more time*.' Monica did her level best to oblige with the duster, but tended to swipe over all the props in the general vicinity, bowling clocks and vases of flowers in all directions. 'Cut,' called Carl Redwing. '*One more time...*' Paul lolled in a canvas chair, drinking Fleurie and scowling. 'This elephant's fucking hopeless,' he said. 'Fucking *hopeless*.' Jerry, who'd pushed the boat out rather on the *Saute de Veau aux Champignons*, sat in his canvas chair smoking and sucking glumly on a Rennie.

At seven o'clock Carl called it a day and everybody went off to the pub. I drove back with Ivan, weaving through the sidestreets to avoid the out-of-town crush heading east. 'I think she did brilliantly,' I said. 'Not easy for her,' said Ivan, nodding his head. 'The lights, you know – she gets hot. We'll need to be careful tomorrow, give her more rest, I think.'

I got back to the flat at nine thirty and called Kath.

'How'd it go?'

'Pretty well, though we didn't get much done. We shot about three takes.'

'And how was Monica?'

'Monica was a darling.'

'I can't wait to see her.'

'Jerry said you weren't coming to the shoot – is that right?'

'I'm afraid so. It's madness here at the moment getting things together for this launch. You think *you're* busy.'

'I am busy. I was up at five today.'

'It's a drag, isn't it?'

'Yes. I still think you should pack it in you know, Kath.'

'I know,' she said gloomily. 'But I can't, not at the moment.'

'This'll soon be over now. We could go away somewhere for Christmas. How about that?'

'That'd be nice,' she said flatly.

'Kath, what's up? Why are you so depressed? What is it?'

'It's nothing, Brodes. It's work. I'll be okay.'

The next day Ivan and I repeated our trip along the river, arriving at the studio at nine.

'Yes?' said the porter.

'Yes?'

'Can I help you?'

'Well, yes. We're here for the shoot, same as yesterday.'

The porter consulted his pad. 'Not on my list,' he said, after a spell.

'Look for Christ's sake! It's exactly the same as yesterday. Just open the barrier, will you?'

'Not on my list,' said the porter.

'Okay, okay. How much do you want? A quid? Two quid? Go fuck yourself,' I said, before he could answer. 'Open it, would you, Ivan?'

Ivan shouldered his way past the porter, ignoring his little shouts of protest, and heaved up the barrier by brute force.

'Oi! You can't do that. I'll *have* you for that.'

'You really should slip him a couple of quid,' said Caroline Silverstone when I told her. 'Everybody else does.'

Scott arrived just as we were commencing on the scene where Monica takes the product and squirts it into the bowl of the lavatory.

'Are we on schedule?' he asked, looking about him critically at the army of T-shirted coffee drinkers.

'Bit behind, I'm afraid. We lost a little time yesterday morning.'

'I know, Jerry told me.' He frowned, and I thought he was about to say it was unacceptable, or at the very least unsatisfactory, but he seemed to think better of it. He walked onto the set and peered into the toilet, then at Monica. Monica looked back at him unwinkingly. 'Morning, Mike,' called Paul, appearing with a glass of orange juice.

'Paul – good morning.'

'Looking good, isn't it?'

Scott made a noncommittal noise. 'Where's the product?' he asked.

'Behind Monica there.'

'Monica?'

'The elephant.'

He rummaged about for a while behind Monica while Paul and the crew exchanged glances. Scott emerged again holding a couple of plastic bottles. 'Will the label be clearly visible when the trunk's holding the bottle?'

'Sure,' said Paul.

'Show me.'

There was a pause while Ivan coaxed Monica into gripping a bottle with her trunk. She waved it in the air like a little flag.

'No,' said Scott. 'That's unacceptable. I want to be able to read the label and the company mission statement.'

'Can't do that, old love,' said Carl Redwing. 'It isn't big enough.'

'That's for you to sort out.'

'Come and have a cup of coffee, why not, Mike,' I suggested. 'Let Carl and Paul discuss it.'

'I don't want a cup of coffee.'

Carl got up and took Scott gently by the arm. 'Let's have a chat about this,' he said.

They strolled off the set, Carl gesturing and explaining. Paul came up to me. '*Get him out of here*,' he breathed fiercely.

'I can't just hijack him, Paul. He *is* the client.'

'But he's going to fuck everything up! He's only been here two minutes and he's already fucking things up! I'm warning you, Brodie ...'

'But what can I do? He doesn't do what *I* tell him.'

'Just...just –' Paul's face worked. 'Just get him to *fuck off.*'

'I think I've cracked it,' announced Carl, returning. 'We'll shoot with Monica, then do a cut away separately, mix it together on Harry, yeah?'

'Harry?' said Scott, suspiciously.

'Computer, love. Does anything. Don't you worry about a thing. Standing by, everyone.'

'I'll have that coffee now,' said Scott.

The scene took five hours to shoot. Monica got the hang of picking up the product pretty early on, but attempts to get her to squirt it into the bowl proved fruitless. She squirted it all right, just not in the bowl. She had herself a whale of a time, sending great swathes of lemon-scented gunge all over the studio. The housewife actress had to change her costume seven times. Scott, who tried to step in at one point, copped half a pint smack in the kisser, and Monica climbed another notch in my estimation.

'Look, this isn't getting us anywhere,' said Paul eventually.

'Monica is tired,' announced Ivan firmly. 'We rest her now.' Monica, who looked anything but tired, half-turned around and demolished a light stack. 'Take five, everyone,' called Carl.

We huddled in a little conference, Scott, Paul, Carl and me.

'We're going to have to use the animatronic model,' said Carl. 'No way are we going to get this one to point it in the bog.'

Scott gave tight-lipped assent, having registered the view that this was, in the final analysis, unsatisfactory.

But our problems were far from over. The animatronic elephant was wheeled

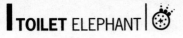

out and set into place, with wires hanging out all over the place. A fat bloke in a Motorhead T-shirt started twiddling some dials on a handset and the trunk extended jerkily. Monica, meanwhile, who was munching down a line of bananas by the exit, stopped in mid-chew and stared at the animatronic elephant intently. The next thing a whole clump of bananas was winging through the air, pitched with clinical accuracy. It struck the model on the thigh, and it pitched over with an expensive-sounding crash. Monica blew a triumphant trumpet blast and reared up on her back legs.

'Get that fucking elephant out of here!' shouted Paul. Simultaneously Ivan was on his feet, barking commands in Russian. But Monica's excitement had been aroused. She lumbered over to the model with surprising agility, dispersing sound men and clapper-boys in all directions, circling the prone elephant and prodding at it with her trunk. It took fifteen minutes of heavy petting by Ivan to cajole her away and into the car park.

'Jesus,' I gasped, when we were safely outside.

'She hasn't seen another elephant for twenty years,' said Ivan. 'Try to imagine how you would feel.'

Scott emerged and eyed the three of us frostily.

'I'm going back now,' he said. 'I can't say I've been impressed by any of this, William. And I can tell you now that we're not paying a penny over estimate for this film, so I hope your insurance is good. Good night to you.'

'Nice man,' said Ivan.

'Yeah, right.'

'You want to have a drink some place?'

'God yes.'

We drove off, Monica and all, and stopped at the first pub we came to. Ivan parked the truck where he could keep an eye on it through the window and we went in.

Ivan's good humour was unfaltering. He regaled me with stories and tried to teach me Russian phrases and swear words. Three pints later my spirits were thoroughly restored. Three pints after that I said, 'Er, Ivan...the police are pretty strict on drink driving over here, you know. Think we ought to call it a day?'

He snapped his fingers. 'You British,' he smiled. 'You can't get drunk on this, this beer. Impossible!' He smacked down his glass and ordered another.

He drove me back to Regent's Square an hour and a half later. His driving, like his general demeanour, was wholly unaltered. I, on the other hand, was as drunk as a pig.

'Dosvedanya, Brodie!' he called, as I swayed down from the cab. 'I see you tomorrow, okay?'

'Dosver...dos...bye, Ivan. Bye, Monica. Take care.'

When I got in the telephone was ringing. It was Katherine. I was too drunk to make a lot of sense, and I can't remember much of the conversation.

CHAPTER SIXTEEN

Want to know something? I think I may be developing an elephant obsession. Remember when I was obsessed with toilets? Well, now it's elephants. On balance I think it's better to be obsessed with elephants than it is to be obsessed with toilets. How does this obsession manifest itself? Well, for one thing I've started noticing a lot of elephants – pictures of elephants – around the place, and picking up on a lot of elephant references. I see there's a brand of bottled beer called Elephant ('A beer you'll never forget'). There are a large quantity of elephant jokes – more, I would calculate, than jokes pertaining to other species of mammal. Why is this? Got any ideas? Elephants also crop up repeatedly in children's books, on posters, pub signs, logos, sweatshirts, underpants. You name it, it's got an elephant on it. There is a thriving elephant industry at work out there. Have a look around...See what I mean? Elephants are news. The papers are bursting with them. You can hardly open a Sunday supplement at the moment without a pair of tusks pronging you off the page. Have you noticed that?

I dream about them. It's weird. Monica's friends and relations troop through my slumbers. Is this the job getting to me? I find the size and number of elephants in my dreams relate fairly precisely to the amount I've had to drink the evening prior. A couple of drinks produces a couple of elephants. A full-blown piss up conjures a herd. After my evening with Ivan I played host to a sizeable family, complete with little baby elephants, brooding cows and gaunt, tragic tuskers...

I have to get out of advertising. It's fucking my mind.

*

'Brilliant,' said Mike Sharp. 'It's brilliant.'

'It's crap,' groaned Paul Short. 'Look at that fucking computer elephant, for fuck's sake...it looks like it's made of meccano.'

'Rubbish,' said Mike, stoutly. 'I think the whole effect is very...very graceful. Graceful and powerful. What do you think, Brodie?'

'Can I see it one more time?' I said. Paul hit the play button again and the housewife sprung into view. '*Housework's a chore! Luckily my cleaning lady*...etc.' There was Monica, doing her stuff. There was a very obvious model elephant doing his stuff. There was the packshot; and there, in a welter of starbursts, was the close, the elephant trumpeting. God it was dreadful. I can't quite convey the depths of its dreadfulness.

'It's okay,' I said, reluctantly.

'Okay? *Okay*? What's with this Okay shit? You two – Jesus.' Mike stormed round the office, waving his cigarette in the air. He stabbed it in my direction. 'You've got to sell this with a bit of conviction tomorrow, Brodie.'

'I will, I will. Don't worry.'

'It isn't okay anyway,' said Paul. 'It's *crap*.'

'Scott wants me to present it to him first of all, then to the MD – Jimmy Gillespie.'

'No problem,' said Mike. 'Gillespie will love it. Scott seen anything yet?'

'He saw the rushes.'

'Like them?'

'Well...'

'Gillespie will adore it,' said Mike firmly. 'Fuck Scott.'

'Talking of Scott...he wants you to come to the sales conference to present it in person.'

'When is it?'

'Week tomorrow.'

'Where?'

'Brighton.'

'Brighton? Why's it in fucking Brighton? I'm not going all the way to Brighton.'

'So shall I tell him you can't make it?'

'Yes. No. Tell him I'll...let me give him a call. Is that the lot?'

'That's it.'

'Right.' He put his jacket on. 'Come on, Paul. Take you out to celebrate.'

'Celebrate what?'

'The ad, you arse. Get a move on. Sell it, Brodie. Yeah? Don't worry about Gillespie. Gillespie's a pussycat. Gillespie will *love* it.'

I stood looking up at the departures board, watching for my platform. It was six twenty-five in the morning, Scott having fixed a nice early appointment with Jimmy Gillespie to show him the ad. By my feet was a briefcase containing a doublehead of the finished film and four VHS copies for emergencies. In my left hand was a danish pastry, in my right a cup of tea from a vending machine. For no particular reason I was feeling quite chirpy. I rather enjoy the ride out west.

Paddington came sleepily to life around me. A fat little businessman in a beige suit with a freshly-boiled, pulpy red face strutted up and down, up and down, consulting his watch repeatedly and staring at the board through round wire spectacles. I watched him for a while, making his little turns in front of me. At one point he unexpectedly gave a loud, echoing fart, and shot me a glance – first startled, then defiant, as if asserting his farting rights and prerogatives, his God-given freedom as an Englishman to fart when and wheresoever he chose. After that he stepped off a little distance and continued pacing impatiently up and down. As soon as the Bristol train was announced he shouldered his way to the front of the little ruck that formed by the gate. I waited till things had quietened up and made my way through in his wake. When I got on the train I found my reservation was opposite his. I gave him a friendly enough look as I sat down, but he clearly didn't have any intention of passing the journey with an eavesdropper to his anus and barged off down the carriage to get another seat. Later, on my way back from the gents, I caught sight of a pornographic magazine peeping glossily out of his briefcase. He caught sight of me catching sight of it and snapped the case shut with a glare. Ease up, you fat old duffer, I felt like saying. It doesn't bother me if you fart and masturbate your way to Cardiff and back.

I wasn't feeling unduly apprehensive about my meeting. True, Gillespie's a big cheese at AKL – *the* big cheese at AKL – but Mike seemed sure he'd buy the film, and Scott doesn't have a choice any more if he wants anything to show at the launch. Bit of a formality all round. I sat back to enjoy the trip, watching the milky fog lifting off the fields as they unrolled past the window. Presently I fell asleep. When I woke up again the train was standing still on the track. I looked at my watch: ten past nine.

'Points failure,' the bloke opposite told me.

'Shit. Know how long it'll be?'

'Sorry.'

'Know where we are?'

'Just outside Reading.'

'Reading? Christ, how long have we been here?'

'About an hour. Got a meeting?'

'Sort of. In forty minutes. In Bristol.'

He gave a glum little chuckle. 'Well, you can forget about that one.'

'Yes,' I said. 'Yes, I suppose I can. You don't by any chance happen to have a mobile phone, do you?'

'No. But I saw a chap down the carriage using one.'

I hoisted myself up and made my way down in the direction he pointed. When I saw who it was I gave a little sigh. 'Completely bloody stuck,' my friend in the beige was saying. He had a prim, high-pitched Scottish accent, reminiscent of my headmaster in Perthshire. 'Could be another couple of hours, aye...that's British bloody Rail for you.' He gave me a testy look when he noticed me watching him and wiggled round in his seat to show me his back. Not much point trying there. I walked on down the train, eventually prevailing upon a highly equipped bishop to lend me his. He proudly demonstrated how to use it and I dialled Short Sharp's number.

'Vanessa? Hi, it's Brodie. Listen, my train's broken down. I'm going to be horribly late for the presentation to Gillespie. Would you phone up Scott and explain? No, don't bother telling anyone else at that end. Okay? Thanks. Bye now.'

I handed it back. 'Thank you again.'

'Are you in advertising, by any chance?' asked the bishop politely.

'I am, actually. How did you guess?'

He made a deprecatory gesture. 'Oh, the conversation, you know. And the tie, if you'll pardon me.' He beamed, pleased with his guess.

'Bit of a giveaway, isn't it?' I said, fingering the splurge of pastels with some embarrassment. 'I don't usually go in for this kind. It was a present from my girlfriend – I'm seeing her later on.'

'Very wise,' said the bishop. He leant forward confidentially and said, 'As a matter of fact, I was once in advertising myself.'

'No?'

'Yes...As a copywriter.'

'Really? Wow.'

'I left in 1962. It's a young fellow's game, you know.'

'You did the right thing. I'm thinking of leaving too... So there is life after advertising?'

'Oh indeed.' He smiled.

We spent the rest of the journey together. He talked nostalgically of campaigns he had penned for long-extinct brands; I told him about Carpet Mania and Toilet Elephant, and he nodded intelligently. Fancy meeting a copywriting bishop? As bishops go, he was one of the best.

'Good luck with your presentation,' he said, when I got off at Bristol Temple Meads. 'What is it they used to say?... Sell it, yes?'

'Bishop,' I said, shaking his hand: '*Cheers.*'

In the queue for the taxis I found myself once more behind my farting friend in beige. He was clearly fretful, bobbing up and down as if he could only just refrain from trampling straight to the front of the line. When he eventually got to his cab he snapped: 'AKL, Union Road. And as quick as you can.'

'Excuse me,' I said, stepping forward smartly. There were no other cabs on the rank and it was too good a coincidence to pass up. 'I'm going there too – would you mind awfully if we shared?'

'Find your own!' he barked shrilly, clambering inside. The cab pulled away. Miserable old git. I gave him a finger, but I don't think he saw it. The supply of cabs appeared to have dried up indefinitely. I stood about at the head of a lengthening queue of lugubrious people with cases and pushchairs, occasionally glancing at my watch. Already I was getting on for two hours late. Scott must be doing his nut. If only that silly old bastard could have given me a lift...At length a taxi arrived. 'AKL, please, Union Road Industrial Estate.' I checked my watch for the fifteenth time as we swung out into the traffic seeping along the one-way system. My cabby, a placid old Bristolian, started chatting amiably over his shoulder. He was retiring next month and going on holiday. Thought he might try Portugal – had I been there? I hadn't, actually... Of course, Spain's nice. It is, yeah... Italy's not bad, he'd been there a couple of times. Mind you...

'I say,' I interrupted. 'You don't happen to know another route do you? This seems a bit slow today.'

'Right you are,' he said cheerfully, and took a left. He carried on talking as we curled up and down side roads, looping and doubling back until I wholly abandoned my sense of direction. From what I could tell we didn't seem to be actually *going* anywhere. Not only that, but my driver exercised a broad old-world courtesy in his motoring, stopping obediently at ambers, decelerating at approach roads, breaking to wave out milk-floats, articulated lorries and crocodiles of children from play schools. When I indicated, in the nicest possible way, that I was in a bit of a hurry, he said right-you-are again, and took off down an even more implausible series of byways at imperceptibly higher speed. Fifteen minutes later we rejoined the one-way system roughly two hundred yards from where we left it. 'Cuts out a nasty section, that does,' he said. 'Right,' I said. 'Right.'

I got to the office at five to one. Scott was waiting in reception.

'Mike – I'm *really* sorry about this. The train was delayed two hours, then I couldn't get a cab -'

He brushed aside the excuses. 'Got the film? Let me see it.' We went into a meeting room and I got out the doublehead. Scott shoved it impatiently into an ancient and dusty video recorder that appeared to be made very largely of wood. He hit play. Nothing happened. 'Sure your tape's working?' he demanded.

'I checked it at the agency. Could be the machine.'

We stood and looked at the video, which was whirring contentedly. Suddenly the screen filled with lines, then the end of the commercial appeared. Scott wound it back and we watched it through.

'Well?' I enquired, once he'd seen it twice.

He looked at me candidly. 'Considering the cost, I think it's poor – very poor. The elephant's still unsatisfactory. However...' he paused lengthily and looked at the blank screen. 'In the final analysis, it will have to do. Come along – we should be able to catch Jimmy before his lunch engagement.'

In the lift I apologised again for my lateness, more for a way of breaking the silence than anything else. Scott isn't one of the world's great conversationalists.

'Luckily for you Jimmy was held up as well,' he said. 'He had a dinner in London last night and caught the same train that you did. Fifth floor – here we go.'

'Ah – Mike,' I said, casual as you like, following him out of the lift. 'Jimmy...Mr Gillespie – he's not *Scottish* by any chance, is he?'

'Mr Gillespie will see you now,' said the vast harridan guarding the leather door. I stood up, taking a deep breath. The fart, the porn mag, the cab, the finger... 'Gillespie's a pussycat,' I told myself, sweating gently. 'Gillespie will love it. Gillespie's a pussycat...'

'You're very late, gentlemen,' said Jimmy Gillespie. He was fussing about with some papers on his desk and didn't look up for a moment. When he did, and our eyes met, there was an immediate flash of recognition.

'This is William Brodie – from the agency,' said Scott.

'How do you do?' I said.

Gillespie stared at me hard, as if I was a defective sample coming off a line. 'Hrrmph,' he said at length. 'Well. Show me the advertisement. Quickly, if you please, I have another engagement.'

I plugged it obligingly into the video by the desk and pressed the play button. Naturally, nothing happened. I have yet to meet the video that works first time when I'm making a presentation. Jimmy Gillespie writhed in his chair as Scott and I slapped it and twiddled with knobs. 'Mrs Gibb!' he called, in a grating voice. 'Ask the engineer to come and make this bloody thing work, will you? Now, if you please.' The video gave a little cough and spat out the tape. There was an uncomfortable little interlude.

'You've seen this film, Mike?' said Gillespie.

'Ten minutes ago.'

'And?'

Scott's expression was that of a boiled herring. 'It's...satisfactory,' he said.

'Satisfactory is it? Aye, well, we'll see. Where's that bloody engineer? Mrs Gibb!'

'I've called him up, so there's no point raising your voice to me,' said Mrs Gibb threateningly. I thought Gillespie would blow a gasket but he just grunted and drummed his fingers on the table. Presently the engineer arrived. He studied the tape for a second, put it in the video and pressed the play button. Immediately the image appeared on the screen. 'Thank you, Carter,' growled Gillespie.

We watched the film in silence. When the thirty seconds had played out I rewound and gave it another whirl. The sound of an elephant trumpeting lingered in the office after I'd ejected the tape.

I looked at Scott. Scott looked at Jimmy Gillespie. Jimmy Gillespie looked at me. 'Is that the lot?' he said.

'That's it, yes.'

'No' very long, is it? What you make it so short for?'

'Well, we...' I looked hopefully at Scott. Scott kept his counsel. 'Thirty seconds is the optimum for most advertising communication. In the opinion of the industry.'

'It is, is it? Well, tell me this then. What's the opinion of the industry about filling a valuable thirty-second commercial that's cost me a lot of money with nonsense about elephants in pink slippers? Eh? Where's...where's the company heritage in that? There isn't even a shot of the new bottling plant. New equipment that we've invested heavily in...just all this, this rigmarole with a bloody elephant!'

Scott coughed. 'In the course of extensive consumer research,' he said in a monotone, 'it was the firmly held opinion of the conclusive majority of housewives in our target that the elephant formed a major symbol of cleaning efficacy and a strong brand mnemonic.'

'Research, you say? Research?' Gillespie stood up and walked round the desk. Scott stood to attention like somebody about to be executed by firing squad. 'You know what I say to research? Do you?' He snapped his fingers under Scott's nose. '*Bugger research*.' He gave us both a glare, first Scott, then me. 'Good afternoon, gentlemen,' he snapped. And then he was gone, out and away, calling for his coat.

I thought Scott might unwind a fraction after that joint dressing down, but no chance. 'So,' he said at length, pursing his lips. 'What are your suggestions?'

'My suggestions?'

'The managing director appears not to find your commercial to his liking.'

'My commercial? But...with the greatest respect, Mike, you've seen and approved everything all the way along the line, from concept to rushes. I really don't think you can...'

Scott held up a hand. His face was a mask. 'I have another meeting,' he said. 'I don't want to argue about this.'

'What do you mean he doesn't like it?'

I held the receiver slightly away from my ear. 'He doesn't like it,' I said. 'He didn't like it at all.'

There was a groan at the other end of the line, as of one in great pain.

'What did Scott say?'

'He seems to see it as our problem.'

'What! Fuck *off*. How can it be our problem? It's his problem, it's his ad.'

'I told him that, but he walked off.'

'I can see I need to make some calls,' said Mike darkly, hanging up.

I found Katherine and we took a walk together. Recounting it all to her suddenly made it seem rather funny. Kath seemed preoccupied, though.

'What's up?' I said.

'I've been promoted,' she said.

'Have you? Crumbs. Are you pleased?'

'No. It just means a lot more work. I'm fed up, Brodie.'

'Then leave,' I said. 'Just leave. Do it, Kath. It's easy.'

'You say that...it isn't. You talk about leaving too, but you don't.'

'I will.'

'Bet you don't.'

'Really, I will.'

'What'll you do?'

'I'll think of something.'

She sat down on a step, clasping her knees to her chest. I crouched in front of her, shivering slightly in the breeze. 'Hey,' I said. 'Don't get depressed. It isn't worth it, any of this. None of it matters – none of it matters at all. Don't you see that?'

'I know,' she said miserably.

'Come here. Come here.' We clung together for half a minute. 'Someone will see us,' whispered Katherine.

'So what?'

She disengaged herself gently. 'You have to catch your train. Sort out your problem.'

'I don't give a damn about my problem. I don't *have* a problem.'

'Come on,' she said. 'I'll run you to the station.'

I got drunk on the train on the way back. There didn't seem any point not getting drunk.

'I've sorted it out,' proclaimed Mike the following evening. He dropped his coat and case on a chair and lit a self-righteous cigarette. 'I took the old twat to lunch and he bought it. Mind you,' he added, rounding on me accusingly: 'He's got a point.'

'What do you mean?'

'Well it is a crap film. It's *crap*. Paul's right.'

I shook my head at his retreating back. One thing you can say for Mike – at least he's inconsistent. You can bank on his inconsistency. It's the only thing he's consistent about.

I have to get out of advertising. It's fucking my life.

CHAPTER SEVENTEEN

Mike couldn't make it to the conference. Hazard a guess at who got to go instead.

It was an overnight affair at the Grand Hotel on the sea front, so I had to leave Toby with Connie. She welcomed him in like the prodigal son, feeding him small, sweet biscuits. Toby has a ball when he stays with Connie.

When I arrived the reception was milling with sales people in grey suits, all trying to check in at once. Jerry was vainly attempting to organise affairs, waving little cards in the air and calling out names. Nobody paid any attention. I paused at the door, surveying the scene.

'Brodie!' shouted a voice. 'William Brodie!'

Ivan fought his way through the crush and gave me a bear hug that cracked half my ribs. 'How are you?' I said. 'How's Monica?'

'Come,' said Ivan. He linked his arm companionably through mine and we walked round to the car park. Monica was standing in her truck facing outwards, chewing hay and from time to time putting clumps of it on top of her head. An uneasy hotel official hovered nearby. 'We've had the prime minister here,' he told me, 'but never an elephant.'

'She's okay,' I reassured him. 'I can vouch for her.'

Monica, to my intense delight, seemed to recognise me. I stroked her trunk cautiously and heard a strange rumbling noise from deep in her interior. 'She hungry?' I asked Ivan. 'Happy,' he corrected me. 'Elephants purr like cats when they're happy.' It made my day. It made my month. I told Ivan about my burgeoning elephant fixation and he nodded approvingly. 'You will learn a great deal if you study the ways of elephants,' he said.

Scott called a meeting at four o'clock to iron out the details for the the following day.

'Jimmy kicks off,' he said. 'Then Jerry will go through pan treatments and flush colorants and the industrial side. One hour for that, Jerry – be sure not to overrun.'

'Right you are.'

'I'll introduce Elephant at eleven thirty. Then William will say a few words of introduction on the advertising and we show the commercial. Lunch, then close. Any questions?'

'What's happening about Monica? About the elephant?' I asked.

'The elephant will be concealed behind a curtain. At the key point in my address I will unveil it. Then it remains in position for the duration.'

'Ivan will be with her on stage?'

'That won't be necessary. I've made it clear I want the animal properly chained – we don't want any repeat of that fiasco at the shoot. Any other questions? In that case, rendezvous back here in three hours for the salesman of the year dinner.'

'So she'll be chained up there for *two hours*?' I asked Ivan afterwards.

'I know,' he said woodenly.

'Will she be all right?'

'She'll be all right as long as nothing upsets her. I will stay close.'

I saw Katherine at seven. She looked beautiful in a deep emerald dress with a single silver chain at her throat. I told her as much. 'Thanks. You look pretty dashing yourself. I've never seen you in black tie.'

'Do you think we can sit together?'

'I don't know...I think the seating's arranged.'

'Can I come and see you tonight?'

'Of course you can. Only be discreet, okay?'

'Evening all,' said Jerry, popping out from the gents' lavatory. He was wedged into tight evening dress with a red cummerbund that made him look like an Easter egg.

'Hi, Jerry.'

'Don't let him chat you up, Katherine. Ha ha.'

'No danger,' said Katherine. Jerry gave us a portly twinkle. Then he turned to me and said, 'Got your speech ready yet?'

'Yes. It isn't mine, though. Mike Sharp wrote it.'

'Well, come to that, Mike Scott wrote mine. Maybe we should swap?'

'Ha ha.'

'Well I'm going to escort this gorgeous young lady into dinner.' He took Katherine's arm and rolled into the dining room.

'Evening, William.' I turned. 'Oh hello, Mike. All right?'

'All set for tomorrow?'

'Yes, thanks.'

He looked me up and down appraisingly. 'I want you to give it all you have tomorrow, William. Really make the most of it for the sales guys.'

'Right.'

He studied his feet for a moment, then looked me in the face. 'I know we've had our differences over the advertising,' he said. 'But at the end of the day we pull together. At the end of the day we're all in the same team. Right?'

'Right,' I said again. He gave a little nod and went to his table.

Same team my arse, Scottie, I thought as I took my seat. You and me won't ever play on the same side.

At dinner I sat next to a pair of ratty little men from the Midlands team, one of whom stuttered. At first my inclination was to sympathise, but everything he managed to say was so staggeringly offensive, so blithely bigoted, that I found myself loathing him by the end of the first course. He ate greedily, shoving the food into his mouth then dribbling slightly with the effort of speech. The other one talked loudly and at length about recent sexual accomplishments on a sales trip to Derby. Before long both were shiny in the face with drink and perspiration. Myself, I went easy on the wine. For one thing it was revolting – it tasted like cheap perfume – for another I was developing an ache about the temples.

'You do the advert then?' demanded the articulate one, hacking away at his steak.

'That's right.'

'Any good then, is it?'

'No. As a matter of fact it's abysmally poor.'

He looked at me for a second with his mouth full, then decided I was joking and gave a shout of laughter. A fragment of potato shot across the table and attached itself to the lapel of a fat man reaching for the salt.

'G-got any tarts in it?' enquired my neighbour to my left.

'No,' I said. 'No tarts. Just an elephant.'

He pulled a face. 'No t-tarts? Woss the point innit if there's n-no t-tarts?'

'I suppose the point's to sell lavatory cleaner.'

'No mate,' said the other one, prodding at his chest emphatically with his knife. 'We sell the lavatory cleaner. It's us that do the fucking selling. You want to try it some time.'

'I don't think I do, thanks.'

'I don't think you do neither. Tough job. Not like poncing about in a pig tail making adverts. Tell you what – I banged this bird with a pig tail the other week. Coventry it was. No, hang on...Corby. Or was it? Wait a minute...' He set about racking his brains for the town. It seemed to matter to him to pinpoint the precise location, almost as if it were a police interview. And where *exactly* did you bang this bird with a pig tail, sir?... The other one leaned over, glass in hand, suggesting names of places with much effort and plenty of winks in my direction... They were trying to be friendly. They were really trying. I think that's what made it so depressing.

I lay in bed with Katherine, thinking of Monica.

'Brodie...' she murmured. She rested her chin on my chest. 'Ivan wouldn't put up with it if he thought it was cruel.'

'That's the thing, though, isn't it? It may not be *cruel* – it's just plain obscene when you come right down to it.'

'Any more obscene than dressing her up for a commercial? Any more obscene than the circus act she does eight times a week? Brodie, she's a working animal. For her it's...it's like it is for us. It's a *job*. And nobody I know is nuts about their job.'

'Nobody you know stands around in chains in front of a gang of toilet cleaner salesmen.'

I lay awake for another hour and a half after she fell asleep, enacting fantasies wherein I murdered Scott, kidnapped Monica and got married to Katherine.

Was it then the idea took shape in my subconscious? Or was it when Scott smiled Napoleonically and pulled that little cord, and the curtain surged up...? Or was it when I stood on the platform under the hot stage lights with the hush descending, and I saw salt tears trickling slowly down the wrinkled map of that old elephant face...

I stood on the platform under the hot stage lights with the hush descending... Scottie's launch speech had been a big success. The applause still hung in the air from when he'd unveiled a real live elephant right there on the stage, clanking its shackles. That was really something. The sales people goggled up in wonder. And finally, he said, holding a hand triumphantly up in the air – to show you the advertising that will make this brand famous, that will take this brand to that number one slot in the market...

I looked out at the audience of hung-over and crapulous sales people holding their cups of coffee and squinting up at me. I looked at Scott and Gillespie and Jerry in the front row, looking back at me expectantly...I looked at Monica, rocking from side to side gently in her heavy bracelets, and felt something irrepressible swell up inside me.

I looked at the page of script in front of me on the lectern. '*Gentlemen,*' it said. '*It gives me great pleasure to unveil to you...*' There were a couple of coughs from out front, an embarrassed shuffling of shoes. I looked out again. 'Gentlemen,' I said, and inflated my chest.

'*Gentlemen...*it says here – it says here in my script what a great pleasure it gives me to show you the advertising for Toilet Elephant... That's what it says... But I've got to tell you, it doesn't give me great pleasure. It gives me absolutely no pleasure at all. In fact, if you want to know the truth, it gives me a major pain in the arse. Can I tell you why it doesn't? Because I think this product sucks. Furthermore I think the company sucks, and so do all of you. And actually, all I have to say to you here, now – on behalf of myself, and on behalf of the elephant back there, is this: *You can shove your revolutionary new toilet cleaner up your smug collective arses.*'

Scott was on his feet, but he didn't know how to deal with this one. There wasn't a chapter on it in his management handbook. Jimmy Gillespie was on his feet too, his little round face apoplectic with anger and bewilderment. A babble of surprised exclamation broke out across the room, a scraping of chairs. And then, even as Scott thrust forward and jumped onto the platform, Monica was on *her* feet, rearing up and bugling wildly, chains snapping like plasticine. And then there was pandemonium.

I saw Jerry scrambling for a fire exit, elbow in the face of a frantic little man who looked like a weasle. All around the place salesmen were crawling underneath tables or fighting to get to the doors. I saw Ivan shouting and raising his arms in the air. And I saw Scott cowering back before the wrath of nature's great, nature's greatest masterpiece.

I walked straight through the back and got in the Beetle. Nobody tried to stop me.

EPILOGUE

That was all last year. Things changed afterwards.

Three things happened, in quick succession of one another. The first was inevitable; the second and third came from out of the blue.

I got fired. That was inevitable. You can't go around insulting your clients to their face – let alone to the faces of their management and sales force. I didn't even bother going into work the following day. I slept in, had a leisurely breakfast, watched some cartoons on the television. The phone kept going, and I assumed it was the agency calling up to give me my marching orders. After a while I unplugged it. I felt extraordinarily buoyant, absolutely bursting with beans. I spent fifteen minutes wrestling with Toby on the carpet, woofing at him and crawling about on all fours. Then we went out for a long grind round the northern hinterland of Kings Cross, in between the building sites and the railway tracks, underneath grimy arches full of garages and tyre depositories. It was a brisk early December morning, with a good stiff breeze and a bit of sun, and we walked and walked until Toby's legs gave out. I carried him back on a bus, grinning at my fellow passengers and the expressions on their faces. The old lady to my left eyed him apprehensively and drew her skirts around her, as if he might at any moment rush inside them. Toby ogled her back stolidly, panting.

When I got back to the flat I found a despatch rider just getting back on his motorcycle. He looked at me through his helmet.

'You called Brodie?' he asked.

'I am.'

'Just dropped off a letter for you.'

I opened it there on the doorstep. A curt typewritten note informed me that I had been dismissed for gross professional misconduct, and would I return any company property in my possession. It was signed by Mike Sharp. With it was a handwritten compliments slip in the same hand: *'Kindly get in touch – I want to talk to you.'* I tore up both.

Feeling suddenly at a loose end, I reconnected the telephone and called the AKL number. Katherine's phone rang four times before a familiar voice answered: 'Katherine Napier's telephone. Hello?'

Affecting a slight Scottish accent I said, 'Is she there, please?'

'Who's calling?'

'Angus McAlistair.'

'Can I ask what it's in connection with?' Typical bloody Scott.

I said, 'It's personal.'

'Then I suggest you call her at home.'

'Could I not have a word – it's important.'

'What did you say the name was?'

'McAlistair.'

There was a pause at the end of the line. I held my breath, wondering whether Scott could hear the crashing of my heart. I heard him calling to Kath, hand over the mouthpiece. Did she know anyone called McAlistair? Naturally, she didn't.

'Who is this?' he demanded.

Fuck it, I thought.

'Hi, Scottie. Brodie here. How are you? Sorry I had to miss the end of the conference – did it go okay?'

'Now you listen to me...' he began.

'Eat shit,' I said, and put the phone down before he could go on, like a naughty schoolboy making an obscene call.

'What you reckon, Tobes?' I asked. Toby looked up at me with enquiry. He had planted himself meaningfully in front of the unlit gas fire to try and get me to turn it on. The phone suddenly went off again, making me jump. I hesitated with my hand over the receiver – Kath? Scott? The office?

'...Brodie? Are you there?'

'Edward! Christ, am I glad it's you.'

'What's going on? Why aren't you at work?'

'I've been fired.'

'*What*? When?'

'This morning.'

'Why? I mean, what did you do?'

'It's a long story,' I said.

It took about fifteen minutes. At the end he gave a long whistle. 'Congratulations, Brodes. Best thing you ever did. Best thing I ever heard. Does this mean they won't be able to launch that lavatory cleaner?'

'God, no. They'll go ahead with it. They've spent too much not to.'

'Hmm. Pity. So what are your plans?'

'I haven't the foggiest. I suppose I'll have to get another job.'

'Not in advertising?'

'Hardly – after that.'

'Any other ideas?'

'No. Have you?'

'Not really. How are you off for cash?'

'I'm okay for a bit, I think.'

'What about your mortgage?'

'It's covered for three months on a policy.'

'Then you're laughing. Take a holiday.'

'Maybe I will,' I said.

We fixed to meet the next day at lunchtime. I tried calling Katherine again, but the receptionist had evidently been tipped off. 'I'm sorry, Mr Brodie,' she said firmly, 'we're not to accept calls from you any longer.'

'Could you just get a message to Katherine Napier? Please? It's really important.'

'I'm sorry.'

Ten minutes later I called back and reran the Scottish accent. But she didn't buy it. I tried again in deepest Welsh.

'Now look here...' she began.

'Listen,' I said. 'I don't want to annoy you. But I really have to talk to Katherine. It's urgent. If you give the message to her I swear I'll never call this number again. Just ask her to call me at home.'

There was a pause. Then she said, 'You promise?'

'Cross my heart.'

'No more calls?'

'No more calls.'

'No more funny accents?'

'Not one. A total cessation of funny accents.'

'All right, then. I'll do what I can.'

'God bless you,' I said.

'I always thought you were a funny boy,' she added, in a kinder tone of voice.

After this, of course, I had no option but to stick around by the telephone. And so it was that I found myself in dialogue with Mike Sharp two minutes later.

'Brodie? We've been trying to reach you all morning. Why aren't you answering your phone?'

'I am, now.'

'What in the name of Jesus Christ possessed you to act like that at the conference? Scott's absolutely livid. There's a good possibility we'll lose the business because of this.'

'I'm sorry,' I said. 'I don't think I can explain it. I didn't do it to mess up the agency's relationship with AKL. But I'm sorry to put you to all this grief. You're quite right to fire me.'

'I want to see you. Will you come in?'

'No. It's nothing personal.'

'Then I'll have to have it out over the phone. Just tell me – was it something to do with the Napier girl?'

My heart gave a sick little lurch. 'How do you mean?'

'Come on, Brodie. Everyone knows you've been knocking her off. Did she put you up to it for a dare, or something. Well?'

'She didn't put me up to it. Nobody put me up to it. I just did it. And Katherine's got nothing to do with this. You understand? Leave her out of it.'

'Don't take that tone of voice with me. I can still make things very unpleasant for you if I choose to. If you ever want another job in advertising you'd better start doing as you're told. Firstly, I want you to stay clear of *everybody* from AKL – is that understood? And that includes Katherine Napier.'

'I don't want another job in advertising. You can stick your job in advertising up your arse.'

'I'm warning you, Brodie. If you do anything further to harm the company's relationship with AKL we'll take you to court.'

'Fine. See you there.'

I cracked the phone down, and stood breathing deeply, trying to steady myself. I felt red in the face and close to crying – with anger, not pain, though I felt frightened. Not by the court threat (though I shouldn't have risen to it) – but afraid, suddenly, for my relationship with Katherine. Our secret wasn't a secret after all...it altered the whole complexion of things, or seemed to.

Still she didn't call me. I became fretful, and nearly went back on my promise to the receptionist. Finally, at six fifty, the phone went.

'Katherine? I've been by the phone all day.'

'I couldn't call earlier. I had to wait for people to leave.'

'Fair enough. I'm really glad to talk to you. I've been fired.'

'Why did you do it, Brodie? Why?'

'Can't you work it out? I thought I made it pretty obvious.'

'Oh Brodie, Brodie...'

'Because of the expression on Scott's face when he pulled that curtain.'

'You're crazy. It was such a stupid thing to do.'

'I'd do it again. I'd do it every time.'

'What are you going to *do*?'

'Don't worry about that. I'll be okay.'

There was a silence at the other end of the line. 'What's up, Kath?' I said.

'They know,' she said.

'What do they know?'

'About us. Scott knows. Jerry knows. Everybody knows. They've been having a go at me about it.'

There was another silence. Then I said: 'They knew at the agency, too.'

'Yes?'

'But so what? I mean, I don't give a shit. Besides, I'm through with all that now.'

'I'm not.'

'It needn't matter though, need it? Need it?'

'I don't know. I don't know.'

But it did matter. It mattered a lot.

That was the second thing – me and Katherine splitting up. It hit me very hard, because I loved her, and because I genuinely didn't expect it. Of course there was more to it – far more to it – than the others finding out about us. But whatever it was I couldn't figure out. She just wrote a note saying in a confused way that she'd had enough and wanted to call it a day, and that was that.

At first I wouldn't accept it. I kept trying to call her at her digs, but the phone just rang and rang. I called the operator, who said it was unplugged. I wrote her a long letter. I wrote her several long letters. I got in the car and drove to Bristol, then on to the Gower, where I met Susan. She was very nice about everything, but very firm with it. Katherine was there, but she wanted to be left alone. In other circumstances I might have ignored her and barged on in, but she said it so gently, without the slightest acrimony, that I suddenly realised it really was over, and there seemed no point.

'Would you just tell her, then – I'd like to talk to her, just once? Would you tell her that? I won't give her a hard time, or burst into tears. I *must* talk to her one more time.'

'I'll tell her. Whether or not she does is with her, I'm afraid.' She took my hand and pressed it. 'Don't be downcast, William. I know how much it hurts. You can go through a dozen relationships like this before you find the right person. You've just got to ride it.'

She was right, of course. But who wants to hear that grown-up, phlegmatic stuff when you've had your heart kicked in?

'What's she going to do?'

'She's giving up her job. I think she might go out and stay with John for a while. Sort things out.'

'What's up with her? Do you know? Is she all right?'

'I don't know. I think she just needs some time alone, away.'

'Give her my love. Give her all my love.'

'I will. Bless you, William – be good to yourself.'

Christmas came and went. I stayed in London on my own in the flat. I didn't have anyone to see or stay with, and anyway I didn't feel like seeing or staying with anyone. Stephen asked me over for Christmas dinner, but I declined, sending a card and a large toy elephant for Rebecca. Edward was out of town. He'd got a job, ironically enough, the day after I lost mine, as a runner-cum-biker with a film production company shooting a series of foot deodoriser commercials in the Lake District. I spent my mornings in bed and walking Toby, and my afternoons and evenings getting drunk. After the initial squeamishness about drinking on my own had evaporated I became something of an expert. The trick was, I found, to get pretty drunk pretty quickly, then try and stay that way for as long as possible. I tried various combinations to this effect. Mixing drinks, especially spirits, I found had disastrous effects, aborting the whole process far too early on. I found the best solution was to kick off with a four- or six-pack of those extra strong lagers favoured by winos and down and outs, then go on to standard tinnies. In this way I could drink more or less solidly from about noon onwards, lapsing into unconsciousness around ten or eleven thirty at night. I kept this up through the New Year and into January, literally without exchanging a word with anybody except the man at the off-licence. The phone went periodically, but I ignored it. On Christmas Eve, drunk as a bastard, I yanked it out its socket and dropped it down the chute to the bins. I think it was originally for ash from the open fire. Anyway, I bunged the telephone down, relishing the descending thumps and tinkles, and the final ghostly crash as it hit bottom. Thereafter I took to disposing of all my cans and bottles that way, deriving anarchic satisfaction from the resultant racket and destruction. Connie was, I assumed, away somewhere, as I hadn't seen her all Christmas, and the ground and first floor flats had been unoccupied for three months, so I didn't have to worry about bothering the neighbours. I revelled in my isolation.

After the New Year London began to heave itself back to life. Traffic once again filled the streets, and the pavements thronged with Sales crowds. It was very cold all of a sudden. I bought a Russian fur hat at Covent Garden market, to keep my head warm during the hangover marches with Toby. I still didn't have any plans, or anything particular to do. My money was holding up reasonably well, but it wouldn't go on that way for ever. Reluctantly, I concluded that I would have to find another job. The problem was, I hadn't a clue what, or where to start. The whole idea filled me with lethargy. Nevertheless, in an attempt to get matters underway, I unearthed my CV from a drawer and surveyed the catalogue of minor achievements that constituted my life to date: O levels, A levels, degree, work experience...Sound Technician? That had better come off. I had included it, if memory serves me right, on the strength of operating the tape recorder for two nights during the 1979 school production of Toad of Toad Hall – scarcely a qualification for, say, getting work in a recording studio. I axed a serious of dubious hobbies and interests along with it, and pondered what to list in their stead. Boozing? Walking the dog? I left it blank.

I bought a newspaper and looked through the jobs pages. Telephone sales positions accosted the eye from all quarters of the page, promising vast salaries and a 'lively and stimulating working environment'. Yeah yeah. I flipped on. *'Have you considered Chiropody as a Profession?'* asked a box, bottom right. Well, put like that...*'If you would like to know more about this satisfying and*

financially rewarding profession, and be able to control your own destiny, write to...'
Control your own destiny? As a *chiropodist*? I chucked the paper in the bin and
turned on the TV.

Later, out of boredom, and for want of anything better to do, I wrapped up
warm and went up on the roof. There was a bitter wind blowing from the North
East, and it was invigorating to perch up on the parapet in the teeth of it. I had my
first drink of the day, a swig of vodka from a flat quarter bottle, which shot warmth
through my stomach and into my limbs. The cold and the vodka combined to
squeeze tears out of the corners of my eyes, which I dabbed away with a gloved
hand. Fairly soon it began to hail lightly, little stinging flints of white that blew
sideways across the roofs, and my nose started to run. I stood to go back down.

That's when it happened. My foot simply sheered away from the brick of
the parapet, and the next thing I was sliding down the incline towards the
gutter fifteen feet below. I remember scrabbling for a hold on the smooth blue
tiles and catching the eye of a pigeon standing on the chimney stack, who
stared at me indifferently as I slithered past, yelping with fear and surprise.
Then my feet were over the edge and into nothing with my padded torso
tobogganing down the same way, and I thought very clearly and lucidly: you
stupid bastard, you stupid, stupid bastard. She'll think you killed yourself – you
have killed yourself...

Miraculously, I clung on at the edge. I wedged my forearms in the plastic
guttering and levered my centre of gravity the right sight of the drop. I hung
there panting, looking up at the cruel eyes of the pigeon, who continued to
monitor my behaviour. '*Bastard!*' I gasped, at the pigeon, at myself. A section
of the gutter cracked under my arms, and I floundered sideways to a firmer
piece. By dint of shuffling to my side I found I could progress slowly, and I gave
all my concentration to the task, blanking out the terror of the drop. I
wondered if any passers-by could see my waving legs, whether I should yell for
help, but I hadn't the breath to spare. My coat was bunching round my neck
and shoulders and suffocating me with warmth, my scarf swaddled the lower
half of my face and tickled my eyes with its fronds... I was convinced I was
about to go at any moment. Then my left foot touched something solid, that
bore my weight, and I was able partially to relieve the pressure on my straining
arms and shoulders.

When I gingerly peeked down, I saw my feet were resting next to a window
box full of withered geraniums. I shoved it roughly aside, then off, hearing a

thump several terrifying seconds later as it hit the pavement. With immense caution I lowered myself, holding onto the bar of the sash, and crouched looking into the glass. As soon as I could penetrate my own reflection I made out the shadowy form of a bed and a dressing table – Connie's bedroom. I eased the sash up and fell inwards.

For the next ten minutes I just sat with my back to the outside, regaining my breath and listening to the decelerating thump of my heart. I wrenched off my scarf and coat and lay down limply on my back, staring up at the ceiling. I'd never felt so acutely aware of being alive, or so acutely glad of it.

Eventually I heaved myself to my feet and ventured out of the door into Connie's hallway. Her flat mirrored mine in layout, but being a floor lower, and not in the eves, enjoyed few extra feet of space here and there. It was curiously warm, considering it was clearly unoccupied, and had no form of central heating. Also, I noticed, there was an odd smell about. I'd noticed it in the bedroom, but vaguely taken it to be a run of the mill old-lady's-flat smell, but here in the hall it was stronger, much stronger, and more unpleasant. I turned about slowly and looked towards the closed door of the sitting room. Suddenly I was afraid all over again. I could sense what was on the other side of the door, but I didn't have the nerve to go past it. I hesitated by the telephone, then picked it up... The sound of the dialling tone filled the flat.

After I'd called the ambulance I hung up again and stood undecidedly by the door. The smell seemed to be getting stronger by the moment, and I felt nauseous. Finally I cupped my scarf over my face, took a breath, and pushed open the door to the sitting room.

Connie was dead. She had fallen from her chair, or getting into it, and hadn't managed to get back upright. An electric bar fire was still burning in the hearth. Her face was away from me, but the exposed skin of her leg was decomposed. I took in the scene in one look, then withdrew carefully, shutting the door behind me.

At the inquest, which I attended five days later, it was established that she died between December 21 and 22, of heart failure, possibly inducing, or possibly induced by a fall. I explained my presence in the flat exactly as it had come about. The story sounded odd in the little coroner's room. It could so easily have been my inquest. Death by falling.

*

TOILET ELEPHANT

Who was it said not to look on death as an end, but rather as a very effective way of cutting down on your expenses? Woody Allen, I think. Tumbling off that roof certainly would have sorted out my financial problems. By the middle of January I had exhausted my current account and gone into overdraft. My bank sent letters, first courteous, then threatening. Cash machines flashed hostile messages when I approached. The mortgage was still covered for a few weeks on the policy, but I badly needed a source of income for the day to day. The toad work was beckoning again. You can give him the slip for a while, but eventually he nails you.

I had another desultory look through the papers, but gave up in despair. The trouble was, I didn't want the kinds of jobs they had on offer. I wanted something solitary and brainless, carrying no or very little responsibility, like driving a bus or sweeping the road. I wanted something where I didn't have to use my head, something where, above all, I didn't have to deal with *people* – managing them, selling things to them, arguing with them, competing with them. Basically I just wanted to be left alone.

Then I hit upon the idea of letting the flat. It was brilliantly simple. The money I'd get back would cover the mortgage and leave a bit besides to keep me going. I put a card up in the University of London Students' Union. It generated over a hundred enquiries. I let the place to a Japanese boy working on his Ph.D., banked the embarrassingly large cash deposit he grinningly handed over, and took myself and Toby off to the flat in Cambridge.

Toby settled happily into his old quarters. He padded around sniffing things and peering under doors, as if expecting my father to pop out at any second. I cleaned the place up a bit and set about a personal relaunch. Connie's death and my near thing had acted as a salutary slap in the face. I'd been carrying on like an idiot. I quit drinking altogether and went for long runs by the Cam. I purged myself of the ton of booze I'd put away with press-ups and crunches. I became something of a fanatic, replacing the obsessiveness of the drinker with the obsessiveness of the health freak. But you get tired of that stuff. After a while I found I could run ten or fifteen miles with ease, pounding monotonously through the flat, frozen countryside. Where do you go from there? It felt good to be fit, but what to do with all that fitness? What happens next? Get *more* fit? What's the point?

I'd always told myself – I think we all do – that if I ever found myself out of work, with my days to myself, I'd use the time productively, do the things you never have time for when you're working: I'd learn the clarinet, go to Spanish lessons, read Moby Dick, write a novel. But you don't. You watch black and white films on BBC2. You mooch about in half-empty shops. You piss away the time. Frankly, the last thing I felt like doing was learning the clarinet or reading Moby Dick.

I got a job. Not that I needed the money – it's amazing how cheaply you can live if your accommodation's free and you stay off the drink. I needed something to do, something unconnected with me and my introspective concerns. I got part-time work as a gardener in the parks and college gardens. It was ideal. Every day I would show up at eight o'clock at a shed in the Botanic Gardens, be told where to go and what to do, and issued with implements. Sometimes it would be clearing debris from the commons and greens around the city; sometimes it would be digging and weeding in trim college rose beds and herb gardens; sometimes it would be pruning dead branches off the huge chestnut trees dotted along Victoria Way and round Midsummer Common. I tended to ailing and frost-nipped shrubs. I came to love the work: it was so obviously a good thing to be doing, and necessary. And I came to love the areas I worked on. I wore an old jersey, donkey jacket and stompy Doc Marten boots, and a battered cap with ear muffs to keep out the cold. My hands grew tough and calloused. I even took up smoking, rolling my own spare little cigarettes from a tin of mild, fragrant tobacco, that yielded a delicious smoke, quite unlike the bitter scent of manufactured fags. To look at me, cupping a flame to my roll-up, leaning on a rake in my working clobber, you'd have taken me for any other ordinary workman – because that's exactly what I'd made myself.

And my thoughts during this time? Naturally, they were still with Katherine all the while, reconstructing, sifting, analysing. I thought particularly about what she'd said that time, about people loving one another sometimes not being enough to make a relationship work. I *know* she loved me. I'd been unsure of it for some time, but towards the end I'd seen off any doubts. And I felt sure she still must. That's why it hurt so badly. That's why I'd so wanted just to have another chance to talk. I still couldn't understand it, so I still couldn't accept it.

The pain of her absence never diminished or went away, although the work helped combat it better than drinking, or running. For one thing it was consistently hard physical labour, digging in hardened earth, bending to scrabble in gritty beds, loading trucks with sacks of leaves and soil. For another it was bitterly cold – the kind of cold that concusses you with its ferocity, its palpable, flabbergasting strength. During the third week in February the Cam froze solid, forcing little troops of ducks and geese into disgruntled exile on the banks, while kids took their place on the river, sliding and whooping, swaddled in lurid padded anoraks. Then it thawed slightly and the snow arrived, and I spent my mornings shovelling pathways clear, gritting paths and footbridges.

I had other thoughts besides. I thought a lot about Ivan and Monica, regretting I never had the chance to say goodbye, wondering how and where they were. I thought about Connie, nagging myself with accusations. If I hadn't been drinking like an idiot, maybe I could have helped her. Who knows? It seemed such a clumsy, unnecessary death. And I thought about Scott, the company man, and Jerry, the company fool, and all they did and stood for...I thought about Toilet Elephant and wondered why it wasn't in the shops. Maybe they'd pulled it after all?

In the afternoons, after I'd returned my tools and had a bath, I'd take Toby for walks across the parks and by the river. Sometimes I would drive us out into the fens and amble at random through the whitened fields. Later, back at the flat, I would put a match to the fire and sit and watch the antics of the flames for hours with Toby basking out in front like a contented seal.

The snow didn't stay long. One morning, after it had begun to clear, I saw a truck drive up on Midsummer Common and men step out with pegs and measures. I watched them for a while as they took bearings and consulted maps. After a bit I approached one of them, a middle-aged, professional man in a hard hat: a surveyor, I assumed.

'Can I ask what you're doing?' I said.

He looked me over, clocking the stained jeans, yob boots and mud-caked hands. 'Certainly you can,' he said, briskly. 'We're taking measurements for the development. Won't be long. You can come back this afternoon if you like, finish off your work.'

'What's the development?'

'Why, the car park.'

'Here?'

'Yes.'

I looked around me, bewildered. All around was common land, deserted and untrammelled, bordered by trees. A couple were walking a dog in one corner, four hundred yards distant. 'You're going to build a *car park*? Here?'

Instantly he hardened, retreating behind an official veneer. 'The plans have all been publicly debated and approved,' he said. 'Now I must –'

'Hang on,' I said. I laughed, slightly crazily, and held his arm. He eyed me with antagonism. 'This is a common...it's not...you can't turn it into a car park. It's common land. It's not yours to turn into a car park. It's not anybody's to turn into a car park.'

'It's everybody's,' he said, firmly, brushing off my hand. 'Besides, it'll be underground. There's been an environmental impact study. There'll only be the ventilation towers and approach road. The common will still be here.'

I felt defeated, at a loss. I wasn't used to arguing with people. I wasn't used to *talking* to people. And plainly it had all happened, been discussed, ratified, approved. Midsummer Common, a chunk of untouched green since Arthur's time was being turned into a car park. A fucking car park.

'Listen,' I said. I so desperately wanted to get through to him. 'Don't you understand – this land, it...it won't be the same when it's covered in ventilation stacks and queues of traffic lining up to park. It'll change completely. Don't you see that?'

'Have you got a car?' he demanded.

'Yes, but...'

'Look. This city has an acute traffic problem. This is essential work. If you feel strongly, write to your MP – but don't interfere with me or my men.' He strode away.

I did write to my MP, and got a letter back, regretfully backing up the local authority decision. *Be assured*, it concluded, *that every effort has been, and will be made to minimise the impact upon the surrounding area...*

Cattle graze on Midsummer Common in the spring and summer, and sometimes horses. What'll they make of the ventilation towers, the tarmac, the queueing motors? They'll accept, the same as the rest of us. Accept and adapt. We'll carry on accepting and adapting as more and more green and untouched places are snipped away to be turned into car parks, until the whole place is theme-parked and concreted.

Is this what the future has to hold out to us: car parks on common land, and toilet cleaners shaped like elephants?

The thought depressed me. But it also stopped me thinking about Katherine for more than half a minute.

★

About this time I broke my solitude for the first time. I was working on some beds in Trinity, turning over the chocolatey soil with a hoe, when a gowned figure walked past, hesitated, and approached me.

'Brodie? William Brodie?' he said. He stared at me short-sightedly through the thick lenses of his spectacles, looking me up and down. I straightened up. 'Hello, Patrick,' I said. The puzzlement on his face lessened slightly and he extended a hand. I took it with my earthy one, and he winced. 'What are you...is this a holiday job?'

'No,' I said. 'I do this every day. Have done for a little while.'

He looked at me as one might look at an invalid. 'Come and have a cup of coffee,' he said. 'Tell me about it.'

'When I come off my shift,' I said. 'Two fifteen?'

'Fine, fine...I'll see you at the lodge, yes?'

'Great.'

'It's good to see you,' he said, uncertainly.

'And you.'

He walked on, looking back one more time with curious eyes.

Patrick – Patrick McIlveney – had been at Edinburgh in the same year as me, reading English. He'd scored a brilliant first, far and away better than mine, and gone on to higher things. Now here he was, doing his higher things in his tweed jacket and cape, carrying a little stack of books. And here I was, digging the flower bed in my Doc Martens. Very Voltairian.

I'd always rather liked Patrick, in small doses. He was a bit intense, and unnervingly hard-working, but he had redeeming characteristics, in particular an endearing set of oddball boys-own enthusiasms, such as a passion for sausages, thick boots and complicated penknifes. Occasionally we would go walking together in the Grampians. Patrick would carry around a great armoury of cooking equipment and brew up tea on hilltops, proudly displaying the lighting mechanism of the miniature stove, and cleaning it afterwards with an oiled cloth. 'You can bring a thermos,' he'd say, packing everything away again after the half-hour operation: 'But it isn't quite the same.'

Five minutes before I was due to meet him I suddenly had second thoughts and wished I'd brushed him off. I'd got in the habit of being alone, of not making the effort of talking and listening to people; I was reluctant to be quizzed about my circumstances. But there was no point in avoiding him. We'd be bound to run into each other again in the college. I decided to make it brief – friendly, but curt, and head home.

In fact I spent the whole afternoon with him in a tea shop. I ate sandwiches and scones and cakes – working outdoors gave me an astonishing appetite – and smoked some of my roll-ups. Patrick, I was amused to see, was sporting an enormous Sherlock Holmes pipe, which kept going out, whereupon he would puff on it prodigiously with a fresh flame to the bowl, sending up great blankets of smoke like a Red Indian. I told him everything. Once I started I found I just couldn't stop. I went from the top, the start of the elephant project, the initial enthusiasm, meeting Katherine, the affair, the culmination, the exile, the gardening job. He listened sympathetically, occasionally prompting me with a question or comment. We drank five pots of tea.

'Doing anything tonight?' he asked, when I'd finished.

'No plans.'

'Come to the pictures with me.'

'Okay.'

'Want to know what's on?'

'Not really.'

'You really are depressed, aren't you?'

'Yes, I'm afraid I am.'

'Tell me,' he said. He traced a pattern in the crumbs on his plate. 'I hope you don't mind if I ask you this...you haven't thought of doing yourself in at all? At any time?'

'Never. Not for a moment.'

He beamed, reassured. 'Good,' he said. '*Good.*'

'It's all crap, you know, that you automatically want to kill yourself when you get depression. I never have. I nearly did by mistake and it freaked the shit out of me.'

'I'm sure, I'm sure,' he said hastily, covering his tracks. 'It's just...well, you don't seem to have much appetite for life any more.'

'That isn't true. I like my work enormously.'

'But you can't carry on doing this indefinitely.'

'Can't I?'

He frowned, blowing on his pipe. 'Maybe you can. But from what you say you never go out, never see anyone...in Edinburgh you were such a lad – always out drinking, going to parties. All that stuff.'

'I came walking too.'

'True. True. But I can't help thinking it isn't very healthy to isolate yourself completely like this. Everybody needs other people.'

'I don't,' I said. 'Not right now.'

We went to the pictures. It was a Laurel and Hardy double bill, full of people singing songs and falling over and poking each other in the eye. It did me a power of good: hadn't laughed so much for ages.

February grudgingly gave way to March. On the first day of the month I had a postcard in a familiar hand, forwarded from the flat. My first mail in three months.

It was from Edward – I'd been wondering where he'd got to. On one side was a picture of an elephant with its mahout. On the other I read:

> *I've fucked off to India for six months. Been missing me? Why not come out too? Crap food, cool elephants. See overleaf. Pip pip. Edward.*

Typically, he'd omitted include a contacting address of any kind. Pity really. A few months in India might have been just the ticket. I put the postcard on the mantelpiece next to a crumpled polaroid of Monica I'd found in the pocket of the jeans I wore to the shoot.

The next day I had another postcard, from California.

> *My dear William,*
>
> *How are you? Where are you? Did you get my Christmas card? I'm afraid I sent them out rather late. Have been trying to call you but all I get is a very odd oriental. Perhaps you are at Cambridge? Would you phone me when you get this? Love from Dad.*

Underneath the signature, in cramped-up writing, was the phone number, obviously scrawled on at the last moment. The world was re-establishing contact.

I picked up the telephone. The handpiece felt heavy and odd in my hand, like a lump of plumbing or a dumbell. Funny to think how often I used to use these things at the office. Awkwar dly I dialled the lengthy number.

'Hello?' said a voice, at length, clear as a bell.

'Hello? Dad?'

'Hello?'

'Dad – it's me, William...I got your postcard.'

'William!' He boomed the name, as if realising his voice had to carry across thousands of miles. 'How *are* you? It's three in the morning here. What time is it with you?'

'Eleven. Sorry to have woken you up. It's nice to talk to you, dad.'

'Don't give it a thought,' roared my father. 'So you're in Cambridge, are you?'

'Yes. I can hear fine actually. No need to speak up.'

'What? Really? Oh, excellent. Yes. In Cambridge? Has your company moved?'

'No. I left them. I work here now.'

'Really? How nice! What as?'

'A gardener.'

'Splendid! A gardener, you say?'

'Yes. I enjoy it.'

'Well, that's good.' He seemed to consider it for a moment then dismiss it from his mind. 'As a matter of fact, William, I...the reason why I've got in touch...that is – actually I've got some rather big news.'

'I'm all ears.'

The receiver coughed, a coy cough. 'The thing is –' said my father again.

'Yes?'

'Well...I'm getting married.' The words came tumbling out in a rush.

It took me totally, utterly by surprise. I couldn't have been more surprised if he'd said he was getting castrated. '*Married?*' I repeated, stupidly.

'To a woman I've met,' amplified dad, unnecessarily.

'Dad, that's...that's great – great! Congratulations!'

'And I wanted to ask,' he babbled on, unstoppably now, 'Would you like to act as best man?'

'Oh, dad...Yes. Yes, of course, I'd love that. What's her name? Where did you meet? Tell me all about her.'

'What?'

'Tell me about this girl? This woman.'

'Oh, of course. She's called Antonia.'

'How old is she?'

'I haven't asked her.'

'Well, roughly speaking.'

'Forty, I suppose. Fifty, perhaps. Maybe sixty. I'll send you a photograph of her.'

'What does she do?'

'She works in a bookstore. She's a widow. You'll like her awfully, William.'

'When's it to be? I'll book a ticket.'

He told me. A second later a little bomb went off in my interior, a controlled explosion that sent out ripples through my body. 'Are you still there?' asked dad.

'Still here,' I said. 'It'll be a pleasure. Count on me.'

May eleven. Well what do you know?

The next day I went into a travel agent and booked a flight. 'How long will you be staying?' asked the girl. Hadn't thought, I said. She gave me an open ticket. I came away slowly, holding it like a charm.

My father's news cheered me up no end. Together with my renewed friendship with Patrick and the gradually lighter days and improving weather my spirits started to approach their old, pre-Katherine levels. True, I still thought about her roughly thirty times a minute, but in a steadier way, a more positive overall frame of mind. Accept and adapt, I told myself. Well, I adapted; I never could accept.

Towards the end of March I was walking with Toby down a quiet pedestrian lane leading to the ferry when a little poster in a window caught my eye. It called for supporters to join a movement opposing the work on the common. I knocked on the door without hesitation. Five minutes later I was drinking tea with a smart middle-aged lady, the chairman of the group. A couple of other rebels were there too – a game old pensioner with a strapping deaf aid, wearing a beret and a cravat, and a nineteen-year-old hippie anarchist with a pink rat called Simon. Simon and Toby eyed one another in mutual trepidation, studiously minding their own business, while we discussed strategy. Later we all went to the pub up the road and the hippie bought me a pint of Guinness. I grasped it like an old friend. He stuck around after the others left and we got plastered together.

A week later I was arrested along with my new-found friends for obstructing a digger. We spent a night together in the cells, being brought cups of tea by wholly charming and sympathetic policemen. 'Wish I could have joined you,' said one. 'I think it's criminal what they're up to.' The next day we were released without charge. It hadn't achieved much, but we'd made ourselves known, and the small amount of publicity it generated helped recruit some new members.

On an impulse I sent a letter off to Susan Napier. I outlined the situation and asked if there was anything she could do about it by way of publicity. Three days later she telephoned. We talked for an hour.

'Are you okay, William?' she asked. 'I was really worried about you after we last parted. I didn't think I'd be hearing from you again.'

'I'm okay. Thanks for your concern.'

'By the way, Katherine told me about what you did at the conference. I think it was wonderful.'

'I didn't do it as some kind of noble gesture. It was childish, really.'

'I still think you were right to do it.'

'Yeah, well. Kind of thing you only get to do once, I guess. I'm glad I did.' There was a short silence. 'How's Katherine?' I forced myself to say. For such a banal query it took a lot of effort.

'She got back two weeks ago. I think she's a lot better for the break.'

'I'm glad.'

'I'm desperately sorry it didn't work out between you two, William. She misses you, you know.'

'I just wish I knew why it happened.'

'I don't think *she* could explain that.'

'It wasn't to be, eh?'

'Perhaps. Trite, I know. I've been there too, you know.'

'Why did you and John break up?'

'I don't think I could explain that.' She laughed. 'Look, I'll chase up those contacts I mentioned about the common – see if we can get a story, yes?'

'Brilliant. Thanks for everything, Susan.'

'Goodbye, William. Good luck. Give me a call in a couple of weeks, won't you? Let me know how things progress.'

'You bet. Bye for now.'

After that I threw myself into my work, putting in as much overtime as possible to raise cash for America. Crocuses started to appear along the river banks, then daffodils. The people walking about the place seemed to be visibly more upright and cheerier in the brighter weather, calling greetings in the cold air. It seemed a pity to be going away just as spring unleashed itself upon the city. It seemed a pity to be going away just as our little guerilla movement got off the ground as well. By the middle of April we'd generated over four hundred members, articulate professional types, who organised well and formed an effective lobby. And then an article appeared in one of the Sundays. It wasn't a long piece, or prominently positioned, but it felt like a real breakthrough. The originator was S. Napier.

A group of us celebrated the piece together over breakfast in town. Afterwards I made my way merrily back to the flat and dialled Susan's number with a flourish.

The phone rang nine times. I was on the point of giving up when it was answered. 'Swansea 77458?' said a voice. But it wasn't Susan's.

I felt my mouth go dry. I stood there dumbly holding the receiver to my ear with my heart pumping out of control in my chest.

'*Hello?...Is anyone there?*'

Very carefully, flatly, formally, I said, 'May I speak to Susan, please?'

'Certainly. Who shall I say?'

'A friend.'

I heard a catch of breath, faintly, at the other end of the line. Then Katherine said: '*Brodie?...Is that you?*'

'Yes, it's me.'

'Oh God.'

'Just get Susan, would you? Please.'

Previously I'd have given anything to talk to her again. Now suddenly my inclination was all the other way.

'Brodie, wait. I...oh God,' she said again.

'Listen, Katherine. This isn't doing either of us much good. Can I just talk to your mother? Then I'll go away again.'

'Brodie, don't hang up. I've been meaning to call you. I treated you badly back before Christmas. I...'

'You don't have to go on. I don't hate you, Kath. I'll never hate you. But please don't let's drag over it now.'

I heard a small gulp. 'Okay,' she said. 'So...so how are you?'

'Fine.'

'What have you been up to?'

'Look, if it's all the same with you can we dispense with the small talk? I'm not up to it.'

'I just wanted to know what you've been up to, that was all.'

'I've been doing some gardening.'

'Yes? That's...what, are you a gardener, then?'

'That's right.'

'I've been learning to type. I'm going to work with Mum.'

'Great. Well would you say to her I called, and thanks for the article?'

'Have you seen it?' she asked.

'The article? Yes of course I have. That's why I'm calling.'

'No, no – Elephant.'

'What?'

'*Toilet Elephant* – it's in distribution. I bought a bottle yesterday for old time's sake. And the ad's on telly – haven't you seen it?'

'I don't have a telly... So they did launch it.'

'You know Jerry got made redundant?'

'No, I didn't know that.'

'And Scott got promoted.'

'Well, well.'

'You don't hate me, Brodie?'

'I said so. Why did you do it though, Katherine? Something I said?'

'It just all got too much for me. What with you wanting to get married, and all the pressure of the project and seeing each other and working together...I couldn't *stand* it. I had to get out. I can't explain any better than that.'

'Uh huh? Fair enough.'

'Brodie, I'm sorry.'

'Forget it.'

'Friends?'

'Yeah, why not.'

There was a slight pause. Then Katherine said, tentatively, 'You want to meet up some time?'

'I...I don't think that would be possible.'

'You *do* hate me.'

'No, I mean I don't think it would be physically possible. I'm flying out to California next week. I could be away half a year.'

'Oh.' She sounded genuinely regretful and my heart softened.

'I could see you when I get back. That would be nice.'

'You can't beforehand?'

I felt a surge, almost sexual in its intensity, spreading up through my body, making me sick with suppressed longing. Could this – could this just be what it sounded like? I cleared my throat. 'Do you...would I...would I be thinking in the right general ball park if I thought you – just conceivably – want to give it another go?'

'Yes,' she whispered. 'Yes. Yes.'

'Jesus, Katherine...'

'Both of us are less crazy now. Don't you reckon?'

'I wouldn't bank on that – I got arrested again last month.'

'Oh, Brodie, Brodie...what about you, though? Are you willing to risk it all over again?'

'Stay there,' I said. 'Fucking *stay* there, all right?'

'What is it?'

'Give me six hours,' I said.

I put down the phone and picked up the car keys. Toby paddled out into the hall and looked at me enquiringly.

'Get your things on, Tobes,' I said. 'We're going to Wales.'

I drove along the M11 at full tilt listening to Beethoven's Ninth on Desert Island Discs, revelling in the throaty saw of the double basses as they ushered in the ode to joy. Nice of them to lay on the mood music.

By the M25 turn-off I overtook a Mercedes doing sixty-five. The driver was talking fiercely into a little cell phone, drumming his fingers on the wheel. I thought to myself – thank God. Thank God I made that call.

Hate telephones? Me? Whatever gave you that idea?

I don't hate telephones. I *love* them.

For the record, Kath and I got married four months later, in California. Dad was the best man. I hear Toilet Elephant lasted exactly nine months in the shops. The competition got their act together and sat on it. Wish I could say I was sorry.

Introducing Ian Shirley – one of the many new authors published by Citron Press, the only publishing house dedicated exclusively to promoting new fiction in this country.

We are determined to give new authors like Ian Shirley a platform for their writing. We are even more determined to give our growing list of loyal readers access to the freshest, most innovative new fiction – fiction that doesn't bow to the latest fashion or formula.

If you believe that new talent should have a voice and an audience please support Citron Press by buying our books.

The face of the future

Support New Fiction by Supporting

CITRON
PRESS

Further Reading
from Citron Press

THE RIVER THIEF *by* BARRY ROSS

From the safe lunacy of Soho to the quaint rural pursuits of 'ye olde drugge deale', my decision to 'find myself' in the country gloriously backfired. Seriously threatened and romantically rebuffed, I wanted out... But someone was trying to steal a river and, stupidly, I decided to stop them...

Funny, inventive and sharp, *The River Thief* is a black comedy thriller with teeth, a bizarre cocktail of drugs, heavies and the landed gentry, with a languid hero caught in the fallout. Seldom has country air stank of such stewed corruption...

ORDER NO. T0109

THE MONDAY LUNCHTIME OF THE LIVING DEAD *by* JEREMY JEHU

Laconic political fixer Rupert Tranquil likes to imagine himself a modern Clubland Hero – a hip Richard Hannay ever ready to render his country 'some small service' if the price is right.
But his agreeable self-deception is shattered when a simple spot of blackmail erupts into a bloody fiasco. Then old university mate, Rick Marchant, begs disillusioned Rupert to save his life. Our hero detects one tiny problem. Rick's been dead for twenty years. Rupert should know. He killed him. The book critic of ITV *Teletext* has created a wittily offbeat contemporary romp for fellow fans of the English thriller in its heyday.
'A terrific read' *Daily Telegraph*

ORDER NO. T0107

FRAGILE STATE *by* DAVID TURNER

'A compelling read'
The List

What do you do when your girlfriend disappears and your best friend commits suicide? Glen McGregor's answer is to get mind-numbingly drunk. But as bad as things are, they can always get worse, and soon he is being hampered in his quest for drunken oblivion by the lies and duplicity of his unsavoury past. Before long he is on a reluctant collision course with the truth, his progress hindered by the MI5, the Metropolitan Police, a plethora of dead bodies, and a desire to run away and hide.
Fragile State is a poignant, richly textured novel about friends and lovers, and the other, darker lives that they may lead.

ORDER NO. T0108

NASTY LOVE *by* SELTZER COLE

'Funny, energising and awash with insights into the modern male psyche. Seltzer Cole has produced a first novel of lively wit and vigour.'
Shyama Perera, author of *Haven't Stopped Dancing Yet*

She's twenty-five, drives a BMW and runs a business, and Chaz Douglas wants her badly. Is his growing fixation sparked by love, or lust for a better life? Swept into a fast-moving and brittle world where promises are cheap and greed is second nature, he quickly becomes backed into a corner from which violence is the only escape. Tracking the flip side of lust and ambition, this is a book where obsession burns and love is nasty.

ORDER NO. J0108S

Support new fiction

CITRON
PRESS

SHADOWPLAY *by* IAN SHIRLEY

'Entertaining...reads like Robert Sheckley with a hint of Robert Rankin'
SFX Magazine

London 2147. When her perfect body is blown to pieces, successful investment banker Helena Svenson is left with few options. With her soul in Purgatory, a special tribunal gives her another chance to enter Heaven. All she has to do is complete one simple task - recover the remains of Adolf Hitler so the Devil can claim his soul. She can't return to her own body, but don't worry, they've located just the thing...
Prepare yourself for a journey through space, time, parallel hells and the most entertaining ride of your afterlife!

ORDER NO. S0103

DEAD SANCTITIES *by* SEAN BADAL

Journalist Vishnu Kolandra'ss upbringing in London hasn't prepared him for the wonderful yet disturbing dichotomy that is his India. Adjusting to the frenzy of new surroundings, Vishnu finds himself encircled by casual acquaintances and developing interests - that is, until his apparently cursory involvement with a corruption and nepotism scandal jeopardises his new career.
Embroiled in something he can neither avoid nor contain, Vishnu confronts the challenge of a labyrinthine present - with the sickening realisation that all the roads of his past have led him to this one surprising destination - an old Indo-Saracenic building in downtown Bombay. *Dead Sanctities* evokes the colour and myth of India with elegance and wit.

ORDER NO. J0107

BOMBAY MIX *by* RICHARD BAUM

A politician stealing money to finance a sleazy TV station, a coconut seller who swaps the sidewalk for the catwalk, a crooked stockbroker trying to stop the destruction of his childhood home   it could be just the story to get people reading The Bombay Nose again. Unfortunately for plumbing journalist David Leadbeater, it could be just the story to land him in jail.
Bombay Mix is a wild satire that lifts the lid on a city driven by money, politics and directionally challenged taxis.
'A lively subcontinental satire in the Rushdie and Irving mould'
The Independent

ORDER NO. Q0113

GOING INDIGO *by* SAM NORTH

'Treads new ground in its off-beat, child's eye black comedy.'
The Independent

Exiled from his small country town by the tragic combination of a missing father and a mother committed to a mental institution, Oliver, a pale bald-headed twelve-year-old boy, arrives at King's Cross Station accompanied by his cat, Flop. He is dreading his new life with a fortune-telling Grandma he has never known. If nothing had prepared Oliver for the stern manners of Grandma Otis's companion Lena, absolutely no one had prepared Lena for this wild neglected child and his scrawny cat. Oliver soon discovers that the new people he's living with are possibly crazier than the ones he left behind.

ORDER NO. J0201

By supporting Citron Press

CITRO
PRESS

Further Reading
from Citron Press

THE ADVENT OF THE INCREDULOUS STIGMATA MAN *by* KELVIN MASON

Scotland, the not-too-distant future: The forces of the right have found a natural ally in the conservation movement. A man is saved from street execution by a supernatural force. Stigmatised, Mick flees for his life with his best friend's girlfriend and her brother, a world-wise dwarf. Kathy and Tam have their own reasons for escaping the sadistic agents of the all-powerful Extended European Community. Kathy is pregnant and believes the baby is Mick's. Mick knows different. The EEC Commissioner is expecting Tam for dinner. The hunt is on. In a cataclysmic showdown the full meaning of Mick's mixed blessing is revealed.

ORDER NO. S0102

CRITICAL MASS *by* FRED BASNETT

The author was a boffin at Windscale during the 1950s and *Critical Mass* is essentially an evocation, lightly fictionalised, of his bizarre interlude there. Many of the people at Beaufort (which is, of course, a wind scale) were young, and the peculiar attraction of the place for them was that working there could earn exemption from national service. But there was a price to pay. All unmarried personnel were confined to an isolated hostel where for every ten men there was just one woman. It is this explosive sexual imbalance that gives the novel its title, its hair-trigger violence, and its black, radioactive humour.

ORDER NO. Q0101

HOW TALL WAS HEMINGWAY *by* KENNETH MCDOWELL

In the heady Seventies, before the savagery of Tory cuts took the soul from the Education System, university life could be Elysian... Mature literature student Stanley Noone, though, is a long way from paradise. Topics on this year's hectic curriculum include his problematic past, sexual insecurities, irritating academics, terrorists and lawn tennis. And Stanley's new life is bobbing well below the pass mark... '**How Tall Was Hemingway?** is a most enjoyable piece of writing and has something that there is not enough of these days, a really strong sense of comedy and farce...a considerable comic talent.' *Malcolm Bradbury*

ORDER NO. Z0104

FLORENCE OF ARABIA *by* DAVID GODOLPHIN

On the Persian Gulf island of Belaj, British air hostesses and Egyptian belly-dancers are busy relieving oversexed citizens of their frustrations and petrodollars. One of the punters is murdered: whisky-soaked publisher Farouk, whose randy wife Nayla is a niece of the Amir, Shaikh Khalid Al-Khazi. Newcomer Cass, an East London housewife, becomes a $500 hooker. Sam, a stewardess with page-3-girl boobs, and bisexual banker Eddy join their Arab boyfriends in a plot to assassinate the Amir in a bizarre bedroom romp. All over Arabia thrones rock, heads roll: democracy dawns!

ORDER NO. Z0103

Support new fiction

Order this
Fresh Fiction
from Citron Press

All Citron Press books are available at bookshops nationwide, on-line from amazon.co.uk, the Internet bookseller, or by ordering direct from Citron Press. To order any of the books detailed above, simply complete the order form below, including the order numbers of your selection in the space provided and post to Citron Press, or phone the Citron Press Hotline.

Citron Press Hotline: 0845 602 2202

Order No.		£7.99	Order No.		£7.99
Order No.		£7.99	Order No.		£7.99
Order No.		£7.99	Order No.		£7.99

*Please note: postage and packaging are **included** in the above prices*

Name..
Address..
....
....
....Postcode..............................
Telephone.............................E-mail.................................

Post your order to:
Citron Press, P.O. Box 88, Southampton SO14 0ZA

Please make all cheques payable to: **Citron Press**

If you prefer to pay by credit card, please complete the following:
Please debit my Visa/Mastercard (delete as applicable) card no:

☐☐☐☐☐☐☐☐☐☐☐☐☐☐☐☐

Signature | Expiry date | /

Visit our website at www.citronpress.co.uk

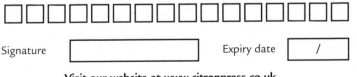

By supporting Citron Press

Your nearest book shop

The most convenient way to purchase innovative new fiction

CITRON
PRESS

WWW.citronpress.co.uk